Y0-EHE-116

THE KING OF CLUBS

THE KING OF CLUBS

JAY BILDSTEIN

as told to Jerry Schmetterer

BARRICADE BOOKS / New York

Published by Barricade Books Inc.
150 Fifth Avenue
New York, NY 10011

Printed in the United States of America.

Library of Congress Cataloging-in-Publication Data

Bildstein, Jay.

The king of clubs: the story of Scores, the famed topless club, and the lurid life behind the glitter / by Jay Bildstein, as told to Jerry Schmetterer.

p. cm.

ISBN 1-56980-073-1 (hardcover)

1. Scores (Club: New York, N.Y.)—History. 2. Music-halls (Variety-theaters, cabarets, etc.)—New York (N.Y.)—History. 3. Striptease—New York (N.Y.) 4. bildstein, Jay. 5. Businessmen—United States—Biography. I. Schmetterer, Jerry. II. Title.

PN2277.N52S363 1996

792.7'09747'1—dc20 95-51181

CIP

First Printing

DEDICATION

To all the girls in my junior high
who fanned the flames
of my adolescent libido.
J.B.

To Honeysuckle
J.S.

CONTENTS

AUTHOR'S NOTE

Many people contributed generously to this book. I'd like to thank my family for their support; Eric Kloper; my agent, Fern Edison; Marina for her generosity; Sheldon Shuch, Ph.D., for his editing skills; Dave Schmetterer for his Mac help, Emily Schmetterer; Frank DeMaio; Lisa Beck; and Sandy Stuart.

A note about the names in this book: Many of the women who earn their livings as showgirls use stage names to protect themselves from those who might seek to damage their reputations and the reputations of their families. They are also concerned about stalkers and others who might prey on them. For that reason many of the dancers written about in this book have asked that their real names not be used, and we have complied.

CHAPTER 1

Opening Night

It was October 31, 1991, Halloween, and it was supposed to be the greatest night of my life. The years of negotiations, of long dreary business trips, of haggling in smoke-filled back rooms and sometimes cold dark alleys next to roadside strip joints, were behind me. So were the nightmares, the awakenings in darkened, musty motel rooms on sheets soaked with my own sweat as my anxious mind and body fought off the fear of failure. But, as I stood inside the main entrance of Scores, the nightclub that was going to revolutionize New York nightlife, to be to the nineties what Studio 54 was to the seventies, I was about to be the clown in the thousand-dollar suit.

We were ninety minutes from opening, ninety minutes from blasting off into a new era of entertainment, and my million-dollar investment was about to go down the drain. I did not have in my hands that little piece of paper known in New York as a cabaret license. It was caught in red tape thicker than an aging stripper's makeup. Without it I would be the laughingstock of New York instead of the King of Clubs.

As I stood waiting, praying for some last-minute miracle that would produce the license, there was activity all around me. A thirteen-man crew was cleaning up the mess left by the painters, carpenters, and electricians who had spent four months turning a warehouselike twenty-thousand-square-foot space into a richly carpeted, leather-and-suede-bordered club for New York's well-heeled young wheeler-dealers. In the dressing rooms fifty of the best-looking girls in the world were putting the last-minute touches on their makeup, removing the tiniest bits of stubble from the deep, inviting corners of their smooth thighs, and adjusting the slim strings of leather and lace that would stand between them and total nudity as they performed for the wheeler-dealers of Wall Street and Madison Avenue, the Hollywood movie stars, and the professional athletes who would be drawn to Scores like teenagers to a *Playboy* centerfold. It was to be the first club of its kind in New York, but it would not last long past opening night without a cabaret license.

The red tape snafu had begun when my architect forgot to get a New York City Public Assembly Permit. Inspections for that permit had to be made before the final cabaret license could be obtained. It did not matter that on my list of VIPs who had accepted invitations for opening night were several city officials, including a deputy mayor who would someday lend his name to an important commission. Because of the oversight we did not obtain that permit until October 30, the day before opening. On opening day I sent an army of lawyers, at $300 an hour, onto the bureaucratic battlefield, trying to push that cabaret license through before 5 P.M.—the hour that $60,000 worth of advertising said we were going to expose the Big Apple to the most wonderful collection of legs, breasts, smiles, and willing hearts that it had ever seen.

No other topless club ever advertised like Scores did. I took out ads on MTV, VH-1, SportsChannel, in the *New York Post* and the *Daily News*, and on radio stations I knew my target clientele listened to.

At 4 P.M. the bartenders set up their stations, while the people from the Squirrel System, the $70,000 computer which monitored every drop of liquor shot through the booze guns and could even take a picture every time the cash register drawer opened, fine-tuned the system. In the back the girls were getting ready, led by Tyler—the nation's superstar table dancer, the girl who set the style for all the rest—as they slipped into their T-bars, or T-backs, those modern day G-strings that barely cover a dancer's crotch and reveal her backside. On the tips of their breasts were the transparent pasties that I invented as a way of getting around the archaic State Liquor Authority laws, which said naked dancers had to stay at least six feet away from their customers, on a platform that was elevated or at least eighteen inches above them.

As I wandered around the club, watching all the activity, realizing that more than two hundred people now depended on me for their livelihoods, I made the decision that I would have to open without the cabaret license and let the chips fall where they may. I had not shared the problem with any of the staff. If Scores had only one night to live, it would be the greatest night in the history of nightclubs.

So despite my worry and anxiety, I was elated beyond measure. For four long years I had worked toward this night, and I was not going to let a bureaucratic snaggle destroy my dream.

In December 1985, I had just gotten back from doing real estate deals in Mexico. The peso was in the toilet. I needed work and was always drawn to high-energy, risky businesses, so I took a position being offered at a commodities firm. I was great at it. I went from being an assistant broker to a full broker in record time. I thrived on the pressure and stress. I found myself to be a great motivator of people and learned to channel my energy into the hearts and minds of colleagues and clients alike. I was far and away the best broker in the company, making money hand over fist as the stock market charged forward. I did so well they gave me my own office in the Wall Street Tower, a prestigious building, which once housed the headquarters of Citibank. It was a beautiful building right around the corner from Delmonico's, a landmark Wall Street restaurant.

Before long I had fifty brokers working for me. They spent an exhausting amount of hours on the phone, typically from 9 A.M. to 9 P.M. They worked six days a week, at an unbelievable pace. An inside linebacker for the New York Jets did not work any harder.

By 1987 it was difficult to get people to speculate. They could put their money into a blue-chip stock and do very well without the risk. My guys' brains were getting fried calling up investors sixty hours a week. I, however, loved the action, the excitement, the deal making. I loved living on the edge, going against the accepted thinking of the time. Damn, I just freakin' loved it.

These brokers would call up people all over the country, sometimes just taking their names from telephone books, and try to persuade them to let us manage their money. We promised to invest the money in commodities: pork bellies, cocoa, coffee, sugar, soybeans, things like that. Even though it was pretty much accepted that 90 percent of the investors would lose their money, a fact shared with potential clients, the brokers could honestly say that if they hit right the score could be tremendous, dreams could come true. These young brokers thought that all they had to do was speak their golden words and they could persuade anyone to do anything. We really believed that, and we lived our lives by that code.

One thing I always believed about managing people, and this really paid off in Scores, was that a business group should look at itself as a family with a common goal. That attitude really helped stimulate production amongst the members of my sales team. I tried to make them feel not just that they would make a lot of money, but wanted and important. One of the things I used to do every Friday was to reward the week's top ten producers. I thought it was important.

At four-thirty in the afternoon I invited those guys out on the town. I picked up the tab, from my own pocket, at the downtown watering holes. We would go to the high-class places like Delmonico's and Harry's at Hanover, Windows on the World, and other places where we could get prime food and drinks. We would eat filet mignon—I liked creamed spinach with mine—smoke $10 cigars, talk about the deals we closed or wished we had. We would always talk about women. It was a typical, though expensive, boys'-night-out scene, sometimes costing me more than $1,000 but worth every penny. I really enjoyed it and it did wonders for morale. I needed those guys to be loyal to me, and they were. Afterward we would go home, some alone, some a little more lucky, and think about how we would make our next million.

About three of those short, angled, downtown blocks from our office on Exchange Place was a topless bar called the Pussycat Lounge. It was directly across the street from the American Stock Exchange. In 1987, at the age of twenty-seven, I had seen the inside of many executive boardrooms, the inside of expensive limousines, and the inside of some fabulous villas and mansions, but only once before had I ever been inside a topless joint. I had always figured them to be tacky and tasteless. Definitely not for me.

That all changed one Friday when the winning guys said to me, "Jay, instead of going to Delmonico's we want to go to the Pussycat Lounge." I was really surprised. "What! Are you out of your minds?" I said. "We are not going to the Pussycat Lounge!"

Truthfully, my first reaction was born out of selfishness. I enjoyed the Friday dinners and storytelling. I wanted the good meal, not some watered-down drinks in a a sleazy joint. So, because I was the head cheese we went again to Delmonico's.

But that next week all I heard were complaints. My family was griping. The guys charged me with only thinking about myself. They wanted to go to the Pussycat. My efforts at morale building were in jeopardy. Finally, I gave in. "Look guys, if that is what you want, I'll make you happy. We'll go to the Pussycat and I'll pick up the tab," I told them.

So the next Friday afternoon we walked into the Pussycat Lounge. It was a moment that would change my life and have an impact on New York nightlife that at that time could not be imagined.

The Pussycat was an old-fashioned, diner-type place. It had a stainless-steel facade beneath a green awning. You could not see through its doors and windows, which were covered with a thick, greenish paint. Right away the place made me uncomfortable. I felt like I was entering a Times Square joint, with its B-girls and drug dealing. Inside there were three gigantic old chandeliers and huge mirrors smeared with some kind of mysterious grease. On a long stage behind the bar eight women go-go-danced, mostly to seventies disco.

The women ranged in looks from two huge broads right near the door who looked as if the Twin Towers had gotten on stage to two at the far end who were genuine knockouts. They all wore cheap, sequined bikinis that fit them badly. It was not a pretty sight.

We made our way past the bar, past a 350-pound black guy who told us in an incredibly scratchy voice to "step right in fellas, step right in."

In a way I felt like I was stepping into my past. When I was a student at New York University in the seventies, I worked as a bouncer in some of the hottest restaurants and clubs the city had to offer, places like Max's Kansas City and the Lone Star Cafe. Then, I was a tough, young guy, a member of the college power-lifting team—that's why I got those bouncer jobs. So, I knew that if a place needed a 350-pound thug at the door, there was a potential for trouble. That was a world I had put behind me, and I honestly was not thrilled to be back. But I had given in to the idea, and I noticed that my colleagues did not share my anxieties.

Instantly they were fixated on the women. They stared wide-eyed, like kids in a toy store. We were all dressed to the nines—the Wall Street look of 1987: $800 double-breasted suits, cuff links, gold watches, Ferragamo loafers, $30 socks from Barneys purchased ten at a time. It was the look taken on by the Michael Douglas character, Gordon Gekko, in the film *Wall Street*, the look that was forever associated with mindless greed and slimy deceit. And, let me point out, that's how everyone in the place was dressed. The Pussycat Lounge may have been a first cousin to the Times Square hustle joints, but the clientele were strictly top-drawer. About two hundred guys from the American Stock Exchange—bond traders, brokers, guys who earned six-figure commissions and made their clients rich—were packed into the crummy dive. And in all fairness there were no B-girls and there was no drug selling. Everyone just seemed to be having a great time.

In the midst of my shock, my calculator mind began humming. I started counting the house. I figured there was about twenty-five hundred square feet packed with big spenders. With beers in hand, they fought their way to the stage behind the bar to stuff money into the bikini bottoms of the unenthusiastic dancers, who showed less flesh than an average housewife at Jones Beach. That may have been a blessing, because many of them were less attractive than the average housewife.

My group, eight of us that night, finally squeezed into the middle of the bar and I gave the drink orders. I called for a couple of Budweisers, a double rock 'n' rye, someone asked for something silly like Pimm's and tonic, which of course they did not have, and I ordered my usual Myers's dark rum and coke, no lime. I got Bacardi and coke with a lime.

But who really cared about the drinks. My guys were in a state of highway hypnosis, although instead of staring at the white line they were fixated on eight undulating dancing girls who were almost ten feet away from them. Their jaws were slack as they reached into their wallets for bills to press into the girls' pants—if they could reach them.

Now, I did say that two of those dancers were great-looking, and I kept wondering what they were doing in such a shit hole. They could have been in the pages of *Playboy*, and yet they were there. One was a Latin-looking girl. She was very slim and had long black hair almost down to her waist. The second was straight out of the cornfields. Her hair was very light blonde, about shoulder-length, and she had bright blue eyes. Both wore French-cut bikini bottoms and nothing else. The Latin girl had small, very shapely breasts; her friend from Iowa had large melons, the kind men love to squeeze. I wondered if they had choices, if there was a better place for them.

And I have to admit that while I appreciated the two women, I also watched the cash registers: five gleaming silver, old-fashioned, noncomputerized NCR registers behind the bar. I was trying to count how much money was being taken in by each bartender. It was just incredible. I could not keep track. Drink after drink, the cash poured in. In the hour and a half I spent at the bar, I estimated that two thousand drinks were bought at $4 a drink. The service was terrible, the bartenders were rude; they didn't even serve what you wanted. The only food available was cold pizza from a place next door. But no one gave a damn.

That following week I was going nuts. I have to admit that for a guy who took great pains to avoid strip joints and topless bars, I found the Pussycat to be great fun. The freewheeling atmosphere of the place was infectious. It had nothing to do with being horny.

There was no sex allowed in the place, which did not even try to create the idea that personal relations with the girls were possible. Hell, they were six feet away from the longest arm at the bar. They only moved closer to make it easier for the guys to stuff money in their worn-out, old bikini bottoms. It was just fun. Anyone who expected it to be different would be greatly disappointed.

But it was something else that continued to gnaw at me about the place, and this was due to my particular personality, which at the time was more directed at making money than making love—that the owners of the Pussycat had to be making a fortune. I wondered, because I am always looking to take things to the next level, how much of a fortune they could make if they cleaned up the joint.

What if they carpeted—I mean good carpet—added some decent food, and actually trained the staff to pursue profits greater than they were making. And, what if the women were better-looking! I knew they could make even more money. And I knew my Wall Street broker buddies would be the perfect clientele for such an upscale version of the Pussycat Lounge, that they would eat it up. Little did I realize the seed had been planted firmly in my mind that four years later would become Scores, the nightclub of the nineties.

Over the next few days, every time the subject of the Pussycat came up with my office crew, I would launch into a monologue about how I missed having a good steak and wondered why I could not have both. Tits and ass and wine and perfume, with some dinner and candlelight thrown in.

I bored everyone with my theory about how much more money could be made by throwing in a little class, more still by throwing in a lot of it. Why run a dive when you could make more money by running a nicer place?

But I was all talk and no action until about three weeks later, when something happened that set me on the course that would lead me to opening night at Scores.

It was the day that Joe Wilson won our contest for Broker of the Month. Now normally, for such an achievement, I would send the winner to Atlantic City with his family, maybe the Poconos skiing; something like that. I'm not a gambler but I liked Atlantic City. I loved being around the action. I could watch craps games for hours, sharing the adrenaline rushes with the high rollers as they bet small fortunes on a roll of the dice. I would not do that with my money, but I was always happy to cheer them on with theirs. I loved the atmosphere of people spending big bucks and having a good time. Even back in college, I worked in nightclubs while my classmates waited tables or baby-sat kids in sleep-away camps.

Anyway, Joe Wilson had a different request. He wanted to take all the guys out to a local watering hole for drinks, and then he wanted to return to the office and have a stripper dance on his desk while he called clients. I had never realized what a horny bunch of guys my brokers were. I was shocked. What possessed this man to think this way? This was a serious brokerage office. Clients relied on us to protect their investments. They would not have been pleased to learn we were watching dancing girls while they thought we were watching the Dow Jones ticker.

But Joe insisted, and he got some of the other guys to back him up, until I finally thought it would be more of a morale problem if I did not give in. Joe was a hell of a great broker, and it was in the best interest of the company to keep him happy. And I admit that in the back of my mind I thought we might be able to get one of those good-looking girls from the Pussycat Lounge. So, I said okay.

Of course, I had no idea how to get a stripper to come up to my office, so I turned that part of the job over to my excellent secretary. She actually found one; I still do not know how. Maybe she called "Dial a Stripper" or someplace like that. At any rate, about two hours later this pretty good-looking woman, Stacy a thin-brunette, wearing heels, a short skirt and neat white blouse, and carrying a boom box, arrived at the office. Make note of the date: It was Monday, October 19, 1987.

My secretary explained to the young woman what we wanted, and pretty quickly she got up on Joe's desk and, to some loud disco music coming from the boom box, began to dance, slowly, with a lot of hip and leg movement. And, of course, she began to strip. As she hiked her skirt up, showing off her great legs and revealing the well-toned thighs above her stockings, Joe almost fainted. He was in a state of near orgasm, trying to look up her skirt. I don't know what he was saying to the client on the phone, who had to be hearing the music and the ranting of the rest of the guys. Surprisingly, the female members of the staff were also clearly enjoying the spectacle.

Pretty soon all the brokers in the office, about fifty of them, were crowding around Joe's desk. And as the dancer let her blouse drop to the floor, the Dow dropped eight points. But nobody was at their computer screens and nobody noticed that the Standard & Poor's Index, which we traded, was on that day going, down, down, down. It wasn't until Stacy was down to her skimpy black lace bra and panties that I realized the market had dived into an historic crash.

Wall Street was in a Dow Jones free-fall. We did not know how bad at first, but it has become known as the same kind of cataclysmic event that occurred thirty years before. It was Black Friday, 1987.

Now, in the midst of this chaos—and I don't mean on Wall Street—the head of the firm walked in with a famous, wealthy real estate developer. I quickly prepared some answers to questions I thought they would ask about how we were going to survive this disastrous day. When they came in, though, they immediately noticed—how could they not have?—the crowd around Joe's desk. They heard the screaming. The two of them walked toward my desk and took a quick look at the sinking line on the displayed graph. They, of course, knew already that the Dow was plummeting. All over the street people were looking to cover their asses, and in my office we were cheering for Stacy to uncover hers. I was sure the old man would think I was some kind of degenerate and would run me out of town.

So what happened? These two wheeler-dealers who stood to lose millions of dollars that day joined the crowd around Joe's desk. Of course, the crowd parted for them, and they were soon standing within a deep breath of Stacy. And as she threw her hip in his direction, my boss started stuffing $10 bills in her panties. We were facing riots in the streets and the whole office was hypnotized from watching this woman take off her clothes.

Freud said it and I have believed it ever since that afternoon: *The two strongest forces are the sex drive and the fear of death.* I knew then that if somehow I could push either one of those buttons, I would have the strongest motivational tool possible.

If something was powerful enough to draw people away from the calamity of this October 19th, then there was money to made from it. So, as the Dow continued downward for the next several months and I read this trend as a protracted recession, I began thinking of going into a business that would be strong in a depressed economy. No real estate, no mutual funds. I remembered an old Depression-era slogan: "Win or lose—drink the booze." When things were hard people sought to have a good time. The seed that had been planted in the Pussycat Lounge now had its fertile environment in which to grow.

Seeing firsthand what took place in my office on Black Friday convinced me I knew what that good time could be. I could provide a place where men who faced the increasing stresses of the late twentieth century could escape for a few hours. A place where choices and options were clear-cut, a place where "feminism" was a dirty word, a place where a man could be a man.

There was no question in my mind that I had a winner. I decided to do it. I did not make any speeches, I just got to work. When I commit to something, I keep that commitment. I decided it was something I was going to do and make happen.

Now, four years and $9 million later, Scores was without a cabaret license and minutes away from its much-ballyhooed grand opening.

Then, at five minutes to five, like in a scene from a B movie, an out-of-breath, $350-an-hour lawyer burst through the club's outer door. In his right hand he waved a piece of paper. "Jay, Jay," he screamed, "I got it." He shoved the cabaret license into my hand, and in a minute the most precious document I have ever possessed was tacked up on the wall over my desk. Quickly, I put my anxiety behind me and went out to check the crowd.

The "crowd," however, consisted of three construction workers, who for four months, had been watching Scores being renovated from their job site across the street under the 59th Street Bridge.

The doorman did not want to let them in because they were wearing their work clothes: jeans, boots, and sweatshirts—not exactly in accordance with our dress code of jacket and tie. But there was no one else waiting to get in, so I overruled the doorman and let them in. They headed straight for the bar and with the order of three beers became my first paying customers. As they settled in, the first group of dancers took up their positions around the club and the deejay cranked up the music. Welcome to Scores!!!

For fifteen minutes, three of the most beautiful and scantily clad women in New York danced to an empty house. They danced to pop rock standards selected to remind the customers of their youth before mortgages and careers had taken their minds off sex; to remind them of the days when the bodies of their girlfriends were still firm, slim, and forbidden fruit. The construction workers caught on right away. The smiles on their faces, the gleams in their eyes, showed me they understood what Scores was about: Lay back and enjoy it!!!

Then a few guys in suits walked in, followed by a few more. Soon a dancer named Joy was invited to a table to give a private performance for a thirty-something guy with a fistful of $5 bills. An atmosphere was beginning to form—but not the crowd I had hoped for. I knew things would pick up around 8 P.M. when the invited guests—ballplayers, society types, and the media—would show up. But I also knew those were not the people I would need to support Scores after opening night.

I was on an emotional roller coaster. Where were my Wall Street brokers, the guys who packed the Pussycat Lounge? The guys who would think they could talk these fabulous women out of their T-bars, the guys who sold fantasies to pensioners, the guys who think they rule the universe? Where were the guys who were going to make me and my Brokers in Bikinis rich?

At six o'clock I walked out into the street. I looked west toward the station for the number 4, Lexington Avenue line, the subway that ran to Wall Street. What I saw was a mob of young men in expensive suits, attaché cases in their hands and Burberry trench coats draped over their arms, walking toward me. I recognized them immediately. The gold Rolex crowd was heading to my club.

By ten o'clock that night more than two thousand men had jammed into Scores. Taxis and limos pulled up constantly. Liquor poured through the computerized booze guns, steaks were grilled, T-bars overflowed with cash. The crowd was in the promised land. For the first time in New York, their fantasies were exposed before them, just a hot breath away, in surroundings fit for royalty. I watched over this scene and knew that at that moment, on that Halloween day, I was . . . the King of Clubs.

CHAPTER 2 Studio 54

Right off the bat I want to tell you about one of the worst nights of my life in nightclubs. It was the night I got shot. During the fall of 1979 I was working as a bouncer in the fabled restaurant-nightclub Max's Kansas City, on Seventeenth Street and Park Avenue South. Today on that site is a Korean deli, but the neighborhood has become home to some of the most trendy restaurants in the city, places where the young advertising executives and models hang out. But in the seventies it was a rougher neighborhood populated by streetwalkers and dime-bag drug dealers. Max's was a place that needed a bouncer.

Actually it had a team of bouncers, mostly guys I booked through a bouncer agency I'd started the year before. I got my friends, most of them brutes from the New York University powerlifting team, a lot of work. They got paid, and I got a piece of the action. So everybody was happy.

Well, that particular night I was actually working a shift myself, and my six-foot, two-hundred-pound solid-muscle body was getting a workout. Max's clientele was on the rough-trade side. They were biker types in thick leather jackets and engineer boots. They liked the music on the jukebox and the cheap steak and lobster dinners. The girls were rough types, too. There were some college girls looking for a walk on the wild side, but there were also many working girls who were bored during the day and liked to swing at night. Some of these girls were real troublemakers. They would wear these really short skirts and sit on the bar stools just daring someone other than their boyfriend to look at them. That would cause a lot of stupid fights. There would also be fights over the low-level drug dealing that went on among that crowd. Sometimes it would just be irrational, drunken shit that caused a brawl.

That evening it seemed a fight broke out every five minutes. The way we handled things was that a bouncer should never have to take on anyone alone. The whole bouncer team would jump into the fray to overwhelm the troublemakers. So I was bruised and sore by midnight.

Later that night, while we were escorting a group of five or six stoned punks down the street away from the club, a car came screeching around Seventeenth Street and someone fired a few shots out the window. We all ducked, and the girls in the bar screamed while everyone scattered. As I hit the ground, while I felt a pinch in my left shoulder; then it felt like it was burning.

Because it was a cool night, and also because my bouncer team liked to affect a tough image, I was wearing a black leather jacket and two sweatshirts underneath. I ripped the jacket open and tore at the sweatshirts until I found the cause of my distress. I was bleeding from a bullet wound in my left shoulder. A friend from the club who came running into the street when he heard the shots and all the screaming threw me into his car, and we drove quickly across town to Mother Cabrini Hospital's emergency room.

To the doctors there that wound was hardly something to write home about, and in a few minutes they had removed a .25-caliber bullet and patched me. The police, of course, were notified, but no one ever came around to question me about it. The shooter was never identified. He could have been someone who came into the club every night; I'll never know. But the important thing is that that incident did nothing to dampen my desire to become involved in the world of nightclubs.

For a college kid I was I having some unusual experiences in those days. For instance, at the time, I was pretty much living with a girl named Liz. I was nineteen, she was twenty-five. She was one of those women who had to try everything.

I arrived at her apartment around five one morning to find her and her downstairs neighbor, a younger girl named Mary, making love in the bathtub. They had tripped on mescaline and had got it in their minds to dye themselves green. What a sight it was to see them rolling around in green food dye, licking and kissing each other as the shower poured down on them. They did not skip a beat when I got undressed and joined them. We spent about five fantastic hours in that bathtub. But that was the kind of life I was living then. I was ready, willing, and able to partake of any opportunity.

It was an attitude that had led me, the summer before I got shot, to seek out Studio 54.

In the seventies and eighties Studio 54 was the place where the Beautiful People went to dance, drink, and meet each other. In my opinion it was the most important club in New York history—until I opened Scores.

There are important parallels between the two clubs. The two genius club guys, Steve Rubell and Ian Schrager, opened Studio 54 when New York nightlife was in the doldrums. The legendary clubs, the places that defined the word "nightclub," like El Morocco, the Stork Club, and the Copacabana, had run their course. They were places where the elite went to see and be seen, but the live action in their rooms usually revolved around a singer like Frank Sinatra or acts such as Martin and Lewis. The great columnists such as Walter Winchell and Louella Parsons held court in nightclubs on both coasts; for the regular clientele it was a matter of sitting at a table eating, drinking, and watching, but not really being part of the scene. For the media-conscious Beautiful People—Andy Warhol and his crowd; Liza Minnelli and her followers; Bianca Jagger, who became a goddess of Studio 54—the old nightclubs were just too quiet.

Studio 54 was a place where the wife of the prime minister of a great Western country was caught on camera dancing without underwear. It was a place where even famous people could not get in without the okay of Rubell, who stood at its door like St. Peter at the Gate deciding who would get a shot at heaven and who would have to settle for the hell of a lesser club like Max's or Xenon or, God forbid, the Limelight. As Scores would do more than a decade later, Studio 54 came along just when New York needed it.

The first person I met who had actually been to Studio 54 was Stan, an accountant who worked for my father's very prestigious firm. My father was a very important man in the world of international business, and I always felt—although, like all sons, never readily admitted—that I got my business acumen from him. Of course, I was always a little more adventurous.

Stan entered my life while I was still at NYU, before I became involved with Max's. I was working part-time at my dad's firm. Most of the time I could be found at the NYU gym working out with weights, learning martial arts, and doing a little bit of boxing. I was a tough kid. When people looked at me they didn't see the straight-A student of the NYU business school, they saw a jock. I looked like one of those marine recruits whom drill sergeants call "young, dumb, and full of cum." Well, looks can be deceiving. It has always been a business advantage to me that people do not immediately take me for a thinking man, but I was never dumb.

Anyway, things at my father's office were usually boring. Basically, I was filing, running errands, and doing some flirting with the young legal assistants and secretaries. The most fun during the day would be listening to this guy Stan talk about his nights on the town. He would always seek me out for talk. I guess he kissed up to me because I was the boss's son and he wanted to be a partner. Little did he know my father!

Stan would brag about who he knew and where he went. He claimed to be friends with Jackie Onassis and Nickey Hilton of the hotel family. As an eighteen-year-old college kid from Queens, I did not know a thing about the level of society Stan talked about. And I wasn't particularly impressed. My family was well-off, and I was used to being around successful people.

But when Stan talked about Studio 54, he really got my attention. That was a place I read about in the newspapers. That was a place Farrah Fawcett went to. There was a picture of her in the *Daily News* dancing at Studio 54. She was wearing little more than a slip. All around her people seemed to be having the time of their lives. To me Studio 54 was a magical place. It was the kind of club I wanted to go to. I hated the bars we hung out at in Queens, and I did not care much for the neighborhood girls. Farrah Fawcett was the kind of woman I wanted. She fit into the fantasies my overworked teenage libido developed one after another. I was still smarting from my breakup with the first love of my life, a girl I met in high school. Emotionally I was not ready for another serious affair, but Farrah Fawcett, come on . . . who needed to be serious! I would have given anything to be in the same room as her. Wow!

Stan's stories of Studio 54 made that summer for me. But I have to say I did not really believe him. He seemed like a regular guy to me. Heck, he was an accountant, not some screenwriter, or artist, or even aspiring actor. Those were the guys who showed up in the tabloids standing right behind the babes. And everyone knew that it was virtually impossible for a mere regular guy to get into Studio 54. Rubell had created an image for the club that made it seem much more alluring than it really was.

He would stand at the door in the middle of a crowd of people begging for his attention and decide who would get in and who would be left on the street. Men and women, some of them very successful in their fields, would scream, "Steve, pick me, pick me; let me in please." Sometimes they would dress in bizarre and revealing outfits to get his attention. Some girl who sat at a reception desk in a dull law firm all day would open her blouse and bare her breasts to the crowd on West Fifty-fourth Street at night, hoping that Rubell would agree she would add a nice touch to the revelers inside. The crowd outside willingly sacrificed their dignity for a chance to be on the "A" list—to be a regular at Studio 54. Not anyone, they reasoned, could get in there. You had to be special. Stan said he and Rubell had been fraternity brothers at Syracuse University and were very good friends. He offered to take me there some night. I said, "Yeah, sure, thanks." I just did not see the ass-kissing accountant as anyone the great Rubell would let in his club.

One Friday there was a picture of Carly Simon in the paper, and Stan said he was there the night before and had actually talked to her. That afternoon, riding the subway back to Queens, I looked around me at all the working people. I noticed how tired they looked and how hot and sweaty we all were. I thought about how people like Warhol and Calvin Klein and Tom Wolfe and Jack Nicholson worked up their sweat at Studio 54. I imagined myself grinding to the Rolling Stones, with Farrah. I saw myself in the middle of a crowd of poppers. I had an image of Jay Bildstein getting out of a limo and being met on the sidewalk by Steve Rubell.

In the admiring crowd were all the girls in my neighborhood who would not give me the time of day. Getting into Studio 54, in my mind, was like being selected to play center field for the New York Yankees—better, because there were no girls on the Yankees.

But later that evening I was back to the reality of a schoolyard in my neighborhood—shooting hoops with my regular crowd. There was my best friend, Peter, and Jack, both premed students, and Buddy, who was studying at the Wharton School of Business, and Matt, who cared more about music than books.

We were playing half-court basketball the way it is played in any neighborhood in New York—rough. No mercy expected or given. Even among us best friends, in that upper-middle-class neighborhood, basketball was played with a vengeance. It was part of being a street kid in the city. We were all in good shape, and we beat the shit out of each other. What we lacked in finesse and skill we made up for in desire. As usual, I was pissing everyone off by running my mouth. Way before it became fashionable in the NBA, bad-mouthing was a requirement on the courts at PS 188.

After the game, sitting on the bench under the one tree the yard had to offer and drinking sodas, the talk invariably turned to women. That night I dominated the conversation as I verbalized my Studio 54 fantasies and told my friends about this guy Stan who actually danced with Carly Simon and saw her tits. The conversation got pretty gross, with all of us bragging about what we would do if we met Liza Minnelli or Cheryl Tiegs on the dance floor at 54. We would show them what real men could do; they'd never go back to those twerpy models and actors they were now hanging out with. At least that's what we thought. Or *claimed* we thought.

Our behavior as that night went on was as adolescent as our thoughts. We went to Jahn's, the famous ice cream parlor, and ordered the Kitchen Sink, which had enough ice cream for ten people. Before we left we made sure to unscrew the caps on the salt and pepper shakers so the next people who used them would ruin their food. Then we trashed the men's room. That was what I was about in those days. A teenage jerk with dreams of screwing Hollywood stars.

After Jahn's, we decided to visit a couple of the bars on Queens Boulevard where we might run into some girls who might, just might, put out. Nobody danced in these neighborhood bars, and the music sucked. We weren't big drinkers, so the scene was pretty depressing. But I always seemed to calm down a little when I was inside a club. Even then I would study the crowd, watch the bartenders, and wonder about how much money could be made in a place like that.

At around nine o'clock I persuaded Peter to drive with me into Manhattan to try some of the bars there. He had the use of his parents' 1977 four-door Chevy Impala for the weekend. Cool we were not. The singles scene was in its heyday in 1978. All along First Avenue there were bars like Maxwell's Plum, T.G.I.F., and Mr. Laff's, where mostly career-minded single men and women could meet each other, or at least exchange phone numbers. At best they could retire to one of their apartments, probably on the East Side, for casual sex. Downtown there were clubs where music set the scene. Fillmore East was still around in the East Village, where harder rock could be listened to, and there were places to smoke dope and drop acid, something we two teenagers from protective homes knew little about. A couple of places in Greenwich Village were still active. And there was Max's. But to my way of thinking these places were hangouts for losers, people without connections, people on the fringes of the real club scene—Studio 54. Everything else was the minor leagues. Such was my sense of values in 1978.

Finally I told Peter that even though I did not think we could get in, I would be happy just to hang out in the street around Studio 54. He looked at me like I was crazy. "That's not a place for us," he said. "Even if we *can* get in, those women will laugh at us. We'll be like a couple of assholes." I was as sensitive as Peter about being the butt of other people's jokes, but I thought that in this case, the potential reward was worth the risk.

"What if we just get a look at Farrah Fawcett or Cheryl Tiegs! Those broads are there every night. Come on. It beats the single bars; we never score there anyway," I argued. I argued and I argued all the way across the 59th Street Bridge and into Manhattan until by the time we reached Lexington Avenue, he gave in.

"Okay, you win. How do I get to the place?" he asked.

That was a good question, because I had no idea where Studio 54 was. So I called Information and got the address. After driving around for about thirty minutes, we found the place. We even found a legal parking spot around the corner on Broadway.

The scene in the street around the club was straight out of a Fellini movie. Peter and I were shocked; we looked at each other in amazement. Usually things do not live up to their advance billing, but that scene was more than we'd imagined.

There were women everywhere, from teenage girls to some a little older who looked like professional models. There were women with their husbands or boyfriends, really beautiful women, wearing the latest sexy styles, the kind of clothes we saw only in ads in *Cosmo* or *Vogue,* when we even looked at those magazines. The clothes were all revealing. There were breasts and legs showing all over the place, everywhere we turned. We got into the middle of the crowd. Everyone was smiling, laughing, and pointing to different people. We heard sighs, and gasps, and "Who's that? Wow! Look at her," as each limo pulled up. I saw Steve Rubell himself part the crowd to usher in some old guy with a great-looking twenty-year-old on his arm.

We saw people in costumes, clown suits, monster masks, and a lot of S&M gear. One girl was naked except for panties, sitting on a guy's shoulders and screaming, "Steve, here I am; pick me, pick me." It dawned on me that many of these people never expected to be picked, that they really were happy just being a part of the crowd. I did not know it, but my nightclub education was really beginning that night.

We stood for more than an hour watching Rubell, every five minutes or so, unhook the velvet rope that separated the chosen from the losers and make a selection for entry. There were women and men in that crowd who would have done anything he asked in order to get in. Without realizing it, Peter and I kind of drifted to the back of the crowd, which actually covered an entire block. We found ourselves, by great coincidence, standing in the doorway of a cleaning store that was owned by Peter's cousin, directly across the street from the Studio 54 entrance. As a game we started counting the number of blondes who emerged from the arriving limos. One stretch job delivered six of the most beautiful women we had ever seen. We were sure they were *Playboy* centerfolds. They had to be. No other women looked like that. Boy, did we have a lot to learn.

Then the most incredible thing happened—something that changed my life forever. We did not notice him coming through the crowd, but suddenly Steve Rubell was standing in front of Peter and me. We were stunned.

"You guys want to come in?" he asked, in such a quiet, unassuming voice that he might have been offering us a cigarette.

We were too stunned to answer. We could not respond.

I remember this like it was yesterday. Rubell then smiled and said: "Come on, follow me."

We followed. Like the two dumb stooges we were, we followed him as the crowd parted and he unhooked the velvet rope, letting us into heaven. We entered the greatest club room in the history of nightclubs. We were too dumbstruck to even say thank you.

There I stood in a powder blue T-shirt, painter's pants, and Puma sneakers in a room filled with tuxedos, evening gowns, diamonds, and Chanel No. 5. To me this was greater than being welcomed in the clubhouse at Yankee Stadium. I turned around to say something to Peter and found myself standing next to Margaux Hemingway. She was close enough to touch. She, of course, paid no attention to me, but who cared. Peter wandered off toward the bar.

On the dance floor, the Beautiful People were moving to Jefferson Starship. It was my favorite band, and I had been disappointed earlier in the week when I could not get tickets to their performance at the Nassau Coliseum.

"I love this; I love this music," I said to no one in particular.

A gorgeous woman—much older than me, I thought, but probably not even thirty-five,—actually responded.

"It's great, isn't it," she said. "You know they're here tonight."

Jefferson Starship was there. I was in the same building as Grace Slick! I grabbed Peter and we went searching for her. We started at the bar and made our way through the entire main room and all the upstairs nooks and crannies. We didn't find Grace, but upstairs we actually saw the Starship guitarist, Craig Chaquico. I talked to him. I told him how great he was. He was so nice. He said he was sorry we missed the concert. He said it like he really cared. It was like we were buddies, pals from the real world.

Then I turned around and saw, of all people, Stan, the ass-kissing accountant. He was there, just like he said he would be. He introduced me to Nicky Hilton. He introduced me to everybody. I guess he really was Rubell's pal. Stan was a part of the scene. I would never look at him the same way again. He had risen a gizillion points in my estimation.

Stan led me to the famous circular bar and ordered two Wild Turkeys on the rocks. One was for me. Next to me was a knockout Latin-looking woman who had to be a model. She was so exotic, merely sitting on a bar stool like this was just another night in her boring life. I could not get my eyes unglued from her breasts, which were almost totally exposed at the top of a little white blouse. Her skirt was little more than a handkerchief. No stockings, just perfectly tanned legs and white high heels. Stan, I noticed, was checking out her legs, and he did this really cool move with his hand as he left us alone. He had the guts to kind of brush her thigh and say, "Hi, good to see you.'" My God, he touched her. My God, she let him.

Somehow I got up the nerve to say, "Hi." There I was in my schoolyard clothes. I had not even showered since playing basketball. She was perfect. I babbled away.

"My name is Jay . . . first time here . . . Steve brought me in. You know Stan, he's a good friend. . . just was talking to Craig upstairs . . . couldn't catch him at the Coliseum . . . Grace isn't here . . . not feeling too great tonight . . . my friend and I have been really checking the place out . . . I'm a power lifter . . . you workout?" My eyes implored her to answer; my body language begged for her. And while I babbled on a guy, an older guy in a great suit, came up on the other side of her and kissed her cheek.

"What are you drinking tonight?" he asked her.

"Brandy Alexander" was all she replied. But I'll never forget the way she said it. I'd never heard two more beautiful words in my life. The old guy pulled out a fistful of hundreds and paid for the drinks. She—I never did get her name,—slowly turned on the bar stool and moved into his world. I bet that to this day if you hypnotized her and brought her back to that moment, she would not remember that I'd stood next to her, a young buck of an eighteen-year-old in such heat that he would have passed out if she'd just once looked his way. Later I tried to explain to Peter how she said "Brandy Alexander," but he just could not appreciate it. Little did I know that in a few years my life would be so filled with women like that that I would have to fight them off.

After the brush-off, however, I was ready to leave. I found Peter making a game of trying to look up Margaux's skirt. As we headed toward the door. Rubell stopped us. Out of nowhere he appeared and struck up a conversation. He asked if we'd had a good time and where we were from. He told us to ask for him anytime we came back. Then he put his hand on my arm and asked if I would come down with him to his private room in the basement. I was appalled. I knew exactly what he was getting at and wanted to break his jaw. I think he read my reaction, and he backed off. He smiled shyly and told us to have a good night and very graciously reminded us to come back.

So, in a way that wonderful evening ended on a downer, as did Rubell and Schrager's entire Studio 54 experience—they both ended up doing time for tax evasion. It is interesting to me that the club that made such a great impression on me, that helped me decide what I would do with my future, ultimately evolved into one of Scores's imitators, a place called Cabaret Royale.

Whatever its eventual fate, Studio 54 woke up New York nightlife when it was needed most. A decade later I would surpass Rubell's greatest accomplishments. I would bring the sexiest women in the country to work in New York and deliver the city's nightclub industry from a deep economic slump.

CHAPTER 3 Alicia

The day after the stock market crash—Black Monday of 1987—I found myself in a state of shock with the worst hangover I ever had. After Stacy the Stripper left, with about $500 stuffed into her French-cut panties, the boss read us the riot act. He was gracious, not blaming us for the intolerable losses our clients had suffered that day; but he knew bad times were ahead, and he told us so.

Privately, he told me that he did not think we could continue with the staff we had and that I would have to lay some guys off. This was one aspect of management I dreaded. That evening, without any discussion of it, we all went to the Pussycat and drank ourselves under the table. It was the first and last time in my life I drank in order to divert my mind from genuine troubles.

For the next few days I was a zombie; I walked around in a daze. Reading the *Wall Street Journal* made me sick. Moneywise, I was healthy. I was never a big gambler in the market or in real estate. I got my satisfaction from being able to pass on my knowledge and instinct to clients, and I enjoyed watching them make money. Of course, the commissions did not hurt.

One thing I noticed: when I told my friends and family about how disastrous a day October 19, 1987 was and about the scene in my office, they invariably wanted to know more about Stacy the Stripper. "Well, how much did she make that day?" everyone would ask. After telling my tale of woe to one of my best friends, his immediate reply was "How can I get in touch with that stripper? Was she really good-looking?"

It began to dawn on me that an economics professor at NYU, who generally was a bore, knew what he was talking about when he'd formulated a theory called the Inelasticity of Demand. What he meant was that there are certain things humankind will always need—for example, things like insulin for diabetics, a cure for typhus or whatever other disease is plaguing the world at the time, and products like toilet paper and soap. He referred to those things as goods and services that people would buy at any price.

Sitting in my dreary Wall Street office a week after the crash, I added something to that list that my professor probably knew about but did not deem necessary to pass on to his youthful students. That item was *sex*. If nothing else, Stacy the Stripper drove that lesson home to me. Sex appeal, sensuality, pretty women, the fantasy of a sexual relationship with an otherwise unreachable woman was something that men could not resist—the men I was thinking about anyway, the men whom Tom Wolfe called the Masters of the Universe. I was thinking of the men who risked millions of dollars a day, high-powered, supercharged men who spent thousands on suits and dinners and thought they could have anything they wanted. Usually they were right, but, I saw an officeful of those men—albeit young ones and not yet Masters, but on their way—throw their hard-earned money at a woman they could not have. I know that at least three of the guys in the office tried for Stacy's private number and failed. But she left them with a dream, if only because she told each one of them that she thought he was really cute.

Despite the ups and downs of the economy, beautiful women are always in demand. Speakeasy whorehouses flourished during the Depression. Entire neighborhoods in Chicago and New York and even some small cities survived because there were men who were willing to spend their money in pursuit of a fantasy, no matter how hard they worked for that money or how sorry they might feel the next day about the way they threw it away.

I reasoned that if I could put the right women together with the right men in the right setting, I could weather any economic storm. I know I am not the first man to have had this idea. Some may call it pimping. And, sure, there have been luxurious whorehouses catering to wealthy sportsmen and businessmen since time began.

But I have to tell you that from the first nanosecond of my idea, I wasn't thinking about the men having sex with these women. What I envisioned was a spiffed-up Pussycat Lounge. The fantasy, I thought, was what these guys were really interested in. I saw in my mind the world's greatest gentlemen's club. A club that would be the inner sanctum of *man*kind. It would be a place where boys could be boys. Where they could watch sports on television, even shoot some hoops, while eating fine food and drinking top-drawer booze, in the company of the most exquisite women in the world.

I saw a place where these captains of commerce and industry could leave their business at the door and enter a world that existed only in the pages of *Playboy* and *Penthouse* magazines. I knew I could use the egos of these men to make myself rich. And I knew that those men would leave the club each night perfectly content without having had a physical union with the women. For the most part my target clientele were married. They were not as much interested in the physical act as in the mental exercise. This club would be safe for them. They would not catch AIDS, and they could honestly say they were there to watch the ball games on the dozens of screens I envisioned surrounding the action. The women would be an added attraction. The women would make them feel like the hotshots they knew they were.

I saw this idea as an opportunity for the women. I realized we were living in an era of increased assertiveness in women. They could earn thousands of dollars a night in my club. They could compete mentally with the greedy yuppies who inhabited the 1980s.

I knew that three of the guys in my office had asked Stacy for her phone number and that she'd given them all the same answer. "You're really cute. Hey, maybe next time," she told them. "Maybe next time." Those three words, I thought, could earn more money for the girls of my nightclub in one night than any number of tricks turned in a four-poster bed in the most luxurious brothel in New York. The men would leave my club with their fantasies intact. "Next time I get that baby's phone number. Then it's dinner. Then I bed the bitch," they would tell themselves as they stuffed $20 bill after $20 bill into her garter to keep their fantasies alive.

But I want to be very clear about something. While I was not planning a sex club, neither did I have in mind a "champagne hustle" joint. I was a victim of the champagne hustle once during the summer I worked for my father after graduating from high school and waiting to enter college, and I found it totally distasteful and demeaning for everyone involved. I did not want to be associated with anything like that, and I did not want to do business with women who would earn their living that way.

That summer, my job mostly consisted of running errands and doing filing. Several times while out on errands I passed a place called the Horse's Rail. It was on Forty-fifth Street between Sixth and Seventh Avenues, just on the edge of Times Square. A neon sign in one window promised "sophisticated entertainment for the discerning gentleman."

Anyone but a horny teenager would have made out the place as a low-life dive. But at that time in my life I was a hormone hurricane. My friends called me Phallus Man and so on that day I threw caution to the wind and became a "discerning gentleman." I paid $5 at the door and walked in.

Inside it was dark and reeked of stale cigarette smoke and cheap liquor. Of course, I thought that was a very adult, sophisticated atmosphere, and I put on my best "grown-up face." There was a long bar and against one wall, there were some booths. Behind the bar was a stage and a dancer, who would have been dancing in the dark except for a small spotlight shining on her. She was wearing something dark that to me looked like a daring bathing suit. Eventually she took her top off to reveal a really unattractive pair of breasts. She seemed undernourished, probably the result of booze or drugs. She wore fishnet stockings. She was doing floor work—that is, she lay on her back, throwing her hips into the air, slowly gyrating them to what sounded like Barry White, though I could not be sure. I was turned on.

At the bar were three women and one other guy. He was staring at the dancer, nursing a beer. The women were staring off somewhere. No one was talking. Before I even sat down the bartender was in front of me asking what I wanted. I ordered a beer. By the way, this was all totally illegal. I was not yet eighteen years old. But I had been allowed in the bars in my neighborhood for a year or so and I never thought about being carded.

I was nervous and excited as I watched the dancer. I figure she was about twenty, a dark-skinned girl, probably Hispanic, and despite her breasts, she did have a nice figure. But between the bathing suit and the fishnets, very little of her actual skin was visible, and the lack of lighting left the eroticism to my imagination.

My imagination was working overtime when Gretchen slinked over to me. She got on the stool next to mine and asked me my name. I told her it was Steve. She said it was her favorite name and gently placed her hand on my thigh. The fire was lit. All of a sudden, this thirtyish, very tired-looking, washed-out blonde became quite attractive to me.

In a flash, the mutant bartender was back asking if I wanted to "buy the lady a drink." I hesitated until Gretchen said if I didn't, she could not sit with me. That should have been my warning to leave, but instead the threat had the desired effect on me and I forked over $6 for a "champagne cocktail." I just wanted her hand back on my thigh.

My excitement level was rising.

Gretchen took one sip of that $6 drink and moved her hand toward my crotch. "You know, Stevie, we could go to a room in the back and have a real good time if you bought us a bottle of champagne."

"The back . . . a real good time!!!" Those were the words I'd been dying to hear. "Bring me a bottle of your best, "I said to the bartender as Gretchen took me by the hand and led me toward the back room.

The back room was even darker than the front. The bartender was waiting by a small booth with a bottle of "Château Dirty Feet," which cost me $60. (I did not normally carry so much money with me, but my father had insisted I buy a new suit to start school, and I had planned to do so that evening with the $100 he'd given me when I arrived at the office that day.) Gretchen and I slid into the booth, which was upholstered in some kind of burgundy-colored vinyl. Soon she was all over me—well, all over me in the sense that she actually sat with her thighs touching mine and her hand occasionally toying with my earlobe. She had a thing for earlobes.

She was looking better and better to me, and eventually I worked up the courage to put my hand on her knee. That's when my little fantasy came crumbling down.

"You know, Stevie, we can't actually do anything, you know, like sex, back here, even though I really like you and all," Gretchen said just as I was about to bust my Levi's.

If there had been any light at all in that room I'm sure Gretchen would have seen me turn red from head to toe. I was totally humiliated. There I was stroking this dirty blonde wig, drinking mouse-fart booze, and expecting to get lucky, at a cost of almost $100, with a tired old B-girl. And she shoots me down in flames. This, you see, is the "champagne hustle."

Quickly, I countered with one of the most stupid retorts I've ever delivered in my life. "Oh, I didn't expect anything," I said. "I'm a sociology student. I'm doing a paper on these types of establishments, and I just wanted to interview you."

I was desperate to maintain some dignity, some sense that I was not the biggest asshole in New York. I guess where there is an erection there is vanity. Anyway, Gretchen was a businesswoman. She told me she would tell me everything I wanted to know . . . but I would have to buy another bottle of champagne. I crawled out of the booth and, trying to look cool, walked out of the Horse's Rail forever. The sunlight outside had never been harsher. Worse still, I had to borrow $100 from a pal in order to buy that suit. Of course, I told my friend that Gretchen had given it up because I was about the coolest guy she'd ever met in a place like that. I had no idea how often I would hear lines like that in the coming years.

So as I began my quest to open the world's greatest gentlemen's club, to make Hugh Hefner look like the bartender at the Horse's Rail, the only experience I had to draw upon was my brief and distasteful encounter with Gretchen, my couple of nights at the Pussycat Lounge, and of course the eye-opening session with Stacy the Stripper.

I began to pay less and less attention to my banking business. Every spare moment I found myself thinking about my dream club. At work I drew pictures in my head of the decor. When I looked at women I tried to imagine them as topless dancers. I was not as much undressing them with my eyes as I was dressing them in my mind. I looked at women in jeans, business suits, jogging clothes and tried to imagine them in evening gowns and wearing fine jewelry.

About two months after Black Monday, I pretty much moved my office to the Pussycat Lounge. It wasn't difficult, since I lived only a few blocks away. I would go either by myself or with some of my brokers. Occasionally I would bring a client who I thought might enjoy the atmosphere. But while they watched the girls, I watched the business.

I tried to count the money going into the registers. I figured profits in my head. I studied the dancers to see how often they rotated and I wondered where they danced when they left the Pussycat. I watched the regular customers to see if I could predict a pattern in their spending—what, for instance, got them to drink more, or what made them give bigger tips, or even what made them send next door for a slice of cold pizza.

The Pussycat was a dive, but it had a certain style that grew on me. The dancers ranged from delicious to dead ugly. The barmaids had some personality and tended to be older than the dancers. The bouncers were rough around the edges, all-business type of guys. They were all black and they dressed like pimps. I thought they'd probably been recruited in prisons. I had no doubt they were armed and would not hesitate to sink a shiv into the ribs of an offending customer, and I'm sure that is exactly the image they meant to portray. But once the bouncers got to know a regular customer, they softened a bit. They were not unlike my crew at Max's Kansas City, except I doubted that any of them attended business school at NYU.

The owner of the Pussycat came in every night around six. He would sit at a table in the back and drink himself to death. He was an unremarkable kind of guy except that he had the biggest potbelly I have every seen on a person. You could tell he was coming into a room five minutes before he arrived. Other than that, he looked like any other businessman. Rumor had it that he'd gotten the Pussycat as a gift from a big mob guy. I never tried to get to know the owner because I reasoned he would not be friendly to the idea of my picking his brain so that I could open my own place and bury him.

What was most significant, though, was that the Pussycat was not a hustle joint. No buy-a-girl-a-drink, no hustle of any kind that I could see. The dancers worked on a stage for thirty minutes at a time. Many would come to the stage in a two-piece bathing suit; the better-looking ones might wear a bra and panties or a sexy bikini. You could recognize a new dancer by her outfit, which would be worn and cheap-looking. As the girls got on the regular payroll and started making money, they would buy more and more expensive costumes. (There was an elderly woman who traveled from bar to bar selling sexy outfits, makeup, and costume jewelry to the girls. She made more money than any of them.) However, no matter what they were wearing, before long the top would come off and they would continue their dance sets topless.

To tip the dancers a customer had to stretch himself across the bar or ask the barmaid to pass the money up to them. The dancers had moves to stimulate tipping. They would catch your eye, then squat down to simulate mounting you. The tips were usually one-dollar bills, sometimes a five, occasionally a ten.

I really did not care for the way the customers at the Pussycat behaved. I thought they made fools of themselves as they leered and gawked and tried to speak to the dancers, who clearly wanted no more from them than their money. I'd see many a millionaire broker acting like a teenager begging a girl to sit with him after her set or to just come a little closer so he could put a $5 bill inside her bikini bottom. It did not make sense to me. I just wasn't about to let my hair down like that. Looking back on those days, I realize that those guys were having a good time. They were more willing than I to leave their inhibitions at the door and to behave the way one is supposed to behave in a seedy topless joint.

My plan was to remain aloof from the dancers. After all, I was there on business. I was the major league scout resigned to spending a few summer evenings at the rookie league in bumfuck Georgia. But that did not mean I had to behave like the local fans.

I was honestly ambivalent about the sensuality of the scene. Sometimes I was tantalized and excited by a certain move put out there by a particularly beautiful dancer, and I might quickly conjure up a scene from the pages of "Penthouse Forum." But when a dancer tried to make eye contact with me, it was a complete turnoff. I was not going to stuff money in her panties. I was not some kind of sucker who couldn't score outside the bar. I was not a pathetic loser like those drooling assholes who came in regularly. At least that is what I told myself. So when a dancer looked at me I would turn away like a shy first grader. Truth of the matter is that I *was* shy.

I was not afraid of women. Hell, I'd been a Manhattan bachelor, a man about town who made a good buck. I loved women. I had dated some truly beautiful career women: brokers, lawyers, an occasional doctor, and one shrink who really got inside me. But I was full of male vanity. I took the lead. Remember that girl at the bar in Studio 54? In my way, I'd gone after her. I'd tried to talk to her while she stared into some distant world that did not include my presence. Because I thought of myself in very traditional male ways, dancers at the Pussycat who tried to come on to me made me uncomfortable. It was not my thing. I would make my move when *I* was ready.

So I employed this stern look and serious demeanor, which I now know grew out of my shyness. But it accidentally worked to my advantage. In contrast to the guys who wanted to be lapdogs for the dancers, I seemed unapproachable. This was a challenge to the smarter dancers. They started flirting with me, winking, making remarks about my aloofness. They saw through me. They knew that despite my $1,000 suit and Rolex watch, I was a bungling, shy kid around the kind of women who fought for survival on the stages of New York's topless clubs.

One day a girl I knew from NYU days showed up on the stage. Her name was Lana. At school she was known as a snob, unapproachable and untouchable. She only dated premed guys and professors. She was gorgeous. Lana looked like what she was: the daughter of a Great Neck psychiatrist. She was about five foot three, maybe 110 pounds soaking wet, but with a great chest. She had long brunette hair, which she wore in a cool ponytail, and had a real sexy but aloof attitude that drove guys wild.

It was the seventies, but she was neither a love child nor an Earth Mother. She was a drama student with her eye on the Broadway stage. I tried several times but could not get close to her. A power-lifting business major did not interest her. People who knew her said she was brilliant, determined, and ready to rip a guy apart emotionally if he did not measure up. Now, however, she was dancing on the ratty stage of the Pussycat, perhaps wearing a better-fitting thong bikini than the other girls but still doing a midafternoon set. The ponytail was gone, replaced by a teased bouffant style that was not nearly as sexy. But when she took off her bikini top, I could not believe my eyes. Her breasts were absolutely perfect. They were gigantic and absolutely perfect. Clearly she'd had breast implants. I could not believe my eyes.

She was enormous—definitely and unnaturally—larger than in her days at NYU.

I was perplexed. Up until then I had not given much thought to the possibility that the dancers were human beings with human emotions, strengths, and frailties. But wondering about how someone like Lana had ended up dancing at the Pussycat made me realize that those girls had lives of their own. Each, I thought, probably had some story to tell.

But I did not linger on such thinking. It is my curse that I am a businessman above all else. I was Jay Bildstein, entrepreneur, not Jay Bildstein, seducer of topless dancers. So it was the barmaids who got most of my attention. They ran the place. They were privy to the secrets I cared most about. I was more interested in learning what kind of cheap rye whiskey sold well than in discovering what forces had led a girl to be dancing under the weak spotlight of a place like the Pussycat. Eventually I would get to know about both, but in those early days I was fixated on the cash flow.

The barmaids became my unwitting teachers about the business of topless dancing. I would deftly ask questions about what was going on in the bar. I asked about revenues, tips, and clients. Most answered in a snap. They thought I was just making small talk.

It was around this time that two people who would play very important roles in my education came into my life. One was an old friend named Bob. He was someone I knew from my neighborhood and from NYU, where we went around the same time. The second person was a barmaid named Alicia.

Bob walked into the Pussycat one day while Lana was dancing. I had not seen him in about four years. It was one of those meaningless things where we'd gotten a little mad at each other and neither had picked up the phone to patch things up. But as soon as he saw me at the bar, it was as if we were the best of friends.

He was there to see Lana. Bob was a great ladies' man. He looked like a Kennedy. He was tall, kept in great shape, had great hair, and possessed a wonderful smile that the girls at NYU could not resist. As we talked, Bob waved to Lana. She nodded back and did a sexy little turn with her shoulder. She was kind of offering her left breast to him.

Bob told me how much he loved topless clubs. He said he spent all his spare time at them and had run into Lana at one in Queens. He said they had dated a few times and were regular sex partners. "Just recreational," he said, "nothing serious." He was surprised that I had not even tried to talk to her. I told him I was surprised that he could actually date these women. "I thought they were untouchable," I said.

"You're wrong," he replied. He then started telling me fantastic stories about the women he met in clubs all over the city. I thought he was full of shit. It seemed like typical braggadocio. I knew him to be great with the ladies, but his stories defied belief.

But we began to meet at the Pussycat regularly, and I watched Bob in action. He did have a style that the girls liked. He did not throw himself at them. He always treated them with respect. He was always upbeat and very complimentary. He tipped them, but not extravagantly. He was such a nice guy, and they appreciated that. In steps, they would first sit at a table with him, then join him for dinner, and eventually date him, and more often than not end up in his apartment in Forest Hills.

Bob took me to topless clubs all over the city. We went to the South Bronx, where the dancers were mostly Latin and black, and sex was available for a price. We went to some places in New Jersey that were usually dives lower than the Horse's Rail, and we went to some so-called upscale clubs on Queens Boulevard where the crowds were more sedate and the women a little better looking. None of the places were anything like what I had in mind for my club. Bob was known in most of the clubs and always seemed able to point to a girl that he'd had sex with.

Just as Lana had made me start thinking differently about the dancers, Bob began changing my mind about the customers. He was anything but a loser with women. He said he dated dancers because they were the sexiest women alive, the closest one could come to the pages of *Penthouse*. He told me I was wrong to think customers never made it with the dancers. Many of the regulars eventually scored, he said; it was just a matter of style.

He said the dancers were worth the chase and worth the money he spent on them. He liked being around them even if he did not score. He loved the flirting and the physical attraction. He said he still dated other women, women he might think about settling down with, but the dancers were the women who really got his blood boiling. He thought my idea for a club was a great one. When I told him I did not think he would be able to score with the girls I had in mind, he laughed. He said I could never convince anyone of that and that this would work in my favor. He also liked my idea for filling the place with sports attractions. "It will be like a frat house with the greatest-looking sorority sisters in the world," he said.

Any doubts I had about Bob's claims of his success with women vanished the day one of the Pussycat's best-looking barmaids came in while we were both there. Her name was Alicia. She was a little older than the other girls, maybe thirty-five, and had a real sophisticated look. She was blonde, maybe five foot three, and in excellent shape. She used little makeup, but her skin was radiant. And as fabulous as her body was, she showed little of it. Most of the barmaids worked in short skirts and revealing tops. They did not wear bras and teased the customers at the bar with "accidental" displays of their breasts, creating an additional reason to tip them generously.

But Alicia usually dressed in tailored slacks and a businesslike blouse. She was so naturally beautiful that she attracted men without needing the usual tricks of the trade. Every regular of the Pussycat—the biggest-tipping customers, the bouncers, and even one or two of the dancers—desired Alicia. But everything about her manner and style sent the same message: "Don't even try; you don't have a chance." As far as I could tell, no one ever got near her. Inside that bar she had tremendous presence and was in command of all she surveyed. Later I learned that she was actually a woman who lived in fear. In her private life she was afraid of her own shadow.

In those days, however, I thought that she was aloof to the scene—that is, until the day she walked in and threw her arms around my friend Bob.

What a greeting she gave to him. A real deep kiss. Everyone in the place stopped what they were doing and watched them. It must have lasted three or four minutes. When they finished she kind of snuggled onto his lap. Bob asked me if I knew his friend Alicia.

"Oh sure," I said. "I've bought many drinks from her."

"Well, Alicia, this is my best friend, Jay. He's thinking of opening a topless club; be nice to him."

"Oh, I know Jay," Alicia said. "He's the grumpy one. Well, I got to get to work." She slid off Bob's lap and after a few minutes showed up behind the bar.

Up until then my relationship with Alicia had consisted of my sitting at the bar with the sullen disposition I had adopted so as not to appear to be one of the foolish regulars, and her either occasionally glaring back at me in her businesslike manner or not recognizing me at all. I was still maintaining my attitude of indifference around barmaids and dancers, not wanting them to view me as a fool. That is what I wrongly thought they believed the regulars to be.

How Bob ever got close to Alicia I'll never know, but it turned out to be an advantage to me. I had not even tried to ask Alicia the kinds of questions I peppered the other barmaids with. She seemed too aloof, too distant. Any glance her way was always returned with a cold stare.

Once, after Bob had not been around for a few days, Alicia asked me if I had seen him. I knew he was banging a dancer at Guys and Dolls on Murray Street, but I answered in my usual abrupt and self-protective way, "What am I, my brother's keeper?" Alicia looked at me like I was a lump of turd on the sidewalk. But after that our relationship began to soften. Alicia began to say hello to me when she arrived for work, and I once broke down and complimented her on a beautiful watch she was wearing. Bob had pretty much disappeared from both our lives; maybe that was the catalyst that brought us together. At any rate, one day Alicia asked me to run across the street to get her a tuna sandwich. Without thinking, I said sure and refused to take her money. When I got back, the ice between us was broken for good.

We both dropped the artificial facades we had established to protect us from each other. We began to talk regularly. She told me about how Bob had charmed her right out of her pants but how she now realized he was a jerk, interested only in the conquest. I told her about the incident in my office the day the market crashed and how that got me thinking about opening a club. She said she had heard that a million times. "Guys want to open clubs so they can make it with the dancers," she said. I never could convince her I was more interested in the money. Whenever I would ask her about the business end of the business she would clam up. Stone cold. She would not tell me a thing about the inner workings of the Pussycat. She even became indignant about it. She thought it was none of my business.

However, as closemouthed as she was about business, Alicia became more and more open about herself. At first we spoke in generalities about the broad issues of life. I would nurse a bourbon and she would carry on about Reaganomics and the defense budget. As it turned out Alicia was very much into language. She had five dictionaries at home. She liked the way I talked. She admired educated people.

She told me she lived in the part of the lower East Side known as "Alphabet City" because the avenues are identified by letters: Avenue A, B, C, and D. It was a rough part of town and reminded me of my days at Max's. The Hell's Angels had their headquarters down there, and I wondered if Alicia was attracted to the leather-and-chains scene.

The answer was no! Alicia was more of a bohemian. She was an artist at heart and loved the offbeat characters the lower East Side attracted. She was also an artist in practice, a very talented painter. And she was interested in literature. She hungered for the education denied her when she'd been forced to flee a tyrannical mother and weak father who molested her. As a teenager she worked as a stripper in the dumps along West Forty-second Street, where performing was mainly a matter of laying down on the stage with your legs spread. She eventually "moved up" to dancing topless at Adam and Eve, a seedy joint on the East Side where business executives made asses out of themselves on their lunch hours. She even revealed how she was raped while working at Adam and Eve.

I became very fond of Alicia and began to think of her as a friend. I admired her quest for knowledge. She also warmed toward me. When she noticed I was not hitting on the dancers, she even offered to fix me up with one of them and was surprised when I declined. After that she began to believe I really did intend to open my own place. If the Pussycat provided me with a look into the world of topless dancing, Alicia was the keeper of the keys to that door.

Alicia's ability to get her life straightened out was inspiring. She had once spent her days in a drug-and-booze induced trance. She turned tricks with customers at the bars where she worked. She could not remember the names of all the men she'd put her faith in while hoping they would lift her out of the sordid life she was living. She was angry at herself for letting Bob seduce her. He represented the hurt in her life.

But she had turned things around. By the time I met her she was a health nut. She did not drink or smoke. She was into herbs and holistic medicine. She worked out regularly, running and lifting weights, and looked it. She had patched things up with her mother, who would even show up at the Pussycat from time to time. Alicia fixed her up with the manager. There might have been rage in Alicia's heart, but there was forgiveness in her soul.

I was absorbed by her paintings. It seemed that all the troubles of her life—her nightmarish home life, her rape, her lack of self-esteem—and her battle to overcome them had been poured into her art.

One painting—I guess you would call it Impressionistic—brought tears to my eyes. It was titled *Pieces of Me* and it was all there. A life in and then out of a wringer. It haunts me to this day. Alicia was a survivor, and it did not dawn on me that her life at the Pussycat might have been a negative. I just believed the worst was behind her.

I began to muse that I would be able to help women like Alicia improve their lives because in my nightclub they would be able to earn tremendous money without getting entangled with the customers. I could not know then that the girls who would eventually work at Scores would have much in common with Alicia. They would be beautiful, charismatic, and sexy beyond fantasy, and they would have these tortured backgrounds that made you cry for them. But I did not realize any of that back then. So, while Alicia eventually totally revealed herself to me, I never saw her as typical. If I had I might have changed my plans right then. But instead, with her help and encouragement, I surged forward on my crash course in the business of topless clubs, table dancing, G-strings, and heartbreak.

CHAPTER 4 Chips

As 1987 came to a close, I began doubting myself. That was very unusual for me. I was a person who was always able to identify my goals and charge forward. I was self-motivated and very successful for a young man. But I was stuck in a rut as far as my dream of creating the world's greatest gentlemen's club went. The problem was, I got no inspiration at the Pussycat Lounge. I was at the point where I knew many of the dancers and barmaids well enough to drop my hard-guy act and let them know that I was really after information. One day I even worked up the nerve to speak to Lana as she was climbing down from the stage after a set. I walked up to the side of the stage and asked her if she was the same Lana I'd known at from NYU. She said she had gone to NYU, and I asked her if I could speak to her for a while.

"Aren't you a friend of Bob's?" she asked.

I guessed she had seen Bob and me talking together, so I told her, "Yeah, I knew Bob at school."

She agreed to have a drink with me. After a few minutes she emerged from the dressing room wearing a short terry-cloth robe and joined me at a table. I was instantly aware that every guy in the place was looking at us.

I did not want Lana to think I was on the make so right away I told her about using the Pussycat as a classroom in order to learn all I could about the topless bar business. "I have great plans for a really special place," I told her.

Saying that turned out to be a real mistake; I could tell by the way she looked at me that she thought I was full of crap, that this was just another line from another hustler. She immediately began to play with me. She let the terry robe open just enough that I could see those fabulous silicone breasts, and she lit up a smile.

"Jay, I could tell you all about the topless business," she said. "Did Bob tell you to speak to me about it? He told me you were a hotshot Wall Street guy."

Now the robe was completely open and Lana was leaning into me as she spoke. Not being some kind of bionic man, I was getting turned on by being so close to this beauty. But I did not want to be so distracted. I kept telling myself to take care of business. And in a sense I was insulted by what she was doing. She saw me as a mark, a jerky guy who was going to lay out some bucks to sit with her at a table in hopes of maybe getting a cheap feel of those terrific tits and perhaps even achieving the ultimate fantasy of taking her home. Well, my yin and yang battled each other for a while. I wanted to touch those breasts, but I knew that feel would not be cheap. Instead, as I had seen many of the big spenders at the Pussycat do, I put my hand inside her robe, slid it down her tight stomach, and placed a ten-spot in the slim band of elastic that held her bikini bottom around her hips.

Then, as she slid a little bit closer, I got up from the table. "Look, I don't know what Bob told you about me, but I am serious about this. Sorry you can't see that," I said, and walked away. I gotta tell you that it was one of the toughest things I've ever had to do. Walking away from a girl like that is not something that makes a whole lot of sense. But it was a turning point for me. It made me realize that I had to get off my backside and begin to get very aggressive about continuing on my quest before more people like Lana took me for a joke. And I was pleased with myself about the move I put on her. I had come a long way from the Horse's Rail, I thought.

The next day when I saw Bob he told me Lana had mentioned our little scene to him. "You know, she's totally fucked up," he said to me. "She doesn't trust any man. She's so used to guys trying to scam her that she puts up a wall between her and every man she meets. The only reason she gets along with me is because we knew each other in school and she thinks I'm great in bed, which I am!" Bob could never resist throwing in a commercial for himself.

He went on to tell me that Lana had been worked over by a professor at school. The guy taught drama and had a reputation for making it with students. He persuaded Lana to try topless dancing as a way of becoming comfortable with opening up her true self to an audience. Only a college sophomore would have bought the rap, and she went for it hook, line, and sinker. The perv professor persuaded her to have a boob job and to turn an occasional trick. He would then demand that she tell him about the sexual encounters as they lay in bed together. By the time she found out he had a stable of girls like her, as well as a wife and kids in Westchester, she was too far gone to return to a "normal" life. She was now a barracuda on the hunt. Bob said that one thing that made her a little different from the other dancers he knew was that she actually saved her money. She gave it to her father to invest for her. "She'll probably make it out of this scene someday," he said.

As Bob and I were talking about Lana, Alicia wandered over on her side of the bar. "You seem surprised by Lana's story," she said. "I figured by this time you would understand the girls a little better."

Alicia and I had already become good friends. We visited art galleries together on weekends, and she invited me to her loft apartment to see her own artwork. She actually had a small group of patrons who regularly purchased her paintings. I am not an art historian, but as I said, I found her stuff moving. Like *Pieces of Me*. Through images that at first seemed disjointed and colors that seemed to clash, Alicia had managed to tell a great deal about her inner feelings, which were so much in turmoil.

I confided to my two friends that I was beginning to lose sight of exactly what I was after. I was not progressing in focusing my idea, and I was depressed about it. Alicia was sympathetic. Both she and Bob thought the concept of a high-class gentlemen's club was a moneymaker. They were always encouraging, and that day was not any different.

They both suggested I get off my ass and get out into the world of New York's sex industry. They agreed I was spending too much time at the Pussycat. At that time there were almost a hundred topless bars in New York. Mostly all of them were pathetic dives in low-rent neighborhoods either above 100th Street in Manhattan or in industrial areas in the Bronx, Brooklyn, and Queens. These were not the kind of neighborhoods I envisioned for my first-class gentlemen's club.

In anything that passed for a decent area in Manhattan, there were only six topless bars: the Doll House near the World Trade Center; the Baby Doll just south of Canal Street; Billy's Topless, near the Lincoln Tunnel, a mecca for blue-collar types; the Kit Kat Klub on Broadway, a champagne hustle joint; the Metropole Go Go in Times Square, which offered fully nude dancers because it did not serve liquor and, thus, was not under the jurisdiction of the State Liquor Authority, and which was also rumored to be the headquarters of Mafioso Matty "the Horse" Ianniello, who ruled vice for one of New York's five crime families; and, finally the Adam and Eve, another all-nude spot on the East Side.

I began to make the rounds of those places. I would visit them on different days and at different times, and it was not long before I realized that there was no bar owner making any kind of effort to create the kind of place I had in mind. All those clubs had plenty in common, and none of it was worth copying. They were all dirty, had overflowing ashtrays, and stunk of stale beer and urine. There was no effort at all to make a real show out of the dancing. Especially in the all-nude places, the girls actually just walked around, squatted on the bar in front of a customer, and collected their tips. They did not even wear G-strings, so they stuffed it into garters on their legs.

The dancers were, for the most part, unattractive. For every Lana there were three really plain girls. The ones that worked the all-nude clubs appeared to be the least attractive. All their faults showed. There was no attempt to cover, with makeup, either their scars, their cellulite, or their bruises and burns. Some trimmed their pubic hair, but some did not even shave their legs. They got their tips anyhow. The better-looking girls like Lana rarely worked the all-nude clubs, because they did not have to. They made good money just by flashing their tits and offering those three magic words: "Maybe next time."

The Doll House, which eventually changed its name to New York Dolls, was the classiest topless bar in a low-class league. It had a bar in the front with a strip stage across from it and a bigger stage in the back that was set in the middle of a group of fairly comfortable easy chairs. It also offered a complimentary buffet that usually sat uneaten despite the price. The patrons were my Wall Street buddies, workers from a nearby post office, and others who served the nearby financial community. Because it was near City Hall, some political staffers and reporters sometimes showed up there for laughs. The Doll House had fewer regular dancers than the Pussycat. It drew more from the girls who worked the circuit of clubs throughout the city. I realized there was not much I could learn from the Doll Houses and the rest of the Manhattan clubs, unless it was about things I should not do in my dream club.

Alicia agreed with me when I complained about the lack of inspiration I was getting from my visits to these clubs. She was not surprised that little effort was made to make them better.

"Why should the owners pump money into these places? They're designed to suck money out. They're always packed with guys willing to spend; why screw with that?" she would say.

More and more, I was learning to respect Alicia's judgment. We had become good friends. I asked her why she thought men who worked hard for their money and had good taste in other matters of their lives would throw their money around in places like the Kit Kat and even the Doll House, or for that matter the Pussycat. Was I being a fool trying to offer more when no one really wanted more?

With this matter, as with most things that concerned the relationship between man and topless dancer, Alicia had once again hit the nail on the head.

"You have to remember, Jay," she said to me, "men will fuck mud."

"Fuck mud!!" I was jolted by the words. I was dumbstruck that she would think such a thing. But why shouldn't she, I considered; that was what years of abuse from her father and then from a series of boyfriends had taught her. The years of watching otherwise very particular men risk their reputations and sometimes the financial stability of their families over women whose attractions were minimal at best had instilled in Alicia the most cynical vision of sexual relations. "Men will fuck mud." Jeez, I'd never thought of it that way.

There was a real awkward silence between us after Alicia said that. Bob was listening in and he also felt uncomfortable. In the background the usual Pussycat disco music was blasting and six girls were doing their thing, and the three of us just sat silently. At that moment I questioned everything I was doing. My plans seemed ridiculous. If Alicia was right, I was wasting good time pursuing something that was totally unnecessary. I could probably make as much money opening up a sleazy dive in a lousy neighborhood.

Bob broke the silence. He had taken the remark personally. "You know, there are some nicer places out in Queens," he said. "Let me take you to Gallagher's."

As if on a personal mission to redeem himself in my eyes, Bob had us in a cab and on the way to Gallagher's in minutes. Throughout the ride to Queens Boulevard, he jabbered on about how Alicia was wrong. "You know me," he said over and over, "I don't jump just any broad. I'm more choosy than you think. What about Lana? What about the great Alicia herself."

I tried to tell Bob that I did not think Alicia was talking about him. "She was just talking in generalities," I said. "Hell, she knows I haven't tried to put the make on even one of these girls. She knows I even put Lana off."

"Yeah, but there a lot of guys like me. We go to these dives because that's all there are to go to. Fuck mud, hell—fuck Alicia!" he said. Bob was mad and never forgave Alicia for the remark. As for myself, I took it as a lesson learned from a wise teacher. I worked the statement around in my mind and accepted the fact that it was generally true. But the men I would attract to my club would be guys who demanded more and spent more.

For them, mud would be something they scraped off the soles of their shoes.

Bob was right about Gallagher's. Compared with the other places it was a paradise. I got my first glimpse into how a little effort could go a long way. It was spotless, clean, well lit, and relatively spacious. The sound system was superb. The crowd reflected the uptick in quality; the guys around the strip stage were a little older, a little better dressed, and a little better behaved than the people I had been seeing in Manhattan. And Gallagher's actually served some edible food. It was mainly franks and sauerkraut, but it was high-quality meat and it was well cooked.

As for the girls, well, they were mainly the regular circuit crowd: floppy, pancake breasts, the washed-out drug addict look, and enough tattoos to grace the centerfold of a biker monthly. I recognized a few of the dancers, and Bob took great pains to introduce me to the better looking ones. One or two were gorgeous. They knew what to do with their hair, and their silicone breasts made me take notice. They were unnaturally large, the way Lana had made hers.

At first the whole idea of breast implants was a turnoff to me. The thought of messing with your body like that actually upset my stomach. And sometimes women made their tits so big I found it comical. But I was a businessman, and I understood that most guys liked giant boobs. And if they were giant boobs that defied gravity, well, so much the better. They gave the women a certain glamorous look, and those with implants seemed to take better care of themselves all around. They were the ones who worked out, knew how to wear their makeup, and generally made a better presentation. So, it was not long before I accepted silicone boobs as an important feature of a topless bar.

The trip to Gallagher's had a positive effect on my outlook. First, it made me realize that I was not off base in thinking that a quality place would be worthwhile. Second, I saw that someone shared my commitment to spending a little to make a little more. On the other hand, it was still light-years away from what I really had in mind.

A few days later, I explained that to Bob. We were walking along the waterfront near my apartment in Battery Park City. For the zillionth time I laid out my plan for a showy, classy over-the-top club. "You know, my new girlfriend has a cousin who is involved in Chippendales. Maybe you can meet him," Bob said.

Chippendales. Wow! A lightbulb went off inside my head. I knew about Chippendales. It got a lot of press. It was a strip club that catered to women. The men were the strippers. I even knew some women who had gone there for bachelorette parties. They told me what great times they had and how gorgeous the men were.

As Bob and I walked, I kind of rambled on. Women are much more concerned with aesthetics. A place has to be clean and well run for them to go back. I thought of times where my dates would be totally turned off to great restaurants because the bathrooms were filthy or crowded. Women were much more demanding about decor. Women would not fuck mud.

I asked Bob to set up a meeting with his girl's cousin at Chippendales.

A few days later Bob and I met with the guy in a coffee shop on First Avenue. His name was Larry Wolf, and his main connection to Chips, as he called it, was with its advertising and marketing. He was very creative and was a partner in a small advertising company himself. He listened to my idea about a men's club and suggested I meet him at Chips one night. We made a date, and two days later we met at the club.

As Larry's guests, Bob, Alicia, and I watched the show from a private VIP room in the Club Magique, which was the name of the disco that housed Chippendales. Actually, Magique was dying at the time. Its day as a disco along the singles strip of First

Avenue known as the Meet Market was passing; only the popularity of Chippendales was keeping the building alive. Chippendales was fantastic.

The club was a full-sized theater. It was fully carpeted. There were real props on the stage, and the show was fully choreographed by the famous Steve Merritt. The women in the audience had the time of their lives. They stuffed dollar bills into to the thong bikinis of the best-built guys I had ever seen outside of a gym. I was a little uncomfortable admiring the guys but quickly got over it as I was caught up in the fun atmosphere of the place. It was fun, not sleazy. These women did not expect to score with the dancers. It was a good time and well worth the money. Even old hard-boiled Alicia got into the mood of the place. She started hooting and hollering with the best of them as one guy, dressed like a fireman, began to reel out his hose. When he went into the audience she stretched her legs out in front of her and faked having an orgasm, as many of the women in the crowd below were doing. It was good to see Alicia letting her hair down. At times I thought she had forgotten how to have fun.

I noticed the booze flowing and the waiters scurrying around like ants at a barbecue. I knew this was the formula I was looking to reproduce. A place like this for men would make me a fortune, I was sure. It would be my dream come true. As I sat there in Chippendales I saw my club in my head. I saw it jam-packed with famous athletes, barons of finance, actors and even actresses, and something funny flashed before my eyes. I saw clean bathrooms. No mud in sight.

Later we all went back to Alicia's loft and of course the talk turned to my club. I explained how I thought copying Chippendales was essential to my concept. Of course, I reminded them, I was going to throw in the sports shtick: televisions and a basketball court. Larry suggested I buy Chippendales. He confided that there were some money problems among the owners and that it was an opportune time to make an aggressive move. But that idea did not interest me much. I wanted a place with my mark. I wanted to be known as an innovator.

To this day, I'm really glad that I did not get financially involved in Chips. Eventually the founder of Chippendales, Somen "Steve" Banerjee, hanged himself in a Los Angeles jail cell. The King of Beefcake, as he was known, pleaded guilty in July 1994 to arranging the murder of Nicholas DeNoia, an Emmy Award-winning producer and onetime husband of actress Jennifer O'Neill. DeNoia was an original partner in Chips and was an innovative choreographer who designed many of the male bump-and-grind acts. He was shot to death in his Times Square office.

As the *Daily News* stated in an article on October 24, 1994, "Banerjee, 48, died at the end of a torn bedsheet in his cell at the Metropolitan Detention Center."

Anyway, by that time Chippendales was already closed, having passed into history as one of the greatest clubs ever in New York.

CHAPTER 5

Show girls

The visit to Chippendales was the turning point for me. I was reinvigorated. After a year of studying the topless club business in New York I'd had finally found a place that at least approximated my dream. I figured that if I could come close to copying Chippendales in the quality of its shows and dancers, I could attract the high-class, big-spending clientele I was after.

Meeting Larry Wolf also turned out to be providential. We shared an interest in the nightclub business, and Larry had a level of experience that complemented my raw enthusiasm. Larry was not a party animal, but he was a fun guy. He hid his serious business mind by constantly cracking jokes. Conversations between us were sarcastic, cynical, and very witty. I liked Larry almost from the moment I met him. It turned out that we even shared the same birthday, although I had two years on him. The only thing we disagreed on was buying out Chippendales. Larry thought it would be a good move, even suggesting we could eventually make it into a club for men with women dancing. I disagreed. Chips had developed a world-class reputation for what it was and to tamper with that would lead to failure. No, I continued to believe the best course of action would be to start from scratch.

Both Larry and Bob kept telling me that the kind of place I had in mind could be found in Houston, Texas. Houston and southern Florida had broken new ground in the topless business and were far ahead of the rest of the nation. Tom Lord, the general manager of Chips, said that Florida might have the best-looking girls, but Houston had the formula down pat. We all agreed a visit to Houston was the next step toward fulfilling my dream.

We met to discuss the trip in Larry's advertising office on the East Side. Bob and Larry both wanted to be partners in my club. I told them there was room for anyone who could meet the financial and administrative responsibilities, and I thought that there would be plenty of money to go around. But I made it very clear, and they did not object, that I would be the boss—first among equals.

We sat around like a bunch of kids that night and talked about how much money we would make and how we would be the major players in New York's nightclub scene. Bob really carried on. He told how he planned to fuck all the beautiful dancers we intended to meet in Houston. He said he was going to persuade them all to come back to New York on a bus and that he would be the only man on the bus. "I'm even going to get a beautiful broad to drive it, and I'm going to fuck her on Route 95," he said.

After a while Bob's boasting began to bother me. The more beer he drank the more he carried on about all the women he had seduced in New York and how running his own topless club would just make things easier. Now, I knew firsthand that Bob had a way of persuading the most beautiful topless dancers, like Lana, and even the more sophisticated ladies, like Alicia, to join him in his

Forest Hills bedroom. I did not doubt his prowess. But what I began to doubt that night was his commitment to business. I admired, even lusted after, beautiful women as much as any man alive, but as far as my topless club was concerned, business had to come first. I began to worry about Bob's involvement. Nevertheless, by the end of the drinking session in Larry's office, our plan was set. We would take a road trip to Houston. We would personally scout out the legendary Rick's Cabaret, in those days the crème de la crème of topless bars—or as they were known in Texas, titty bars.

Around this time—it was March 1989—I was spending less and less time at my investment banking and more and more as a motivational speaker. I had a natural talent for motivating people and even developed a philosophy I called Supreme Esteem that I enjoyed spreading. I was making a little money working for a temporary services company, doing sales and motivational work both for its staff and its clients. A woman named Cathy was the president of the company, and she was constantly pushing me to get into it full-time. She said I got stunning results with her on the sales force assignments she got for me and wanted to increase my commitment to her company anytime I was ready. Well, she was pretty stunned herself when I called to cancel a booking so that I could fly down to Houston with Larry and Bob to study the titty clubs.

"Jay, you never fail to amaze me," she said. "You're a successful investor, you have a great head for business, you're a natural-born entrepreneur, and you have this terrific gift of being able to teach others how to improve their lives. What the hell do you care about topless clubs?"

Her questions were on the mark, and as good as I was at explaining things and analyzing people's motives, I could not really explain why I was so set on this nightclub odyssey. But it had been a driving force within me since my college days, when I worked at Max's Kansas City, and of course since that fateful night at Studio 54, which I had never forgotten.

Even as Cathy tried to talk me out of it, I daydreamed of standing astride the entrance to my club like Yul Brynner in *The King and I*—a modern Alexander the Great, master of all I would see in my club, the King of New York Nightlife. There was no turning back for me.

So, on a Friday night Larry and I met at Kennedy Airport for our American Airlines fight to Houston. Bob did not show up. He offered some weak explanation about some family commitment and I sympathized with him but realized that he was not in it for the long run. He liked to talk about opening a great new club and he certainly used the idea as a come-on line with plenty of New York's dancers—not that he needed a new come-on line—but it was clear to Larry and me by this time that Bob's interest lay in getting laid, and that was that. I'm not saying I blamed him. To this day I have never met a man more successful at bedding the most beautiful showgirls in New York. Bob with his Kennedy good looks—even if today he looks more like Ted than John-John—is a legend in New York. But it is too bad he could not look beyond his dick, because he could have been part of the exciting and successful adventure Larry and I set off on that night. And he would have gotten laid plenty, also.

Larry and I talked all the way across the country, terribly excited about what we were doing. We talked about possible locations. We agreed the club should be somewhere on the East Side, which always had a reputation as having the classier places in town. It should be big, we agreed. And we talked, really for the first time, about how much money our club would cost and where we would raise it. Larry knew from his connection to Chips that it did not make sense to cut corners. The whole idea of our club was that it would offer something different and special. We were in agreement that as long as we were raising money from sources other than our own savings accounts we would go all out and try for more than we really needed. Although even by the time we got off the plane we were not sure of how much cash and promises we would need, I thought it would be catchy if we spent $1 million so our place could be known as a "million-dollar club."

We landed in Houston about 8:30 P.M. and took a cab from the airport to the shopping district known as the Galleria. We asked the driver if he knew the best titty bars.

"You guys don't really want a titty bar," he told us. "You should hit some of the show bars like Baby O's and Rick's Cabaret," he said.

It was the first time we'd heard topless clubs referred to as "show bars," and before long we knew what the driver meant.

We quickly checked into a Holiday Inn and were able to walk to Baby O's. As we approached the entrance I noticed that right next door was a sports bar that was doing great business. I pointed that out to Larry, who did not completely share my desire to mix sports and girls. "You see, they go together like beer and peanuts," I said. He nodded in lukewarm agreement as we paid the $5 cover charge and walked into Baby O's.

We were awestruck. A beautiful middle-aged woman in an evening gown led us to a cocktail table near a small stage. On the stage was probably the most glamorous-looking topless woman I had ever seen up close. She was dancing to some soulful music, maybe Smokey Robinson or Barry White, I don't really remember. The important thing was that she really was dancing; her moves matched the music, and the music was not blasting customers out of their seats but was being used to add to the overall sensuality of the place. That was something that struck me right away. There was an immediate good feeling about Baby O's, no sense of slime or sleaze. The club was decorated in a style of understated elegance. It was like an upgraded Houlihan's restaurant. Wood paneling and hunter green wallpaper gave it the feel of a gentleman's study. In a back room were blackjack tables where games were being played with phony money; no one really won or lost anything, but the dealers were much better-looking girls than you saw in Atlantic City or even Las Vegas. It was all a far cry from the black walls and grease-smeared mirrors of the Pussycat Lounge.

All around us, thirty or so women in various stages of undress—some in just G-strings, some still in their evening gowns—were dancing and posing and even laughing. If they were acting, they were great actresses—they really seemed to be having a good time. None of the sullen glares or disinterested attitudes of the New York dancers was present here.

The women were dancing on small tables set in the middle of a few comfortable chairs. This was something that was not allowed in New York. In New York the State Liquor Authority regulations stated that if a dancer was topless she had to perform on a platform or stage at least eighteen inches high and six feet away from the nearest patron. The rule was taken very seriously. That's why all the dancers I had seen up to that night were on stages behind a bar, unless they came down to try a "champagne hustle." That rule created a significant physical and psychological distance from the customer, and as far as some of the New York dancers were concerned, the farther away the better. Not so in Houston. In Baby O's the stunning, breathtaking women were allowed to perform topless a hot breath away from the panting customers. The initial shock of the scene was something I had never before experienced.

Larry and I sat with our mouths open. We watched in utter amazement as a roomful of women wearing five-inch "fuck me" pumps, with perfect all-over tans and perfect breasts, some even naturally so, and perfect manicures and pedicures, toyed with the libidos of Houston's big spenders. Their hair looked like they'd just left the stylist. Their perfumes—I thought I smelled Chanel No. 5, Opium, and Poison—filled the room. As they gyrated inches from a customer's face, they dropped their silky evening gowns to reveal toned and supple legs. They wore the tiny G-strings that were called T-backs or T-bars. Some wore ankle bracelets or gold chains around their waists, but for all practical purposes these women—who might have stepped out of the pages of *Playboy* or *Vogue* or even *Ladies Home Journal*—were NAKED.

Watching all this, I sunk into my own private fantasy. My highly disciplined businessman's mind turned to mush. From deep inside my soul, a passion I rarely experienced outside the privacy of a lover's bedroom overtook me. I was hopelessly lost in an orgiastic tornado that was carrying me to a world of commercial eroticism so far beyond anything available in New York that I might as well have been on Neptune.

One moment I was having sex with the blonde in the corner, my hand wrapped in her long, soft hair, my face buried in her breasts. Then I was on the stage with the Eurasian girl and she was climbing up on me, her legs wrapped around my shoulders, my teeth nipping at the thin cloth that folded into the slit between her legs. In an instant the Eurasian, with her silky black hair, vanished, only to be replaced by the brunette with the longest legs I had ever seen.

As my fantasy grew hotter, the brunette left the loser she was dancing for and raced across the room to me. She used those legs to straddle my face, and she was not even wearing a T-bar. I ogled these women like an infant looking for a baby bottle. I wanted to touch them, lick them, crawl across the deeply rich carpeting to serve them.

Could this be the great Jay Bildstein, the man who would not grovel, the man who refused to even acknowledge the beautiful breasts of Lana of the Pussycat Lounge. Was this the man who would resist even an Alicia in order to make his point that he was all business when it came to the sex business?

It was Larry's laugh that broke the spell. He was laughing at me. He was laughing so hard he had a pain in his side. He was holding one hand on his ribs and pointing at me with the other.

"Fuckin' A, Jay, isn't this fucking great!!! You should see yourself—you're hooked, man, fuckin' hooked. This is it—FUCKING PARADISE," he howled. "We're gonna be rich."

Larry shook me out of my daydream. I turned to him and began babbling away. A stream-of-consciousness monologue came rolling out of my mouth. "I'm going to rule this business," I shouted over the music. "My concept is right-on! These women are going to beg me to work in my club. I'll be the center of the showgirl universe. They will seek me out!"

Larry put his hand on my arm to calm me down a little. I was having an attack of megalomania, and as he was to do many times over the course of our relationship, Larry brought me down to earth.

"Jay, Jay," he said, "chill out a little, we need to talk all this stuff through." He was right, of course—I was acting like a schmuck. It was the first and last time I lost my cool over topless dancers. But looking back on it, I understand how it happened. After months and months of touring the depressing topless clubs of New York, I had begun to wonder if I really had a workable idea. Walking into Baby O's proved to me I was on the money. To borrow a line from *Field of Dreams*, I now knew that if I built it, they would come.

We stayed at Baby O's for a few more minutes. We checked out the rest rooms, took a businessman's look at the bar, and studied the clientele. Mostly they appeared to be out-of-towners, traveling businessmen who were probably staying in nearby hotels. And they were very free with their money. I figured a lot of the bills were being charged to corporate credit cards. Baby O's would appear as a restaurant on the bill and passed off as travel and entertainment. The crowd was not the type that could reach into their own pockets and slip a few hundred dollars to a girl named Mitzi. They were a little different from the customers I had in mind for my club. These guys were not Masters of the Universe, although they certainly knew how to have a good time.

From Baby O's, Larry and I went to a nearby roach coach for some coffee. As soon as we sat down in the booth, I once again began talking. I knew I was preaching to the choir—Larry was unconditionally convinced my concept would be a great success—but I had to talk about it. I was like a fullback who'd just scored the winning touchdown in the Super Bowl. I wanted to repeat the experience, over and over and over.

"Oh Larry, oh Larry, oh Larry," I kept repeating. "This is it, this is it. Studio 54, move over. Steve Rubell, you're a piker."

"Larry, did you see the money changing hands—or, uh, moving hand to belly? Did you see the bills that were being stuffed into those bikini bottoms? We're not even going to be taking any of that money. You saw the booze flowing, the food being ordered, and there must have been a hundred customers in the room—each one of them paid five bucks just to get in."

As I blabbered the waitress came over and without even thinking I loaded up on grease. I ordered a bacon blue-cheese burger and a side of Texas chili. Incredibly, I decided to wash it all down with a chocolate milk shake. (My propensity toward diner food was one of the things that remained from my days at Jahn's on Queens Boulevard.) Larry ordered a more sensible English muffin and coffee.

I don't think I gave Larry the opportunity to say two words. He was great, the way he just smiled and humored me. I guess it was his experience at Chippendales that enabled him to take a more professional posture than I was taking. For me, the change in life would be much more dramatic. I was putting the boardrooms and bullshit of Wall Street behind me. In exchange I would be making a fortune while surrounded by provocative women and high-powered businessmen and sports stars.

Well, Larry could not shut me up, but the chocolate shake did. About halfway through it, when the cold ice cream hit the hot chili in my excited stomach, I gasped in pain. Without a word I leaped from the table and headed to the diner's dingy rest room. Sitting there, on a filthy commode in a cramped and smelly room, I swore two things to myself; no more Texas chili, and my club would feature comfortable and clean toilets. By the time I returned to the table Larry had paid the check and was anxious to get going. It was still only about nine o'clock at night, so without another word we headed to Rick's.

We walked over, and the exercise helped settle my stomach. After paying a door charge we entered another world. Rick's, believe it or not, made Baby O's look like a Houlihan's in Forest Hills. We stood at the entrance to the main room and saw in front of us about fifty women who could have been answering a call from central casting for "blonde, beautiful, and built." At least ten of them could have been centerfold models. It was complete sensory overload. If it had not been for the pain in my stomach, I would have lost my mind. We had entered the promised land. This night was turning into more than I could handle.

We compared ourselves with the rest of the crowd. The men were generally younger than the group at Baby O's, and some of them were with dates. They appeared to be a sharper, more athletic, and better-looking group. We had heard that Houston's professional athletes hung out at Rick's and that when Hollywood stars were in town they also stopped by. It was not hard to see why they chose the place.

Larry and I represented a different look. I was wearing a chalk-stripe navy blue Tiger of Sweden suit with cherry cordovan loafers and a red tie. Larry was wearing a gray double-breasted suit, a chines collar shirt, and no tie. His expression said, "Party down." Mine read, "Pass the Pepto Bismol."

The walls inside the entrance to Rick's were covered with framed newspaper and magazine articles that raved about the place. There were also many pictures of the rich and famous, including their greatest admirer, Robin Leach, enjoying the delights of the dancers. I thought that if a place in Houston could generate that kind of publicity and celebrity attention, my club in New York would surpass it a hundred times.

A stunning hostess efficiently appeared at our side and led us into the main room. It was decorated like Rick's in *Casablanca*. It was much lighter in color than Baby O's. The walls were painted white and they were highly lacquered. There was a grand piano in the middle of the room, and a topless showgirl who looked like Tanya Roberts was dancing on it.

We were guided to a small cocktail table about ten feet from the piano and settled into two extremely comfortable deep-cushioned chairs, the kind you never want to get out of. Our heads were spinning like Linda Blair's in *The Exorcist*, as we feasted our eyes on the pulchritude that surrounded us.

Nothing I had ever seen before prepared me for the scene in Rick's. For $10 anyone who wanted could command the most beautiful women in Houston, maybe the most beautiful women in America, to put their bodies through a series of spins, turns, pirouettes, and other sensuous moves that have never been named. I noticed that some of the dancers touched the men—slightly, maybe just a hand on a thigh or an almost accidental brush of breast across chest, but there *was* touching. I watched one guy—he looked like a cornball to me in his polyester slacks and shirt and those gray-colored shoes usually seen only in tuxedo rental places—pay for three dances in a row, and I noticed that with each dance the girl got a little bit closer. She also let him run his hand over the back of her leg and through her hair. I wondered just how far they would go in Rick's and what we would be able to get away with in New York. Already I knew that having bare-breasted women so close to liquor-consuming customers was going to be a problem with the New York State Liquor Authority.

Larry and I were in a trance as we sat and watched what was going on. He later told me there was not a woman in sight that he did not want to have. I agreed. I believe that if it hadn't been for my horrible stomachache I would have reached out and grabbed someone. It would not have been proper etiquette, but I was beyond caring. To me this was a paradise for men. I wondered what it would take to get one of these magnificent creatures into bed. I was sure money would do it; after all, why else would they be table-dancing? But, I thought, it would take a *lot* of money. Not even the great Bob, the supreme seducer of New York's topless legions, could sweet-talk these women into bed. The magnificent Lana would be lost in this crowd.

Most of the girls wore garters around one thigh, and I saw that they were overflowing with cash, mostly ten-dollar bills, but there were plenty of fifties and hundreds, I was sure. A quick calculation convinced me a girl could probably make a thousand dollars a night at Rick's. I did not know if the management got a cut from the girls or not. I did not plan to do that in my club, but it really did not matter. Just on the admission fees of $10 and the booze and steaks that were available, Rick's was clearly a gold mine. No one came there expecting not to spend money. In New York the crowds would be even more affluent and willing.

My daydreaming was interrupted by the arrival of a waitress. She was wearing a black leotard and if she'd been anywhere else on earth I would have thought she was gorgeous. But in comparison to the dancers she was on the standard rating system made popular by Dudley Moore and Bo Derek in *10,* maybe a 7. Every dancer in the place was a solid 10.

"Hi, my name is Dorkas. What can I get you guys?" she asked.

Larry ordered a Wild Turkey on the rocks and I, in deference to my aching stomach, tried a Baileys neat. As soon as the waitress turned to walk away Larry and I shouted in unison; "Dorkas? Did she say her name was Dorkas?"

We started laughing like two kids in junior high school who've just watched the principal slip on the ice. We rolled in our seats, tears came to our eyes. "Dorkas,—I can't believe it," I said. "Dorkas!" Larry said. "I can't believe it." We barely had ourselves under control when she returned with our drinks. It turned out that she was very nice. She asked our names and where we were from and the requisite "Have you ever been here before?"

We grilled her right back. Remember we *were* on a fact-finding trip, and we wanted to know everything there was to know about Rick's. By the time the night was over we learned she was twenty-three years old and a student at a community college who would not be a dancer for all the tea in China. She took more orders for drinks, and when she noticed we had not motioned a dancer to our table she asked if we were too shy. "I'll be glad to bring one of the girls over," she offered. But, for the time being, we passed.

Actually, I did not mean any disrespect to Dorkas, but I was trying to catch the eye of the waitress at a table about ten feet away. She had these tremendous long legs and long brown hair, almost down to her waist. I was always partial to brunette hair and long legs. She had both.

After we'd flirted a few minutes, she came over to our table.

For some reason this waitress, who was really a fresh-faced teenager, decided to hang around us and talk. Her name was Tina. She said she was nineteen and had been working in Rick's for only a month. "The money is great," she said, "but it is hard work. You guys are very demanding."

Dorkas came by and gave us all a real dirty look, but Tina did not seem to mind. She just continued blabbing away with us.

She said she was trying to decide whether to become a dancer or join the army—quite a wide range of thinking, I thought. She seemed to be a typical teenager with typical teenage problems. Before long she was complaining about her parents. She was not trying to hustle anything from us, and we continued to order from "old" Dorkas. Since my bout with the chili from hell was fading into memory, we added steak sandwiches to the order. Even after a manager came over and told Tina she was needed at one of her tables, she came back to us.

She was very impressed by us. I think mainly it was the clothes we were wearing. What passed for business attire on Wall Street was "going out" clothes in Houston. Nearly all the men in the place were dressed very casually by New York standards, and I don't care what kind of suit you wear, if you have one of those cowboy bolo ties around your neck, you look like two bits.

Eventually Tina settled into a seat with us—something that would not be allowed in a New York club, and that was frowned upon by Rick's management as well—and we told her about our plans. She was fascinated by Larry's tales of Chippendales. She said she would definitely come to work for us in New York.

Then she uttered some words that I would hear time and time again over the next few months. She cupped her breasts in her hands and said that she thought she "couldn't make a penny with these little boobies."

It was the dilemma that haunted showgirls and showgirl wanna-be's throughout the country. "To augment or not to augment? That is the question."

It was easy to see why girls asked. Rick's and Baby O's and even Gallagher's were places right out of a Dow Corning class-action suit. Most of the women were Memorex, not real. Boob jobs are such a fashion in the topless business that a girl can't get a job if her tits were real.

That night in Rick's I was still a believer that augmented breasts, if the surgery is done correctly, are a sight to behold, things to make a grown man's heart boil with desire. But I was not a fanatic on the subject. Alicia, who was one of the most beautiful and sensuous women I ever met, kept her breasts in their natural form, and even gravity's relentless pull did nothing to diminish her beauty, at least while I knew her. During my career in the topless nightclub business, I eventually embraced more than a thousand women with fake boobs, and I always felt that something was standing between us.

Anyway, Larry and I both told Tina she looked great the way she was—the first time we used what would become the party line for us. From that point forward, we always discouraged dancers from getting implants. We tried to convince them that they looked great, with killer bodies and beautiful faces. These were absolutely gorgeous women, and sophisticated men, we told them, would appreciate them without silicone. Of course, the girls knew that most of the men they would be dealing with were not exactly sophisticated. Over time I began to wonder about the ethics of the medical community, especially plastic surgeons who encourage women to supplement their natural beauty.

I met countless women with incredible bodies who were getting boob jobs, liposuction, tummy tucks, collagen injections in their lips, cheek implants, nose jobs, and even teeth caps. The irony is that these women did not need the help. But it pointed to their insecurity. They competed with each other about who had the best hair, the hardest tummy, the biggest tits, best ass, even the best tan. As I was to learn later, these dancers, even those in the upscale places who were admired by big-spending hotshots, had very low opinions of themselves. Tina was a typical young girl struggling with life's typical problems. But she thought she was nearly worthless. The only life she saw ahead of her was as a topless dancer or an army private. Things got pretty glum around our table as Larry and I considered Tina's predicament, and it was a relief when Dorkas finally told her to take care of her own tables.

"So aren't you guys having a dance?" Dorkas challenged. Larry turned to me and said it was time to find out what all this fuss was about. He motioned two very buxom beauties to join us.

In a flash, a twenty-something blonde had her arm around my shoulder and her boobs, which were bursting out of her slinky metallic gray dress, in my face. "I'm Julie," she cooed. "What's your name?"

"Jay," I told her, and she positioned herself in front of me, her screaming legs brushing my inner thighs. She slid out of the dress, as the the Beach Boys' "Kokomo" came over the speaker system and whipped her long blonde hair into my face. She was amazing: intoxicating perfume, long French-manicured fingernails, ruby red lips. Slowly she stripped down to the tiniest bikini top and an almost nonexistent T-bar. As she danced, a warm flush came over me. I sat, self-conscious at first, but completely mesmerized. Then I went over the edge into the abyss of runaway senses. By the time she removed her top I was gone. She wiggled her sensational butt just inches from my face and then slid to just inches of my lap. She danced for three and a half minutes.

When the song ended, even though another started right up, she sat in my lap while I placed a $10 bill in her garter. To my surprise—and I guess this is why Rick's succeeded while other places flopped—she started making conversation with me. It was pro forma, to be sure—"Where ya from, what ya do, first time here?"—but it was nice. At least at first. After a while, because her delivery was so mechanical, I began having visions of the Horse's Rail and the champagne hustle. That broke the trance, so I did my best Texas accent and said: " Julie gal, you're dynamite, but my stomach's hurtin' a whole lot, so why don't we save the jawbonin' for another time." She sashayed off without a word.

That was my first and last table dance. Thinking back on it later, I realized it had been frustrating not to be able to take advantage of Julie's proximity and bury my face in her lap. I wanted to kiss her beautiful lips and caress that fabulous butt. Given this incredible frustration, I really could not see what the great attraction of table dancing was.

Across from me, a dancer named Maria was finishing up with Larry, and he asked her to stay for a second dance. Maria was the best-looking woman in Rick's, and that is really saying something. She was perfection in stiletto heels, with a body like steel cable and perfect, though Memorex, breasts. She had long brown hair, which Larry and I both liked, and these really soulful brown eyes. Larry was really into it; he had a much better time than I did. He had her dance a third dance for him, and this time you could see that she was much more free with her hands and body, actually rubbing her leg in his crotch and using her hand around his neck. After the third dance this goddess sat with us for about fifteen minutes, nursing a cranberry and vodka, which Dorkas had waiting for her.

We blitzed her with questions. We told her our plans, and she seemed to believe us. She told us she'd just broken off with her fiancé, that she'd even had to return wedding presents. She was warm and friendly and she hid the hustle very well. She was exactly the kind of woman we wanted in our club. Two and half years later, Maria showed up to work for us in New York. That was when we knew we really had made it.

I learned a lot that night about table dancing. Most important, I understood why Larry liked it so much and I did not. I was frustrated because I wanted to have the girl to myself. I did not want to be hustled; I wanted the chance to make love to her. I knew that would never happen, at least without the outlay of thousands of dollars, and it frustrated me. Larry was much more urbane about the scene. He took it for what it was: Just lay back and have a good time. It was a very enjoyable experience—why ruin it by being obsessed with wanting more?

He was right. Over the next few years, I watched both philosophies at work. I watched many men believe they could buy their way out of my club with a girl on their arm. Some of those guys left angry, never to return. Others kept coming back, night after night, never giving up the belief that they would score where no one else could. They were good customers. But the best customers were the guys who knew the score—who enjoyed the sexuality of the moment and were willing to pay for the experience. The girls liked those guys better, and so did the management.

Rick's Cabaret was so successful that on October 13, 1995, it became the first topless bar to go public, as shares began trading on the NASDAQ stock exchange at $3 apiece. It had brought in almost $3 million in revenue the previous year. Eighteen of its dancers went on to appear on the pages of *Playboy*, including Anna Nicole Smith, who legend has it, met her late husband, the multimillionaire Houston oil tycoon J. Howard Marshall, at Rick's. Not bad for a titty bar.

As we were leaving Rick's, Tina, the young waitress, stopped me at the door and asked for my number in New York. I gave it to her and got hers in return. It was a great ego boost to have a girl like Tina reach out for me. But the real ego trip was just beginning.

CHAPTER 6 M. J.

For all the sexual excitement of the evening, Larry and I still went back to our hotel rooms alone. That was okay with both of us. We had decided when we set out on the trip that we were going to be all business. For the most part we stuck with that. The only exceptions, I think, were the first few minutes in Baby O's, when we were overcome by seeing what a really successful topless bar was like, and Larry's total immersion in his table dance at Rick's Cabaret.

My complaining stomach kept me up much of the night, but emotionally I was feeling top-notch. After all, up to this point I'd had some anxiety that I was fooling myself. Deep inside me, even when I gave my best pitch to friends like Alicia and Bob, I'd had a nagging feeling that maybe I did not know what I was talking about. Maybe, I'd sometimes reasoned, topless bars were meant to be sleazy rip-off places; maybe that was their natural place in the feeding chain of the sex industry. Who was this guy, Jay Bildstein from Queens, to change all that?

But it is not my nature to dwell on failure or to spend much time doubting myself. So that night I fell off to sleep totally content in the knowledge that I was right. I still had a long way to go to get my club on the street, and realistically I knew there would be circumstances I could not control, but no matter what happened from there on, after that night in Houston, no one would be able to convince me that my concept was not right on the money.

When we met in the hotel restaurant for breakfast the next morning, Larry and I knew things had changed. We were no longer pursuing something that existed only in my mind. Larry felt all along that the Houston show bars were what I was envisioning, and he'd been right. But he did not spend time gloating. Right away, over black coffee and granola, we started planning our next steps.

When we got to the airport, as a gift to ourselves and in keeping with our high-flying mood, we upgraded our seats to first class. We agreed that we had to project a high-class, wheeling-'n'-dealing profile. We were not money-burning fools but sharply focused businessmen who knew how to live and knew what people liked—and what they'd pay for.

Sitting in the deep leather first-class seats, I felt like an adventurer who had just met a grueling challenge. Larry and I were the Sir Edmund Hillary and Admiral Richard Byrd of the gentlemen's club business. Not that a night in Rick's Cabaret was exactly the challenge of a night on the icy slope of Mount Everest, but no man's goal is less important than another's. However, now it was time to evolve from an explorer to a builder.

Back in New York, I escalated my club activities. I began reaching out to people with money to invest. I did not have a real figure in my mind, but I thought that my concept of a "million-dollar club" was on target. To do it right and to be able to honestly use that slogan, I was convinced I would have to raise at least $1 million. That was no small feat, even for someone with my investment experience. If I could not reach that goal, I could kiss my dream goodbye.

Surprisingly, most of the businessmen I approached with my plan were extremely negative. I thought that men, mostly because they were men, would quickly get caught up in the concept. The truth is they did not. All types of savvy investors threw all sorts of negatives at me.

They had a number of reasons why a club like mine would not succeed in New York. I was told that so many topless clubs were currently meeting the needs of the target customers that a new place would have few prospective spenders to choose from. Another well-respected restaurateur I approached thought that to run an upscale club I would have to charge upscale prices. And why would someone pay that much when they could go down the block to their local topless joint to get their jollies?

It was clear that the people I was calling on did not understand the sexually engrossing effect of what I had seen in Houston.

There were also the skeptics who claimed that the politicians and cops would find a way to close down my kind of club. They believed that little sleazy joints were able to survive because they did not attract attention. A lavish, high-class club, they believed, would attract a different and more intense kind of scrutiny that had not been seen since the days of Minsky's, the legendary Roaring Twenties burlesque house.

Those familiar with the bar business said I would be constantly hassled by the State Liquor Authority. If that was not enough to dissuade me, they added, then I should consider the probable involvement of the Mafia, which was said to control all the bars and restaurants in New York. If I did not pay direct tribute to a mob crew, I would have to at least buy all my services,—everything from liquor to linen—from mob-controlled businesses, and that meant inflated prices.

At least that was what the conventional wisdom believed.

So, my first days back from Houston were filled with naysaying and skepticism. However, my personal philosophy sees adversity as a challenge. So the more negatives I heard, with the image of Rick's in my mind, the more determined I became. It did not hurt that my work as a motivational speaker and sales training expert was taking off. As I filled my days with helping people accomplish their dreams, the rest of the time I just practiced what I preached: I proceeded with great resolve.

I formulated several different strategies for raising the capital that would be needed to make my dream become a reality. I could utilize a private placement, people who would trust me with their money for a guaranteed return. I could form a limited partnership, with me at the helm and a few investors who would trust me to make the right decisions with their money. I could enter into a joint venture with an existing club, as Larry wanted me to do with the Chippendales group. I even entertained the idea of getting a bunch of my stockbroker buddies together to create a public offering—to sell stock to whoever wanted a piece of the action. For a while I pursued all these strategies simultaneously, figuring the cream would rise to the top, that the plan that held the most promise would emerge and present a clear path to follow.

Meanwhile, there was another important question. Every potential investor I approached asked me the same thing. They wanted to know where I would locate the club. And I had to admit I did not have the answer. In New York, location said a lot about your establishment. The kind of clients I wanted were upper East Side types. Guys who lived on or around Park, Fifth, and Madison Avenues. Maybe some a little younger who lived off First and Second Avenues. I was not shooting for the bridge-and-tunnel crowd who drove in from Queens or New Jersey. I wanted regulars who could walk home from my club or who had a limo waiting outside.

One day I was bringing Cathy, the woman whose company I did some motivational consulting for, up to date on my plans.

Cathy was a dynamic businesswoman, and it was of no little concern to me that she thought my plan was nuts.

"Listen, employment is my business," she would tell me. "I match people with jobs every day of my life. It is my business. Forget about opening any type of nightclub. Your life is in public speaking, motivational speaking, sales training. Stick with what you know and are good at."

Cathy's words rang true. I knew that my ultimate destiny was in doing the things that she recognized as important, but as I told her that day: "Cathy, I am on an irreversible course. I have not heard one word of encouragement from anyone but the irrepressible Larry Wolf, but I am not dissuaded. Believe me, I have seen this dream. I have touched it; I can smell it. It will be real."

Well, in the face of that kind of determination, Cathy decided to help me. She suggested I call a friend of hers who had great knowledge about the nightclub business. He was a real estate broker named Jay Cummings, and he handled many of the property acquisitions for New York nightclubs.

Coincidentally, I had heard of Cummings before from Bob. The two of them hung out together during summers on Fire Island. Early on, Bob had mentioned him as someone who might want to get involved in a good deal. I had not been seeing too much of Bob since he punked out on the trip to Houston, so I called his office to see if he could rebrief me on Cummings.

First, of course, I had to fill him in on Houston. I told him all about Rick's, emphasizing the beauty of the dancers. He went into his shtick about how many of them he would have scored with if he had been there and how he would have made sure Larry and I were taken care of also.

Just to break his chops a little, I told him we did get lucky with a couple of the dancers and that it was the wildest night either of us ever had. He went for the bull, hook, line, and sinker. We talked a little more about the great club we would have in New

York, but by this time I had already written Bob off as being a partner. Finally, Bob once again confirmed Cummings's reputation for me, and I hung up, promising to give him a call when the money men were set to meet.

My next call was to Jay Cummings himself. Cathy's name got me past his secretary. From Cummings's voice I could tell he had a great deal of respect for her. Cathy, like Alicia, was a women who combined brains with beauty and a great personality.

Quickly I filled Cummings in on my dream and my desire to find just the right location. He agreed to do some research and meet me in about a week. "If Cathy thinks you're on the ball, you must have something going for you," he said.

Within the week he called me back, and we met in front of a large garage on West Fifty-seventh Street near Eleventh Avenue, across the street from a club called Emerald City, which had had a previous spectacular existence as the Red Parrot.

Cummings's physical appearance was as impressive as his reputation as a real estate dealer. He was about six foot one and had thick curly brown hair. He had the athletic look of a tight end. I knew he was in his midforties, but he appeared to be a decade younger than that. Later I learned that he was very careful about his diet, shunning fats and sweets, and that he was a workout freak at the Vertical Club on Sixtieth Street, around the corner from Chippendales. He would time his workouts so that he could be home by 7 P.M. to watch *Jeopardy!* on television. I admired people with that kind of discipline. He was a unique character, and he knew the players in New York's nightclub scene.

It was a bitter cold day when we met, and we walked through the huge garage wearing heavy overcoats and gloves. The multifloor space was obviously too large for my needs. It was also too "raw." It had only the most basic heating systems, as our freezing bones could attest to, and hardly any plumbing. The floors, ceilings, and walls were simply bare reinforced concrete.

The location was also too out of the way for what I perceived to be our clientele.

Cummings said he agreed with my assessment but that he wanted me to see it anyhow. It turned out he had plans of his own for the space. He had a very creative mind and tremendous energy. I really enjoyed listening to him describe a multilevel entertainment facility he had in mind for the space.

He envisioned an ice skating rink, bowling alley, volleyball court, restaurant, nightclub, gym, and even some kind of golf driving range, all under one roof.

Cummings was like a Hollywood agent who was not satisfied just selling his client's work but wanted to be a producer. He was filled with the idea of operating a nightclub himself. All the years of setting up other people in business had made him think he could do it better than anyone else.

I was beginning to learn that people in any way connected with the nightclub business were never satisfied. They always wanted to open a new place, a bigger place, a classier place, a quieter place—anything but what they had. So much of the thrill was involved in just getting a successful club off the ground that you found yourself craving that adrenaline rush over and over again. Larry was like that. All he ever talked about was buying Chippendales. One of the biggest problems I had while working toward my dream club was keeping all the players on the right track. If I hired someone to put down the carpeting I did not want to hear about the club he planned to open. People had to work toward my goal.

At first Cummings seemed more interested in selling me his idea than finding a location for mine. Eventually we talked about that. He said he'd checked out my background and found out I was an investment broker and someone who could raise money. He thought I would be just as interested in investing in his good idea as starting my own place. He seriously underestimated my determination.

Anyway, it turned out that Jay Cummings was quite a visionary. In 1995 a group of investors opened a facility called Chelsea Piers on Manhattan's West Side that was very similar to Cummings's concept. It even had a golf driving range.

Following that meeting on blustery West Fifty-seventh Street, Cummings and I spoke every day, sometimes two or three times a day. Our common bond with Cathy made us feel as if we knew each other longer than we really had. It also established a level of trust that sometimes takes businessmen years to develop.

During the time that Cummings and I were scouting locations, Larry called me to say that he heard from Tom Lord, one of the Chippendales managers, that the legendary Michael J. Peter was in town. Lord, who had tried to get me to come in on a deal to buy Chips, remembered my resolution to open my own place and offered to set up a meeting.

Peter was the man who revolutionized the topless club business in Florida. He turned a sleazy joint in Orlando into a place called Thee Doll House, and things took off from there. He owned high-class strip clubs all over the Sunshine State, and from all reports they rivaled and in some cases surpassed Rick's Cabaret. I jumped at the chance to meet him. Bob got back to Lord, and a meeting was set up for that very evening at Hot Rods, a disco-nightclub on West Twenty-eighth Street.

We were met at the door by a hunk of granite—obviously a bodyguard for "M. J." Peter, as he was known in the business—who courteously took us to an upstairs office for the meeting. We were invited to view the performance of Gary U.S. Bonds and his band, who were in New York trying for comeback.

Bob and I were led directly to a small table where Peter was sitting with one of the most beautiful blondes I had ever seen. She was dressed immaculately in a black tailored jacket over a short black skirt. She wore horn-rimmed glasses with really big lenses. I think she wanted to appear more like Peter's assistant than his squeeze, but her tremendous mane of champagne blonde hair gave her away as a showgirl. Even Bob, the master cock hound, was impressed. He actually poked me in the ribs and threw her a glance as we sat down. I thought it was a pretty amateurish move for an expert like him, but I could not blame him. She was spectacular.

Peter was pretty impressive-looking himself. His deep tan offered proof of the time he spent in Florida, making millions off horny guys and luscious women. He had a trimmed mustache and wore an obviously expensive and excellently tailored business suit, a gold Rolex, and several gold bracelets. I did not care for so much jewelry on a man, or on a woman, for that matter; but along with the stunning blonde at his side it all added up to a picture of a successful club big shot—which he was.

Bob made the introductions very efficiently, and I thanked Peter for seeing us. Quickly, I told him that I had an interest in opening up a club in New York and wondered what he thought of the idea. I just gave him an outline of my concept. I had enough business experience to know that Macy's does not tell Gimbels. After all, in a sense I would be competing with Peter, even though our clubs might be fifteen hundred miles apart.

He was very polite and obviously relished the image of grand impresario. He told me how he was a graduate of Cornell University's Hotel and Restaurant School, the finest school of its kind in the country. He took great pains to point out that he wasn't just some shlub who wandered into a topless bar and decided to buy it so he could fuck the dancers. He told me how important it was to keep my mind on business.

"It's not always easy," he said as he leaned over and kissed the blonde on the cheek. She got the message and almost climbed into his lap. Personally, although I certainly admired the woman, he did not have to grope her to impress me. I was much more impressed by the man's business credentials. Bob, however, was drooling.

After a while, Gary U. S. Bonds came over to the table, and Peter introduced him to the group. We all sat and bullshitted for a few minutes, Peter invited us to visit one of his places in Florida, and then Bob and I left.

The next morning I was awakened by a call from Jay Cummings.

"Jay," he said, and I sensed an urgency in his voice. "Did you meet with Michael Peter last night?'

I knew Cummings was wired into the nightclub business, and this proved it. His intelligence gathering was as good as the CIA's, probably better.

Cummings was really agitated. "Jay, I hope you did not tell him much about your plans. What did you say?"

I began to sense a problem. I'd never heard Cummings so concerned.

"I didn't say much, just that I planned to open an upscale gentlemen's club in New York and that I admired what he had done in Florida. Actually, he did most of the talking—told me his whole background, including what college he attended."

"Well, I hope he did not take you too seriously," Cummings said. "Our only hope is that he thinks you are a dilettante and he does not have to move quickly," he said, calming down a little.

"Jay, what's going on? Could you please tell me why you are so upset about this." I asked.

"Yeah, I'll tell you, and I hope I am wrong, but I know my information is good. Peter is in New York to scout out a location for a club of his own. And from what I hear, his clubs are the kind you want to be the first in town to open."

The news shook me. With the telephone in my hand, I got out of bed and began pacing the room.

"Well, maybe we have to move a little faster," I said.

Cummings, now completely in control of himself, responded, "I'll see you this afternoon."

CHAPTER 7 Gigi

I might have been more concerned about the potential of a Michael J. Peter club in New York if I'd had more experience in the nightclub business. As it was, I did not really know enough about him to be too concerned. But Cummings persuaded me to take the situation seriously, and we turned to the always helpful Tom Lord for information.

Larry, Cummings, and I met in Lord's office, and I really got a mouthful about Peter and his clubs.

As I already knew, he'd started out by turning a sleazy joint in Orlando into a gentlemen's club known as Thee Doll House, which served as the foundation for other clubs. But I did not realize the extent of his business or the range of his innovation.

Lord said Peter had moved his base of operations to Fort Lauderdale, where he ran Pure Platinum, a club that, by any measurement, matched or bettered Rick's Cabaret. It was an all-nude club where the dancers did not wear even the skimpiest T-bars. Their dances ended with them in their birthdaysuits teetering on ultrahigh heels.

Tom Lord was turning out to be a real asset to our operation. He was full of knowledge about the topless business and knew many of the players personally. He was also a real New York character. One of his strange habits involved his dry cleaning bill, which according to his contract was paid for by Chippendales. It ran about $4,000 a month, as he had underwear and even handkerchiefs dry-cleaned.

He had visited many of Peter's clubs, which he explained offered different styles. For instance, in some the girls would wear evening gowns, complete with garter belts and stockings, whereas in others bikinis and other beach-type clothing would be the girls' starting point. Another thing all his clubs had in common were outstanding-looking women. He was famous for being fastidious in selecting dancers and personally chose each dancer for each club. Part of the folklore that surrounds Peter is that he personally scoured whorehouses around the South, seeking out very young girls who were smart and had special personalities. According to legend, he would "buy" them from madams. He would then teach them how to dress and behave with the kind of big-spending customers who came into his clubs.

Whether this was true or not, it was a good idea to be very selective in recruiting for a club. That was something I had also made up my mind to do. After all, after the evening gown, or French maid's costume, or even jeans and T-shirt are on the floor at the customer's feet, what remains must be candy for the eye. If I was seeking a premium price from a big spender, he had to get his money's worth from the minute he walked in until the minute he walked out.

Peter also added other values to his clubs. He created the Doll of the Month, an award that went to a dancer selected by management. She received a gold key, which she wore around her neck as a status symbol. He also added merchandise to his clubs: hats, T-shirts, and even baseball-style trading cards that featured his dancers. A Pure Platinum calendar was a best-seller.

Lord knew so much about Peter because he was trying to broker a deal between the still unconfessed Somen Banerjee, who was running a Chippendales in L.A., and Peter. Lord believed Peter wanted to be the number one strip club owner in America. The rumor was that he desired to own two strip clubs in every state.

Cummings said he heard Peter had already looked at a site at 333 East Sixtieth Street in the shadow of the 59th Street Bridge that was currently operating as the Great American Clubhouse, a sports bar that among other things featured female boxing matches.

Prior to that ownership, the site had been home to Club A, a superexclusive nightclub owned by an Argentine millionaire. It catered to only the wealthiest jet-setters. It was even a step above Studio 54 in its level of clientele. I was there once when it was the most admired club of the eighties. I double-dated with a college friend. My date was a gorgeous Asian girl named Tina who is now a doctor. I remember being impressed by the crowd, which was mostly Eurotrash guys and their American girlfriends, who I took to be call girls. They were beautiful. The place reeked of money, and I remember thinking how I would have liked to own it.

Strangely, it did not last that long, a couple of years at most, and I could never figure out why. Possibly it was that when dealing with the jet-set crowd you have to be constantly innovating, because they are a restless bunch and are not loyal. Club A's $30 admission charge and $15-a-drink tab made sure the average Joe could not become a regular customer, and that must have also contributed to its demise.

I appreciated everything Lord told me about Peter. I realized that someday I would be competing against him in New York. There was no way such a brilliant and focused businessman would not try to tap into the lucrative New York market. But I thought there was a difference between the types of clubs he ran and the club, still unnamed, that I had in mind.

Obviously, the basic attraction would be the gorgeous women. But I wanted a club that catered to all of a man's desires. I wanted my customer to have all his favorite toys at his fingertips. In my mind that meant more than just girls. It meant that in addition to bright eyes and smooth thighs, he would have access to his next favorite things—balls. That is, baseballs, footballs, and basketballs, with hockey pucks thrown in for good measure.

From day one it had been my concept to include sports with the girls. That night in Houston when Larry kidded me about a sports bar being right next door to Baby O's, I saw it as an affirmation of my perception. If you think of one of Peter's clubs, like Pure Platinum, as kind of a living *Penthouse* magazine, then my club would be the *Sports Illustrated* of clubs. Of course, it would be the *Sports Illustrated* swimsuit edition.

I explained this to the people who were then my closest advisors: Larry Wolf and Jay Cummings. They listened politely, but the looks on their faces offered nothing but skepticism. Cummings broke the spell with a line that I will remember for the rest of my life: "What are you gonna call the place, Mitts and Tits?" We all broke up laughing, and Mitts and Tits became the working name of my club.

As we broke up our meeting, we agreed to stay away from Mr. Peter. Cummings said that if Peter approached him to help find a location, he would not turn the business down—after all, at this time he had no financial or emotional stake in my club—but he agreed to give me first shot at any hot properties that came on the market.

Larry once again suggested we join up with Chippendales. Tom Lord said that he would be anxious to join us as a partner if that is what we decided to do.

After the meeting I decided to walk over to Cathy's office on Forty-second Street. I walked around New York a lot. The exercise helped me keep my weight down, and I also found that while walking I could not be interrupted by a telephone call (I had not yet gotten my first beeper), so that I could work things out in my mind.

I distinctly remember laughing to myself as I walked past a sporting goods store on Forty-second Street near Grand Central Station. The store's window was filled with all kinds of equipment: skis, footballs, basketballs, baseball mitts, and sneakers in all sizes and colors. "Mitts and Tits, Mitts and Tits"—the name resounded in my mind. Cummings had gotten something going with that idea. Although I would never use the word "Tits" in the name of a business that was shooting for a high-class clientele, I was absolutely certain that I would keep to my plan for a sports motif and that the name would have to reflect that.

Cathy was waiting for me with her coat on, and we went to a nearby restaurant for lunch. It was a place just south of Times Square that catered to the garment center lunchtime crowd but that at night was a well-known "cheaters bar," a place where garmentos could meet their secretaries for a little hand holding and promise making. It also attracted from the outer boroughs single women on the make for young executives. On Saturday nights it catered to transvestites.

Over lunch I brought Cathy up to date and once again thanked her for opening the door for me to Jay Cummings. I told her about "Mitts and Tits," and to my surprise she endorsed the name. I guess she did not get it. I realized again that it was still not clear to a lot of people how different I wanted my club to be. Even my close associates were having a hard time separating a classy topless club filled with stacked showgirls from the sleazy places they were used to. I told Cathy I would have to take her to Rick's

Cabaret so she would get the idea. Then Cathy asked me something that I had not given too much thought to.

"How are you going to get all these beautiful girls to come work for you, Jay?" she asked. "After all, they don't know you from a hole in the wall, and they must be constantly preyed upon by all kinds of con men and phonies. What are you going to offer them?"

The question was a good one and caught me off guard. I was surprised at myself for not have ever really considered the issue.

"I'm going to offer them the chance to make millions in New York City," I said.

"Yeah, but why do they need *you* to do that? The way you describe these girls, they could probably pull in big bucks dancing or turning tricks for escort services in any city."

"First of all, Cathy," I responded, a little upset that she still had the wrong idea about the table dancing scene, "these girls do not turn tricks. They don't fuck. Now, I'm not saying they are not businesswomen and that a good night's pay is something they will walk away from. But the table dancing, topless showgirl scene, in the high-class places, does not include prostitution. The management does not even take money from the girls."

Cathy was surprised. She had the average New Yorker's concept of what topless dancers would and would not do. But I knew that even at the Pussycat Lounge, the dancers did not turn tricks. Even Alicia at her lowest points, stuffed with drugs and in desperate need of money, had not done blow jobs in the back room.

"So you are telling me that these rich guys can't get laid in these places," Cathy said.

"For the most part that is true," I answered, "but in the sex industry nothing is for certain." In the coming months I would learn to live by those words.

"Well, you really are going to have to do a lot of public relations to convince people of that," Cathy said. " And to tell you the truth, I don't know why those kinds of guys would go to the place—certainly not for the basketball games on television." By this time my usually enjoyable meal with Cathy was not so enjoyable.

I changed the subject and we made it through the bacon cheeseburgers, Caesar salads, and pecan pie desserts without any more talk of breasts and thighs.

As we were leaving the restaurant I spotted Bob at the bar. When I waved "Hi" he beckoned for me to come over. I made a dinner date with Cathy for the next week, and she excused me from walking her back to her office.

Bob was at the bar with a coworker of his named Hal. I had met Hal before—the three of us had gone bar-bouncing on a couple of occasions. He was a cocksman of some repute. He was in Bob's league, maybe even a step ahead, because while Bob was a great seducer Hal was the kind of guy women chased after. He was usually in the enviable position of being able to pick and choose among several women. They all seemed attracted by his Gregory Peck looks.

I once witnessed Hal get picked up by two Dutch models. They spotted him at a bar where we used to spend some time. First they bought him a drink, and then they walked over to where he was standing and began talking to him. Soon one of the tall blondes had her hand inside his shirt, and the other had her tongue in his ear. After a few minutes of intense conversation they invited him back to their hotel room, where they had a three-day ménage-à-trois. A great thing about Hal was his aptitude for telling stories, especially those recounting his sexual adventures. He thrilled us for months with his descriptions of what went on in that room.

Part of "the Legend of Hal" that I knew to be true was that he kept an eighteen-year-old Puerto Rican girl in his apartment as a virtual slave. She washed his clothes, cleaned the apartment, and bathed him daily. And of course, she fulfilled all his sexual desires.

I filled Bob in on my meeting with Cummings and told him about "Mitts and Tits." I could not resist once more repeating the lie about what a great sexual adventure the trip to Houston had been.

Hal was not sure what we were talking about, so Bob told him about my plans for a club and what I had been doing to learn the topless nightclub business.

"What a great way to make a living," Hal said. "Hey, have you been to the Harmony Club yet?"

I said I had not been there and knew it only by its reputation, which was pretty low.

"Naw, it's a great place. Let's go down there a little later; I'm sure you'll learn some helpful things," Hal said. I said, "Okay, one more trip to one more topless club can't hurt."

We were about halfway through a fifth of Wild Turkey when Bob started chatting up two young women sitting at a table near the bar. Of course, they could not resist him, and soon the three of us had joined them at their now very crowded table. They were a couple of happy-go-lucky girls who worked in the neighborhood and had stopped off before going home to Brooklyn. Their names were Sandy and Rhonda; big hair, bubblegum pink nail polish, and impossibly tight jeans.

They quickly fell for Bob's bullshit and Hal's good looks. Bob began telling them all about me. He said I was a big-time entrepreneur who was going to open a major new nightclub in New York. "A really high-class strip joint. The three of us are going to an important meeting about it tonight," he said.

The girls were not too impressed. I'm sure they were hoping we were three neurosurgeons awaiting appointment to Mount Sinai Hospital.

"Can you make a lot of money in the nightclub business? I heard those places are always folding," Rhonda asked.

"You can make a fortune with the right club," I said.

Another thirty minutes of inane conversation had passed when Bob finally said, "Well, guys, I guess it's time to head for our business meeting."

We got up to leave, but Rhonda was not letting go of Hal so easily. "Maybe we can drop you off," she offered. "Our car is right across the street."

Bob, not wanting to let two possible scores escape his address book, jumped at the invitation. In minutes the five of us were jammed into Rhonda's compact car heading for the lower West Side, where the Harmony Club was located. A large bag of videotapes that Hal had purchased for his niece made conditions even less comfortable.

Bob was giving directions, and he pointed out the large office building that housed the Harmony. "That's the building; our meeting is on the fifth floor," he told Rhonda, who rolled to a smooth stop right in front. As he was getting out of the backseat the door handle tore a hole in the bag of videos. Sandy got out of the car and made a big deal about helping Hal wrap the bag again. Bob got the home numbers of both girls before they drove off toward Brooklyn.

The three of us took the elevator to the fifth floor. Once there we paid $10 each for admission to a large dark theater that reeked of ammonia and was suffocating under a thick blanket of cigarette smoke.

Under the glow of red lights a young woman was dancing nude except for a tiny G-string covering her crotch. Men sitting in club-style chairs around the stage were offering dollar bills for her to come over in front of them and spread her legs. In the aisles other girls were performing a "Mardi Gras" act, parading around, sometimes topless, stopping at customers' chairs and offering a dance for $15.

To blend into the place the three of us took seats in the chairs, which were revoltingly dirty. A short, dumpy Asian girl quickly zoned in on me and asked if I wanted a dance. I declined. I was pretty turned off by the available talent, and what the girl was doing on the stage did not interest me at all.

To me the sensuality is in the mystery. Once a dancer exposes herself completely, in my opinion, she loses much of her erotic charm.

The Harmony was a no-booze club at which the dancers actually got into the lap of the customer and dry-humped him until he either came or went. It represented the basic difference between lap dancing and table dancing, which places like Rick's Cabaret presented, and which of course my club would feature as well. A table dancer may not actually be perched on a table when she is doing her thing, but she almost never actually sits in the customer's lap. However, if she has done her job right the customer will leave feeling she touched him all over every part of his body.

But the next girl who came over to me was quite a different story from the first. She was an absolutely stunning Latin girl. She said her name was Gigi and asked if she could dance for me.

I really could not resist. In a flash she was in my lap, with her hand out. I gave her $15 and her top came off as if by magic. Gigi was really charming.

"Don't you think I have soft skin?" she asked. "I have the softest skin of all the girls here," she said.

I was sure she did, and I told her so.

"Don't you love my breasts? They're small but pretty, aren't they? You are allowed to touch them. And you can kiss my nipples if you don't get saliva on them."

"You really are beautiful," I told her.

She began rubbing herself in my lap. For a moment I was able to put the sights and smells of the surroundings out of my mind. She was very exciting. A little bundle of beauty, about 105 pounds with a small, pouting mouth.

The music stopped and she put out her hand again. I gave her $20. Next to me Bob was having a great time with a tall black girl.

"Do you want to come?" Gigi asked as she increased the friction in my lap. Only a thin pair of panties stood between her and totally nudity.

I said it was not my scene to have sex so publicly. "Well, just groan a little, make some noise like you are enjoying it," she said. Then she stood up for a minute and "adjusted" her panties so I could see her bush.

I really was taken in by her eagerness to please. I asked her how she got such soft skin.

"I'm a vegetarian. I never eat meat. I'm studying nutrition at NYU."

"Are many of the girls here college students?"

"A few, the smart ones," she replied.

"How come you work here?" I asked. "You're so beautiful you could make good money working in a topless bar like the Pussycat Lounge."

"Can the men touch you in that place?" she asked.

I said they could not. "But they would give you plenty of tips just to look at you and talk with you because you are so young and beautiful and smart."

"It's not for me," she said, then threw her arms around me and gave me a big hug. When the music stopped she put out her hand again but I said I would look for her later. She gave me a kiss on the cheek, put on her top, and walked away.

I would think about Gigi often over the next few years and come to realize that despite her fabulous looks she suffered from such low self-esteem that she could not imagine that someone would pay money and not demand to touch her or to have her touch him. She was very endearing, and I really hoped she was a college student.

All in all, I found the Harmony Club revolting. Once again it hit me that someone—in this case, Hal—did not understand what I was shooting for. If he did he would not have brought me to the place. It was as different from my imagined club as Siberia was from Key West.

But I did reflect that even in that dump there was a diamond like Gigi working. I knew I had to remember that.

When a two-hundred-pound woman who may or may not have been wearing a G-string,—I could not tell because the rolls of her stomach hid her crotch—asked me if I wanted a dance, I actually felt lunch coming up.

I just waved her off and turned to Bob to suggest leaving, but I could see he and Hal were totally engrossed. It was amazing to me. But I guess those two guys would chase any pussy, anytime.

Suddenly there was a commotion near the elevator and a woman was screaming: "I'm looking for a fucking thief named Hal. Where the fuck are you, you prick!!"

It was Sandy from Brooklyn, along with her friend Rhonda.

The three of us jumped out of our seats and started for the elevator. Sandy was screaming at the manager. "Three guys came up here for a so-called business meeting. One of them stole my wallet."

"Hey, there they are," they shrieked in unison as we charged up the aisle.

Rhonda spotted me first, "Hey Mr. Big Shot is this your 'business meeting'? Where the fuck is the wallet?" she bellowed.

I tried to calm everyone. I was completely embarrassed, first to be seen in such a dive and then to be humiliated by those two girls.

There we stood, the five of us, in the middle of the lobby, surrounded by the manager and some of the nearly naked girls, arguing over the wallet, when two police officers stepped out of the elevator. They had been called by the manager.

Sandy locked right onto one of them. "Officer, this fucking piece of shit, pervert, creep stole my wallet," she said, pointing to Hal.

Hal was stepping forward to defend himself when the bagfull of videotapes burst spewing its contents to the floor. Abruptly there were about ten tapes with titles like *Bambi*, *Cinderella*, *Alice in Wonderland*, and *The Wolf and the Hound* at our feet.

Everyone shut up and stared at Hal, who now appeared to be the biggest pervert since Fatty Arbuckle.

The first cop was actually laughing when he took a small brown wallet from his jacket pocket and asked Sandy if it was hers.

It was. The cop had found it at the curb in front of the building. She must have dropped it while helping Hal with the videotape bag after it ripped.

The cops suggested we all leave. The girls sheepishly apologized, and the dancers went back to dry-humping. The manager supplied a new bag for Hal, and we all got into the elevator together.

As we rode down, the irrepressible Bob suggested to the girls that we all go for a drink. To my surprise, they agreed. I guess the lure of Bob and Hal was too much for them to resist.

We went over to the Cedar Tavern in the Village. Within minutes the girls made it plain that my company was not really needed or desired. I got the hint and bowed out, saying I was going to head over to Alicia's studio. As I stood up to leave, Rhonda grabbed my sleeve.

"Let me ask you one thing," she said. "How come a nice guy like you wants to own a place like that? You gotta be able to do better."

CHAPTER 8

Dear Diary

I headed straight to the shower when I got home. I was able to laugh about the incident in the Harmony, but just being in the place had made me feel dirty. I wondered about the women who worked in places like that. I wondered how they started out. Had any of them ever worked in Rick's or Baby O's? Is that what the future held in store for the beautiful showgirls I saw raking in thousands of dollars? I really did not think so.

I knew that women like Lana and Alicia had not always been cannon fodder for places like the Pussycat Lounge, but I found it hard to imagine that they could fall much farther. How wrong I was.

I fell into an uneasy sleep, visions of beautiful women dancing all around me mixing with images of men from Chippendales and harlots from the Harmony. They were all laughing at me. They were making fun of this dilettante who thought he could conquer the hard-assed world of the showgirls. I saw myself being smothered by the large woman from the Harmony; my head was buried in her gigantic breasts. The fact that I had not yet raised one penny toward opening my super club kept running through my dream.

The persistent ringing of the telephone saved me from further agony. I was sweating and breathing hard when I answered the call with my trademark greeting: "Talk to me."

"This is officer Elwick, from the Spring Valley Police Department. I'm trying to reach Mr. Jay Bildstein," said an official-sounding voice on the other end.

Quickly gaining my composure, I said I was Mr. Bildstein and asked what was up.

"There's a woman named Tina Arnold being held here on two hundred dollars bail. Prostitution charge. She says you'll come up to bail her out."

"Tina Arnold." I thought hard. "I'm not sure I know Tina Arnold," I said.

Police Officer Elwick turned from the phone, and I heard him yell: "He says he doesn't know you."

Through the phone I heard the voice of a young woman. "Tell him it's Tina from Rick's in Houston."

Before Elwick turned back to the phone, I realized who it was: Tina, the fresh-faced young waitress who was trying to decide between a boob job and the army. I remembered she had asked for my telephone number.

I interrupted Elwick and without much thought said I would bail Tina out.

"I'm sure you won't be sorry," Elwick said with a chuckle.

I took my rarely-used Jeep Cherokee and drove to a small town about thirty miles north of New York City. On the way I examined my motives. First of all I was still a man. Tina was a gorgeous young woman in need, and I could reap the rewards of saving her ass.

But I also realized that I was increasingly becoming a part of a world that six months ago for me did not exist. The apparitions of my dream were becoming the realities of my life, and I was enjoying it.

As I drove along the New York State Thruway, I ran the group through my mind, like a film strip. Alicia, a stripper and topless dancer who overcame alcohol and drugs and was now an artist with a growing reputation; Lana, an ex-classmate who had everything going for her and who was now a cynical, man-hating topless dancer with fake tits; Bob, who had emerged as a friend with great stories about fantastic conquests; Larry, the advertising genius; and, finally, Jay Cummings, the real estate wheeler-dealer. They represented a different world from the one I had lived in for more than twenty-five years. But I realized that it was a world I enjoyed. It was not accidental, I thought, that I'd been drawn to Studio 54 as a teenager and that during college I'd hired out my muscle to nightclubs—maybe there was some kind of karma at work here.

I was starting to see myself as a character in a movie. I was like the intelligent and heroic sergeant, keeping a platoon of misfits alive and finding a way to make them rich. This was turning out to be much more than a business venture. It was changing my whole life. My quest to become a successful nightclub owner—actually, the most successful nightclub owner in history—had turned into an excellent adventure.

It was about 5 A.M. when I got to the police station. Tina was in the waiting room entertaining a group of young cops with stories about how much money she made as a dancer at Rick's Cabaret and how they should look her up if they ever got to Houston.

When I walked in she greeted me like a long-lost boyfriend. She threw her arms around me and gave me a big, wet kiss, right on the lips. I did not mind a bit.

I paid her $200 bond, and the desk sergeant gave her a date to appear in court on charges of soliciting for the purpose of prostitution. He returned a small overnight bag to her and wished her well. We left the building to a chorus of "See ya soon, Tina. We're all coming to Rick's next month."

Tina sat very close to me as we began the drive back to New York. She was wearing sneakers and jeans and a short Houston Oilers jacket. She looked like a high school kid out on a date. The only thing different about her from the last time I saw her was her hair, which she had dyed a bright, reddish blonde, almost orange. As far as I could see, her breasts were still all hers.

"So, Tina, I see you did not join the army. It's good to see you, but it's quite a surprise," I said as I aimed the Jeep toward the Tappan Zee Bridge.

"Oh, wow! Thanks for coming to get me. You won't believe what I have been going through. Things are great. There's a spot open for me in this club in Fort Lauderdale, but I want to get my boobs first," she said, apparently oblivious to the fact that a few hours before she had been arrested for prostitution.

She nuzzled up against me, putting her hand on my thigh. "Listen, I really appreciate your help—let me pay you back," she said, and started unzipping my pants.

I pushed her away, not an easy task, and asked her to first tell me what she had been up to, how she had ended up in the Spring Valley police station. I was concerned about my own reputation. The cops clearly thought I was some kind of sucker for this girl. But I was not so hot for her that I would make a foolish mistake.

For the rest of the trip she filled me in on what had happened to her. A few days after we met in Houston, she was befriended by a wealthy oilman who hung around in Rick's. He made sure she was assigned to his table, and he tipped her large sums. Then he asked her out to dinner.

The night they were supposed to meet, her father went into one of his periodic rages and punched her around. When she showed up for dinner she had a black eye and swollen nose. The rich oilman persuaded her to leave home and move into an apartment he kept in downtown Houston and to put off her army plans until "you get yourself together," as he put it.

The first demand the oilman made after she moved into his love pad was that she quit her job. He promised to get her a spot as a table dancer in Fort Lauderdale at one of Michael Peter's clubs.

In the meantime he bought her some great clothes, and she became his regular companion in the swing clubs of Houston. Finally the oil man took her on a business trip to Buffalo, with him. One morning he got a phone call from his wife and had to return to Houston right away. He left without a good-bye. Mr. Oilman did pay the hotel bill, but Tina was left on her own. She decided to hitch her way to New York and made it all the way to Spring Valley before a cop looking for a freebie arrested her because she would not put out.

"You should have joined the army in Buffalo," I said.

"Well, I'm not quite ready for that. First I want to make some money and get an education, and then I'll be able to go to officer candidate school. Besides, I have to get back to Houston to make sure everything is all right with my oilman."

"Tina, you're just not experienced enough to handle the life of a showgirl," I said. "But I don't blame you for hanging in there. There's a ton of money to be made, and you'll end up in charge of scumbags like the oilman." I had no idea at the time how many stories like Tina's I would hear in the next few years.

As soon as we got to my apartment Tina headed for the bathtub where she spent about an hour washing away the New York Thruway. I called Bob and told him Tina from Houston was in town. He came over in a flash and took her away to his apartment.

That was okay with me. I was exhausted from all the excitement that had begun the night before in the Harmony. I passed out and this time slept without the vision of a two-hundred pound woman smothering me with her bosom.

The experience with Tina invigorated my failing spirit. Over the next few days I resumed my search for investors in my dream.

I basically wanted to find one individual who would fund the entire project. I had hoped that my network of contacts, which was pretty extensive, would accomplish that. I just needed to reel in one big fish who would be lured by the profits and glamour of owning the world's greatest gentlemen's club. I had the plan, the vision: women and sports, combining to make an upscale paradise for men. All I needed was the money.

I have always been a voracious reader of self-help and motivational books, and much of what I learned from them helped me make it through this very frustrating period. One book in particular stood out in times of trouble. It was *Think and Grow Rich* by Napoleon Hill. Another helpful text was Herb Cohen's *You Can Negotiate Anything*. Lessons learned from both helped me sell a lot of orange juice futures in the eighties when bundles of money could be made just by buying blue chips such as General Motors.

I committed large tracts of these books to memory, and to a lesser extent the classic *The Power of Positive Thinking* by Norman Vincent Peale. Although Peale might not have approved of owning a gentlemen's club, he would have approved of the amount of faith I had in myself.

But it was Hill's book that most influenced my life. Hill said that thoughts have a very real, tangible existence. He said that more gold has been mined from the minds of men than from any gold mine.

So I needed money, a partner, and some investors to make my project come to life. But each business meeting was ending on the same note. I was hearing the same cacophony of negativity.

"No one will be interested. There's no shortage of topless bars in New York" was the message I was being sent.

I was also hearing, over and over, that the government would never let it happen and that I needed to be connected to the Mafia. Many people, I believe, would have given up by this time. But Hill's words remained in my head. As long as I maintained the thought I could make it a reality.

Many nights I lay wide awake in bed, drained by my efforts but too charged up by my vision to sleep.

By the summer of 1989 word around the industry in New York was that M. J. Peter intended to open up two clubs simultaneously. One location was on the West Side, on a site that had once been a successful club named Visage; and on the East Side he had his sights set on the former Club A site, now the Great American Clubhouse.

If I was to move, I had to start right away and move fast. I had to start making some compromises. I could not let Peter steal my thunder. I reached deep inside myself and dug into the teachings of Hill and Peale. I became as resolute as a professional paratrooper. I did not welcome the war, but I was prepared for it.

We were all prepared for it—Cummings, Larry, and myself. We were so anxious to get rolling, it was eating us up. Cummings was especially hungry, because he had just been screwed out of two commissions by some club owners he'd brokered deals for. He was a good guy who'd been stabbed with the short end of the stick by two slimeballs. He was frustrated, angered, and somewhat embarrassed by his situation. And he had rent to pay and a pretty high style of life to support. I knew he could not waste much more time on Mitts and Tits.

Larry continued to show loyalty to me, but he constantly harped on the idea of taking over Chippendales, and the longer that I could not put my deal together, the more ammunition he had for refocusing our attention. He even went so far as to suggest we do both deals—starting, of course, with a takeover of Chips. I knew he was getting antsy, and deep inside me I feared losing his support, both emotional and creative.

But I was not helping the situation. It was on my shoulders to get investors, and I was not making any progress. The road was considerably rougher than I had imagined. Finally, after one really disappointing meeting with a potential investor, I agreed to let Larry see if we could put a deal together to take over Chips. If we could not, I added I'd even consider Larry's plan of opening a competitor to the male strip club. I rationalized that it was a great business, and I could make some money while cementing a reputation as a club owner. I believed, for a short time, that it would be my eventual route to Mitts and Tits, figuring there might be some synergy between a men's strip club and a women's strip club.

Larry was still doing advertising for Chips, so he knew from the inside that Somen Banerjee was letting it deteriorate. He also knew that Banerjee had discussed a takeover deal with M. J. Peter, so he was certain the time was right. On top of it all, Cummings was picking up vibes in the real estate market that there was a group that wanted to buy the building that housed Chippendales and build a supertower of condominiums on the site. Somewhat reluctantly, I had to admit that Larry was right about making a move on Chips.

We mapped out a strategy of getting the top Chips dancers and the fabulous choreographer Steve Merritt to join our venture and work for us in a new venue. We were prepared to offer them bigger salaries or even equity in the project, if that was what it took.

So Larry put together a meeting with dancers Michael Rapp and Eddie Prevot. They were both worldwide stars of male stripping, great-looking guys with terrific personalities and real dancing talent. We knew that if we could get them to join us, the female clientele would follow them. We met in a coffee shop, and Larry laid out our plan to open a competitor to Chippendales. At first,

Rapp was reticent. He had heard it all before. He was a legitimate star, making a large salary and in wide demand. But he did not impress me as being very adventurous. He seemed content with his situation at Chips. (And with his situation at home: He was married to a gal named Nancy who was one of the best-looking women in New York.)

Prevot was much more enthusiastic. He was a fascinating guy. In addition to having the kind of looks women swooned over, he was really intelligent. He had a degree in engineering and tons of creative ideas of his own.

He also saw the handwriting on the wall for Chips. He realized Banerjee was letting the place go, and he knew about the possible real estate deal that could bring the club tumbling down. He helped persuade Rapp to get on board, and after a few more meetings, the two agreed to star in a spectacular new upscale review that we would produce.

Next Steve Merritt, the choreographer, agreed that he would leave Chips if we put a deal together.

During one great meeting with Merritt, Larry, Cummings, Rapp, and myself, Prevot laid out a brilliant idea to do an actual show instead of a strip revue. He explained that women needed a lot more romance and sentiment than men to get turned on. He told me to stop thinking that a club that featured men was the same as one that featured women.

His idea was for a show he called *Dear Diary*. It would revolve around the finding of a diary by a beautiful woman. She would be the narrator, and sitting in a corner of the stage she would read the most intimate fantasies of the diary's writer, a woman. The fantasies would be acted out by the dancers, starring Prevot and Rapp, in a series of vignettes.

Through Broadway contacts we even got to meet Jacques Levy, one of the writers of the scandalous and nudity-sprinkled *Oh! Calcutta!* He agreed to fine-tune Prevot's script.

Well, it was a great plan, and we certainly had a top-notch team ready to break through with it. Once again, though, the weak link was in my area of specialty—financing. We figured that it would take about $500,000 to put *Dear Diary* together in the high-class manner in which we wanted to present it. We were not talking about Mitt and Tits at this point, but we still did not have a backer for anything.

It was Cummings who made the big breakthrough. He arranged a meeting with a major force in the nightclub business named John Juliano, owner of the Copacabana and Emerald City. We met several times at the Copa. Juliano was a cordial gentleman who knew the club business inside and out. He was really impressed by our ideas and thought we could put *Dear Diary* into his Emerald City location. He had no compunction about taking on Banerjee or anyone else involved in Chippendales. He was strictly business. I tried to persuade him to put up all the money, but he was understandably cautious about that. After all, I was the leader of the group and I had no experience in owning a nightclub. No pay, no play was his policy. He said he would finance half the project, but he wanted us to put up the other half—in other words, carry our own financial risk.

Well, we did not have his kind of money, so we had to continue our search for investors. But now we had much more to offer. We had a cofinancer, two genuine stars, a world-famous choreographer, and a Broadway playwright to offer up.

Cummings, Larry, and I started meeting with anyone we knew who could possibly be persuaded to invest. Cummings knew a lot of rich men from Fire Island, where he spent his summer weekends, including one of the owners of Nautica, the clothing company. I had a brief meeting with him but got a no thank you.

Around this time I ran into an old college friend of mine named Jody Blanco who was doing very well in the public relations business. She set up a meeting for me with a close associate of hers named Les Garland, who was one of the founders and programming director of MTV. He was a fun guy and a creative legend long before I came into his life. He liked Eddie Prevot's idea of backing the show with rock music and agreed to help us promote *Dear Diary* and to get us access to the many important celebrities he knew well. Those kind of contacts would help feed Jody's public relations machine.

Now, with help of Juliano and Garland, I was really getting to meet high powered investment types. I found these people to be open to many ideas, and I never missed the opportunity to pitch Mitts and Tits. Everyone liked the concept, but the name turned them off.

While we continued to pursue more money, we also carried on our creative meetings. One missing ingredient was a really special woman to take on the role of narrator. We wanted a knockout. Eddie Prevot came through again when he showed up at a meeting with a tall honey blonde named Kelly. She was a former Las Vegas showgirl and musicians' assistant. She was very classy, with great posture that made her look even taller than the five foot eight she really was. Her success in Las Vegas gave her a confidence and presence that even surpassed that of the girls in Rick's Cabaret. I found myself irresistibly drawn to her. It was very hard to keep my mind on business when I was near her. I was overjoyed the day she said she would like to be a part of *Dear Diary*.

The arrival of Kelly also seemed to change our luck. All of a sudden we were running into people who wanted a piece of the action. No doubt her presence at meetings had something to do with that. Finally we settled down to serious discussions with a group of attorneys from Hewlett Harbor, Long Island.

They agreed in principle to finance the *Dear Diary* deal. They drew up papers involving all parties: Rapp, Prevot, Garland, Merritt, Levy, Juliano, and most importantly (to me), the magnificent Kelly.

At the same time I was getting really close to bringing a group of Asian investors on board who were mostly interested in Mitts and Tits.

As I envisioned things at that time, *Dear Diary* would put the last nail in the coffin of Chippendales. Then when Chips closed, I could put Mitts and Tits in that building. Wow! It was happening.

CHAPTER 9

Ups 'n' Downs

Things were really going great as 1989 came to a close. Here's an example.

One day, Kelly and I went to visit a photography studio in the hopes of finding a first-class photographer who could help us develop a certain style for everything connected with *Dear Diary*. We wanted everything to have a particular image.

Kelly was turning out to be a real find. She was as smart as she was beautiful. During her years in Vegas, whether working as a topless showgirl or with a magician as the beautiful damsel who gets cut in half, she always kept her eyes and ears open. She learned a lot about what goes into making a successful show, and she was willing to share that knowledge with me because she knew I was the kind of guy who remained loyal to people who were loyal to me. She always told me I would make it big and she wanted to be along for the ride. I just wish she'd been as generous with her nonstop body as she was with her mind.

Kelly was tall and sinewy. Her breasts were on the small side, but they were so perfectly shaped that it took awhile to realize they were not 38 double Ds. Not that it mattered to me. She was a perfect package in many ways. For instance, that day in the photo studio she was wearing tight jeans and a navy blue blazer. Her honey blonde hair was in a long ponytail. She wore penny loafers and white socks. It was not the glamorous look I really loved, but she was so classy she pulled it off. Everywhere she went men did a double take, even when she dressed down.

Anyway, while we were waiting to see the photographer, I noticed a picture on the wall of a woman in a shiny black latex, full bodysuit. The woman had long black hair and was wearing very high heels. The look on her face read, "Surrender to me—you won't be sorry." It was a real fetish picture, and I have to admit it turned me on.

Kelly noticed me staring at it.

"See something you like?" she said to me.

"I sure do, I should be so lucky to have a woman dress like that for me."

"Hey, you can never tell. When is your birthday?"

"January." I said. It was just one month away.

"Well, I'll get dressed up like that for your birthday. We'll do the whole scene. It will be my present to you."

I knew from the way she said it that Kelly was not joking. I got hot on the spot and was about to say something stupid when the photographer appeared and saved me. That's the way things were going in December 1989; fortune had turned my way.

My name began popping up in gossip columns as the man to watch in the nightclub business, and people were actually beginning to seek me out for deals.

One idea I was approached with was based on MTV's *Club MTV* concept. The club would be called *Downtown Julie Brown's*, and through Les Garland . . . we learned that she herself wanted to be active in it. We threw a quick proposal together to open such a place at the site of the Roxy disco, but it turned out that Julie Brown was more interested in opening up a blues club in Los Angeles. Without her aboard, we did not want to get involved. So the idea died. But that is the kind of stuff which started to come my way that December.

People were starting to appreciate my foresight and vision. Of course, behind all the wheeling and dealing I was getting involved in was my gentlemen's club. All roads would lead there.

In the middle of all this activity Jody Blanco called one day begging me to take some time out to meet with a friend of hers, a psychic who had an idea for a restaurant.

We met in Jody's apartment in Gateway Plaza, not far from my Battery Park City pad. I persuaded Jay Cummings to join us.

A friend of Jody's named Gary was there in addition to the psychic, whose name was Jeff. Gary and Jeff had an idea to open a combination pasta restaurant/comedy club. Jeff the Psychic said he might be able to get Al Lewis, "Grandpa" from *The Munsters*, to front the place. He already had a restaurant in Greenwich Village, which was doing very well. I thought the idea was interesting—comedy clubs were really a successful trend—but it did not seem to be the kind of venture that would lead in the direction of my gentlemen's club, as I figured doing something with the MTV crowd might.

I was really feeling full of myself. Here was a group of people who thought I was a major player in the New York nightclub scene, and they wanted my opinion on a idea they had.

I began to expound on a theme I used in my motivational sessions and had applied to my entertainment ventures. I went on about how sex and death are the two main drives in life and how they are manifested as the emotions of greed and fear.

A gentlemen's club, I explained, was sexy. It would help satisfy man's insatiable appetite for young, firm, fresh, nubile, and willing flesh. It would be a place where men of all ages could feel young, virile, powerful, even immortal.

A club for women would offer the same thing but in a different way, I went on. Clubs like Chippendales and shows like *Dear Diary* present a more romantic scenario and cater to more subdued sexual urges, yet if done properly they let women feel eternally desirable. Any club that focused on those emotions, I assured them, would be successful.

I went on about how a club could also capitalize by having a big name or personality attached to it.

Cummings had heard all this before, yet he seemed to be listening intently. Jody was hanging on my every word, and Jeff and Gary were positively transfixed. Boy, was I turned on by having such an interested audience. But in the end I made it clear that I did not want to get involved with Gary and Jeff's plan, as I envisioned myself becoming a much more exciting guy than some pasta joint owner.

After all, we were about to sign the contracts on *Dear Diary,* and the Hewlett Harbor group also seemed interested in Mitts and Tits. We'd even begun to stitch together some of the vignettes for *Dear Diary*. I loved the creative time with the dancers and Kelly. They were top pros and I appreciated their talent. I have always been someone who enjoys watching a top-flight professional work, whether the person is a carpenter or a brain surgeon. I appreciate skill and education. Kelly had both attributes, as well as that great beauty. Oh, I was counting the hours to my birthday.

On top of all this was the rumor that M. J. Peter was having trouble putting together his financing, so that we were actually gaining on him. One night, walking to meet Kelly for dinner, I stopped in front of the Great American Clubhouse (the former Club A) on Sixtieth Street, which was one of the places Peter was trying to move into, and stood in front of the doorway. I focused my eyes on the entrance. I could see myself standing there as the owner of the greatest gentlemen's club in history—master of all I saw. It was a spiritual moment for me. I was filled with the feeling of success. And my birthday was coming closer and closer.

Then, the next day, all hell broke loose.

Larry, Cummings, and I met with the attorney who was putting the deal together with the Hewlett Harbor group. He was the son of one of the big investors. He was not a particularly impressive fellow. As an attorney his credentials left a lot to be desired. He did not practice law but rather, from a seedy office on a seedy block on Eighth Avenue, put deals together for his father's friends. For most of October and November he kept putting us off with complaints that it was hard to get everyone together around the holidays. But he continued to make promises that everyone would deliver their shares and that by early 1990 we could get *Dear Diary* off the ground.

To be fair, he had spent a lot of time and energy drawing up contracts, an investment deal for Cummings, Larry, and myself, and a creative deal for Levy, Garland, the dancers, and Kelly. So I had reason to believe he was working as hard as he could on making the dream a reality.

Then, that day, all of a sudden he started making demands on the contracts that were different from what we had always agreed upon. All of a sudden the Hewlett guys wanted a bigger percentage. They wanted to boost their take to 30 percent as opposed to the 20 we'd talked about, and even worse they wanted us to personally guarantee their investment, which would be nearly a half-million dollars. We argued about it all that day and the next.

What they were really asking for was a 30 percent piece of whatever we made without risking anything, since they wanted us to guarantee their investment. I thought it was ridiculous and was angered by the way they sprung their demands on us at the last minute.

I realized these guys were just a bunch of barracudas who were looking to take us to the cleaners. I do not blame them for trying to make the best deal for themselves; no one invests in a business to lose money. But we'd always been up front about the risk, and if they did not want to take it, they should not have led us along.

Anyway, we finally stomped out of Junior's crummy office in a huff, agreeing amongst ourselves not to do business with that bunch. But that really left us out in the cold, and I spent the rest of the day fulfilling my obligation to let the rest of the gang know the money had fallen through.

On hearing the news, Garland, Levy, and Merritt said they would have to move on to other projects. That really hurt, because having those names attached to my idea gave me a cachet of respectability that was going to be hard to replace.

Prevot and Rapp took the news very hard. They were really going to hit it big with *Dear Diary*. For instance, they were going to get $500 a week during the rehearsal period, then salaries of $80,000 each during the run of the show, plus the opportunity to work the audience so that horny women could stuff money into their bulging pouches.

That evening, during a meeting with Larry and Cummings, it became clear that they too would have to get on with their lives. Even the Asian investors backed out when they heard the news; at least, they explained, they did not want to carry the financial burden alone. The biggest blow came when Kelly said she would now have to take a job back in Vegas. She promised to try to get back for my birthday. All of a sudden, and with no way to explain it, everything had fallen through; gone south, in the toilet.

By the end of the year Larry was back in his advertising business full-time and Cummings was selling real estate. *Dear Diary* became a great idea that never happened.

These developments shook my usual resolution. I have to admit I gave serious thought to abandoning my idea altogether and just going back into the investment brokerage game full-time. I had no heart for working out; I was eating junk food; I even passed up an evening with Tina.

Alicia was a great comfort to me during those days. She was someone who knew what it was like to be way down, and she sympathized with my situation. She was smart enough to realize that it was not the end of the world and that I should try to learn something from the experience. I was shooting for something really big, and that usually means the flip side is a long hard fall.

Christmas is usually such an exciting time in New York, even for non-Christians, but that year, for me, it passed in a blur of depression. Even Bob's stories about his latest conquests could not bring me out of it, and one night I refused to meet him and Lana at the Pussycat Lounge for a drink.

New Year's Eve was a complete downer, and I stayed in a funk until the first week of January, when Jody's friend Jeff the Psychic called.

"I want to set up a meeting with an attorney I think you should meet. He's working on a restaurant/club deal."

My first impulse was to refuse the meeting. The attorneys from Hewlett had screwed up my whole plan. I felt attorneys were just out for themselves. But I forced myself to keep my mind open, and I said okay. After all, what did I have to lose. I agreed to meet at Grandpa's restaurant in Greenwich Village.

The night of the meeting came, and I could not really get up for it. I decided to take a totally cynical stance on whatever went down. I did not even dress in my usual businessman's uniform of suit and wing tips. I just threw on some jeans, a sweater, and a baseball cap and walked over to Grandpa's.

Something Jay Cummings used to say to me was ringing in my ears as I entered the restaurant. "Just remember," he used to say, "attorneys are deal breakers, not deal makers." That had certainly been driven home by the experience with the Hewlett Harbor humps.

When Jeff the Psychic saw me approach the table he almost spit out his orange juice. My whole attitude—clothes, body language, the look on my face—said, "Fuck you, Mr. Park Avenue Attorney, I don't give a shit what you have to say."

The well-dressed man at the table with Jeff rose and offered his hand. Jeff introduced him as Michael Blutrich of Blutrich, Falcone & Miller. I knew who he was and I knew the firm. They were Park Avenue hotshots. Most people who did business and brokered deals in New York knew they were politically connected to Governor Mario Cuomo. In New York connections mean everything, and they connected on the highest level. It was widely believed that if Cuomo failed in his political life he would become a partner with Blutrich, Falcone & Miller. It did not matter if this was true or not. Just the fact that people believed it added to the influence of the firm.

If Blutrich was bothered by the way I was dressed, he did not let it show. He was a cherubic, cheerful fellow in his late twenties like myself, and I immediately took a liking to him. But I wondered what he wanted with me, a recent failure in the nightclub business.

CHAPTER 10

Manhattan West

While we waited for our food Jeff the Psychic explained why he thought Michael Blutrich and Jay Bildstein should get together on a project. He told of a restaurant project in Los Angeles that was in danger of folding. He reminded me of a little speech I made the first time we met when he asked if I would be interested in joining in a pasta restaurant/comedy club restaurant.

I remembered telling him that if I was to get involved in something like that it would be due more to the connection with "Grandpa" Al Lewis than to the type of restaurant it was.

That night in Jody's apartment I was riding high, my dreams of *Dear Diary* having not yet been shot down, and I expounded like the impresario I hoped to someday be.

I'd told the group, which included Jody's friend Gary and Jay Cummings, that with the economy heading for the doldrums, a successful restaurant or club would need some real sex appeal and star power to make a dent in the business. We were not talking about strip joints or table dancing gentlemen's clubs; rather, Jeff and Gary were interested in high-concept restaurants.

"Jay, I remember you talking about how a famous personality could be used to create a theme," Jeff said.

In spite of the bad mood I was in, and despite the presence of Blutrich, which I still did not understand, I started talking about my nightclub theories. I figured that if Jeff had promoted me as an expert, I'd better be able to put forth my ideas at the drop of a hat. Besides, I am the eternal optimist, and just talking about clubs raised my spirits. In spite of myself, I opened up to Blutrich.

Jeff, who had heard it all before, egged me on.

"A restaurant fronted by a big name that might be used to create some kind of theme would give people a sense of belonging, a place to migrate to," I said. I was beginning to wonder if Jeff was trying to snare Blutrich in his pasta/comedy idea. I was not sure "Grandpa" Al Lewis was that big a name. As I was going on about how people loved big celebrities, the linguine and Caesar salads arrived, and Blutrich interrupted me.

He had been sitting in a kind of stunned silence, but now he got right to the point. "Look," he said, "I have dumped all kinds of big money into a restaurant in L.A. I got talked into it by some people I used to do business with in New York. Right now I feel upside down in the project; I don't know if it's coming or going, and I'm about to lose big money. It's over five thousand square feet. It's called Manhattan West, it's on Restaurant Row, you know, La Cienega Boulevard; a great location—and it was just rated as the number one new French restaurant in town."

The conversation was becoming very interesting to me. I could see that Blutrich, like many good attorneys, was an engrossing storyteller. He really had my attention.

"The food in the place is great," he continued, "and it is possible I am going to get the maître d' from Nicky Blair's, the city's top spot right now, although that appears on shaky ground."

I had, of course, heard of Nicky Blair's; some top Hollywood stars were rumored to be its backers. I'm not talking about a couple of Chippendales dancers. Everyone from Streisand to Spielberg turned up in the gossip columns in connection with Nicky Blair's.

Blutrich went on: "The trouble is, I am not pulling enough bodies through the door to carry the nut. They killed me on cost overruns in the kitchen. The place has been running over budget since we opened it six months ago, and it does not show signs of improving."

He explained he had two partners, whom he identified only as Steve and Richie. Richie was dating Cathy Moriarty, the beautiful blonde who was great as Jack La Motta's wife Vicky in *Raging Bull.*

Great, I thought, someone is pitching me another losing proposition. Could this be Prevot and Rapp all over again, and this time without even the luscious Kelly to keep some birthday fantasies cooking for me?

We were into some veal parmigiana when Blutrich finally got to the heart of the matter.

"What my associates want to do, Jay," he said, "is abandon the French restaurant crap and run away from the snotty Manhattan West theme. We want to set up a new place with a bigger draw."

He said that Steve and Richie had worked out a deal with former National Football League star Lyle Alzado, who in his All-Star career played for the Cleveland Browns, Denver Broncos, and Oakland Raiders. He was a beloved sports figure in all those cities and enjoyed a national reputation as a tough, exciting, big-play player.

Alzado, according to Blutrich, had agreed to license his name to the restaurant, which would be turned into a freewheeling, rock 'n' roll sports bar. The football great would lend the club all his trophies and awards and other memorabilia for display purposes, and he would contact his pro athlete friends in all sports for some of the same from them.

In addition, Richie was promising that his girlfriend would serve as a hostess when her film work permitted.

"The location is actually better suited for a place like that," Blutrich said. He explained it was the former site of Alan Hale's Lobster Shanty, which was successful for more than fifteen years.

Blutrich had actually eaten at the Lobster Shanty with his wife years earlier, and they'd even seen Alan Hale there. He, of course, was best known as "the Skipper" from *Gilligan's Island* and was popular with two generations of television watchers. Tourists could not get enough of him.

"I think it will be the same with Lyle Alzado. Everyone visiting L.A. will want to come meet the famous football legend, and they'll eat and drink while they're there. It will be great," said Blutrich.

All of a sudden I was back in the ball game. He had not said anything yet, but I knew Blutrich wanted me in on his deal. The only thing was, I was not sure how I felt about that.

"The place is three thousand miles away, but I am convinced it will work with the right amount of money and the right people involved in it," Blutrich said. He stopped talking and stared right at me.

After a moment or two he started up again. He was playing me like I was the jury and he was delivering closing arguments.

"You said Al Lewis was potentially the most interesting part of a comedy club/restaurant deal, didn't you?"

"Well, yes," I stammered.

"And didn't you tell Jeff that you'd be interested in any deal that had either sex appeal or a big name attached?"

Again I stammered a lukewarm affirmative answer.

I felt like I was in an episode of *The Twilight Zone*. If Michael Blutrich was such a big shot attorney, why was he making such a strong pitch to the relatively unknown Jay Bildstein? I figured Jeff had given him an exaggerated view of where I stood in the nightclub business.

I could not comprehend what he needed with me. After all, he had already poured a small fortune into Manhattan West, and now he had Lyle Alzado and Cathy Moriarty aboard to try to salvage something out of the disaster. Plus a guy like him should have had many routes of investment, a lot of access to money.

That is what I was thinking, and because I was basically in such a shitty mood that is what I told him. I dug up a line I thought was from one of the *Godfather* movies and in my most humble voice asked: "Why are you bestowing this good fortune upon me?

"I mean you are a big, successful Park Avenue attorney and you are presenting me with a deal that sounds very strong. To what do I owe this generosity?" I was thinking there was something wrong with the picture before me, and I really was nasty to Blutrich. He would have had every right to just get up and leave the table. I am eternally grateful that he did not, because as things turned out that meeting in Grandpa's was the catalyst that finally led me to my dream.

Blutrich answered my questions like the stand-up guy that he is. He said that he had run into so many calamities with the Manhattan West project—everything from the wrong kind of pizza oven to mistakes in the earthquake protection engineering—that he was left high and dry in the favor department. He had exhausted his regular network of contacts, both political and financial, and he was still facing ruin.

He knew Jeff because he had an interest in psychic phenomena, and he said Jeff had spoken highly of me. He asked around and found that I did indeed have a reputation as an on-the-ball investment guy.

"Jeff thinks you are a guy who can make things happen, and despite the way you are dressed tonight, I have learned to trust his judgment," Blutrich said.

Jeff broke in to emphasize that the restaurant was undergoing its transformation from Manhattan West to Alzado's even as we sat there, making it clear that Blutrich and his partners were serious about trying to recover and make a go of things.

"In a couple of weeks they are going to have a grand opening, a real Hollywood-style bash," said Jeff.

Blutrich nodded his head in agreement and asked me to consider what he'd said and to come to the opening to see what I thought of the place before we engaged in any further talk of committing money.

"Yeah, come to the opening," Jeff said. "Alzado is going to round up all his ballplaying buddies, Cathy Moriarty is bringing her actress friends, and don't forget Stallone."

Stallone. My ears perked up.

"Yeah," Blutrich piped in. "I did not want to mention it because it is far from a done deal, but Sylvester Stallone and his mother are clients of mine, and I have spoken to her about getting him to at least come to the opening, if not to invest himself. She is going to try to get him there as a favor to me, although I don't think he will be investing."

Now I was impressed. If they could bring Sylvester Stallone around, even a few times a year, that would translate into big business.

"Look, guys," I said, softening my hard-ass attitude a little bit, now that I judged them both to be sincere, "thank you for thinking of me. I will think about what you said tonight—I promise to give it some good, hard thought—and I will get back to you as soon as I can."

I had not really touched my food and I passed on the espresso as we all shook hands and I left.

Their deal sounded very exciting. It incorporated major elements of my overall philosophy—but then again, so did the dear departed *Dear Diary* and of course the still-in-the-dream-stage Mitts and Tits, or whatever I was going to call my gentlemen's club.

The relationship between Blutrich and Jeff the Psychic was not clear to me. And while I do not need much help in blowing my own horn, I had to be realistic and believe that Blutrich knew at least as many high-rolling investors and entrepreneurs as I did. After all, he was an important, successful, and gung ho guy who obviously liked to put his hand in business deals.

Hell, I thought, I should jump at the opportunity and stop being so cynical.

The next day I continued to have mixed feelings about the meeting with Blutrich. On the one hand I was happy that I was not knocked completely out of the box. It was good to know that there were still people, important people at that, who were interested in dealing with me on a restaurant or club project.

But still, what Jeff and Blutrich were talking about was a long way, both geographically and conceptually, from what I had in mind as New York's ultimate gentlemen's club.

The thing that appealed to me most about their Alzado's plan was the opportunity to get involved with legitimate, big-name celebrities. Lyle Alzado was hot commercial property, and Cathy Moriarty was as desirable a Hollywood actress as any. I could even picture her as a hostess in my club. Imagine customers being greeted and led to their tables by a hot number like Moriarty.

Adding to my indecision about Blutrich was the undeniable fact that my reputation as a motivational speaker and sales trainer was growing by leaps and bounds. As the new year began my Supreme Esteem philosophy was being booked all over the country. I had plenty to keep me busy.

A week went by and I did not reach out for Jeff or Blutrich. I have to admit I got a little apprehensive about not hearing from them. Maybe, I thought, I'd seemed cooler to their proposition than I really was. Or maybe Blutrich took a look at me in my jeans and sweatshirt, put that together with my cynicism, and decided I was not worth the effort.

But the next week Jeff called me. He was as friendly as could be, thanked me profusely for taking the time to meet with him and Blutrich, and asked me if I had thought about their proposition. I found myself very relieved that Jeff called. It was like when you are playing hard to get with a girl and a lot of time goes by, and just when you think you blew it, she calls. But instinctively I decided to continue to play hardball.

I cannot explain why—maybe I was still gun-shy over the *Dear Diary* defeat—but I just had a gut feeling that I would be better off in the long run if I once again put Jeff off.

"I'm sorry, Jeff, but I am into other things right now. I really do not have the time to get involved in a project three thousand miles away," I said. "I'm just not up for a new adventure." As I spoke, Jay Cummings's words about attorneys being deal breakers ran, once again, through my subconscious.

Jeff tried again to persuade me to at least come out to the grand opening but then finally hung up with the promise to stay in touch. I did not know Jeff that well but I guessed I'd really impressed him with my "sex and death" lecture the night Jody introduced us in her apartment.

So, there I was in mid-January 1990, a few days before my thirtieth birthday, hanging up on the chance to do a deal with Michael Blutrich and Lyle Alzado. I knew I had come to a point in life where I had to either refocus my attention on getting my table dancing club opened or get on with other things. My dream was on the line. Unfortunately, I did not have any clear plan of operation.

About a month later, with no progress made, I was meeting with a sales group in lower Manhattan. I was in great form as I laid out my particular brand of motivational strategy to them. Their firm was paying me top dollar to give its salesmen a kick in the ass and I went on for more than two hours about how they should not lose sight of their goals and should not let adversity turn them away from their desire to be successful. When I finished I got a standing ovation and a few of the salesmen even asked me for my autograph. One woman among the group asked me for my telephone number, which happens more often than you would think during these presentations.

As I left the office building to meet a friend for dinner, I found myself across the street from the Pussycat Lounge. I stopped and stared for a minute or two, and my own words resounded in my head. It dawned on me that I was losing sight of my goal. I was being paid large sums all over the country to help others succeed, and I had given up on myself. It did not make sense. I crossed the street, and for the first time in many months I entered the surreal world of the Pussycat.

Alicia was there when I walked in. At first she pretended not to see me, then she decided to ignore me. After I sat down at the bar and ordered a cranberry juice, though, she did come over.

"Well, well, Bildstein the Great returns. Long time no see or hear, big shot—where have you been?" she said. Her tone of voice captured her anger at me. She was mad that I had fallen out of touch, and she let me know it.

When she came up for air, I explained that I was feeling like crap and told her about how *Dear Diary* had gone into the toilet and how I was just floundering around with my gentlemen's club plans.

I thought I might get some sympathy from Alicia, a person who knew what it was like to be caught on the other side of success, but she laced into me even harder. She called me a bullshit artist.

"I knew you would never do it," she said, scowling. "It was just a line. I can't believe I even put any credence in what you had to say in the first place. You're just another loser with a line."

I realize now that her words expressed her own disappointment. She was really rooting for me. But at the time I was livid, I was beside myself with anger. Who was this barmaid in a scuzzhole to call me a loser!

Who did she think she was! Fuck her, I thought; fuck everyone. Fuck me!

Her words were like a knife slicing into my heart, not because I felt like a loser, but because I had come up dry in my quest for a club. And here was someone of questionable accomplishments challenging my ability to achieve.

I was reminded of a feeling I once had in a physics class back in Martin Van Buren High School right before a certain test. The teacher, Mr. Gottlieb, said he expected the class to do miserably on it.

"I expect most of you to fail my exam next week and I know that Polly will get the top grade," he said.

He really pissed me off. I was seething at his presumption. Who the hell did Gottlieb think he was predicting that Polly would beat me out on his test? I decided to make him eat his words. I went home and studied harder than I ever had before. The result: Bildstein 96 percent, Polly 85 percent. Everyone else failed. I was number one, she was number two. Suck on that, Gottlieb, I thought.

That same rage overtook me that day in the Pussycat. Who was Alicia to predict what Jay Bildstein could or could not do? Bildstein could do whatever he set his fucking mind to do.

So, I smashed my money down on the bar and muttered something like "Nice to see you" to Alicia and stomped out. My relationship with Alicia would never recover from that moment, but the incident was what I needed to get back on the track. All of a sudden I could not wait to get started again. I stopped at a public telephone on the corner and called an investor I had met a few days earlier. I pitched him the gentlemen's club idea and said I would get back to him.

That evening I began contacting potential investors at a furious pace. I was still not getting much positive feedback, but it felt great to once again be in the hunt.

Two more months passed and I continued to work on my dream. I was so resolute, I scared myself. I knew I would pursue my goal until the day I died.

Then, in April, Jeff called. He wanted me to come to another meeting with Blutrich. This time it would be in the attorney's Park Avenue office. I agreed, thinking my standoffish position the first time around must have worked to my advantage. People always want what they can't have, which is a good thought to remember if you ever want to open up a table dancing club.

We met in Blutrich's office the next day. Without ceremony he began to tell me how great Alzado's was doing. He said he and his partners wanted to expand the place and he asked if I would be interested in getting involved now that the concept had proven a success.

He told me about all the celebrities who'd showed up opening night. (Apparently my not being there did not put a damper on the party.) A picture of Mickey Rourke riding his Hog right through the club made the national wires. Al Davis, owner of the Raiders was there. Whoopi Goldberg and Sylvester Stallone's mother showed up, although not Sly himself.

I told Blutrich that my situation had changed and I had some time and some new contacts and that I would be interested in seeing the club firsthand. He offered me the run of the place. "Go hang out there for a few days," he said. "I know you will be impressed."

I agreed. In early May I flew to Los Angeles. It was a trip that was to change my life forever and put me on a direct course to the opening of my dream club.

CHAPTER 11 Alzado's

As a matter of survival, I decided to take the plunge with Michael Blutrich and Lyle Alzado. I accepted the fact that I was not having success raising the money for my own club, and it made sense to get involved with something that at least was a real working project.

It was now May and the restaurant on La Cienga had been booming since January. Also, Blutrich had impressed me as a no-nonsense guy. He was on a different level from the crowd around *Dear Diary*. Despite all their success, they never operated on a Park Avenue level. There was always an undercurrent of homophobia surrounding the male dancers, and while their show was top-drawer and they had great talent, investors were always wary of their lifestyles. It was interesting how many men thought the male dancers were gay. I think other men were jealous of the way the Chippendales dancers perfected their bodies and stayed in great shape. Women did not talk about strippers and topless dancers the same way, although I was to learn that many of the Chippendales dancers did lead a gay lifestyle.

I was certain that Blutrich was not the type to be spending $4,000 of the company's profits on dry cleaning bills every month, as Tom Lord had done.

So in mid-May, Jeff the Psychic and I met at JFK Airport for a trip to Los Angeles. Blutrich had indicated he was willing to foot the bill for the trip and a few days in L.A., but I decided to pay my own way. My thinking was that he had sought me out as full-fledged business partner so I should carry my own weight. I believe, though, that he paid the way for Jeff. I was still not clear about their relationship, but I would learn later that Blutrich had many diverse interests and enjoyed the company of psychics. Sylvester Stallone's mother, his client, was a person who claimed psychic powers.

Jeff was a pretty popular person in the world of psychic phenomena. Many of his clients were American Airlines employees. Because of that we were given the red-carpet treatment at the JFK terminal. He seemed to know everyone in the airport, from flight attendants to pilots and porters. We were ushered into the Admiral's Club, where we were surrounded by people thanking him for all the help he had provided them. One gushing young woman, in a crisp flight attendant's uniform, almost burst into tears when she told him that everything he'd said had turned out to be right and she was back with her boyfriend. Jeff responded like some kind of royalty acknowledging his subjects.

Personally, I did not believe in psychic phenomena on demand—that is, in a business sense. I do believe that some cosmic forces might come into play, out of the clear blue, in our lives. My own inclination, as a teenager, to be drawn to nightclubs, seems, in retrospect, to have been some kind of cosmic attraction. Some people do have what we call native intuition or gut feelings that seem to help them make the right choices, but I believe this is more a matter of education and experience rising from the subconscious than anything else. I do not believe that those who claim psychic powers on demand, like some of the charlatans in show business, are in any way legitimate.

Jeff and I reposed in our cushy first class accommodations and talked about psychic powers as we flew across the country to our destiny. "If you can do these psychic readings," I asked him, "why can't you predict the eighth race at Belmont or the next bullish trend in the stock market? Better still, why can't you just tell me the name of some fledgling company that sells for about two dollars a share and is going to be bought up by IBM?"

I really needled Jeff about that kind of stuff, and his response was always the same: "It would violate psychic spiritual doctrine" to use his powers for that sort of thing.

That answer, of course, would always cause me to increase my needling. I would only shut up when some gorgeous flight attendant stopped by with free drinks to pay homage to her spiritual leader.

I will say that Jeff did have excellent intuition about many things. He was levelheaded and knew enough to trust common sense. I guess so few of us take the time out to do the same that someone who does seems more levelheaded and serene than the rest of us.

We landed in L.A. at 11 A.M. West Coast time. I had not been there in several years, since I'd had dinner with my ex-wife in the Lobster Shanty, and everything felt very new to me.

After retrieving our baggage we made our way, via shuttle bus, to the Hertz area, where our brand-new white Lincoln Town Car was waiting. Our adrenaline was really flowing. During the forty-minute drive out to La Cienega Boulevard my mind wandered back to Baby O's and Rick's Cabaret. What I wouldn't have done for the company of a couple of those dancers—or even old Tina, who I had heard was working in a strip joint in Los Angeles—right then. I decided to drop in on her if I got the chance.

Glamorous Los Angeles passed in a blur as Jeff tooled the Lincoln past Bullocks, the Beverly Center, and other landmarks like Ma Maison Hotel.

My excitement increased as we got a good look at the Hollywood Hills, where superstars like Madonna had their mansions. Maybe this town, I thought to myself, would be the catalyst to break the inertia my own project had fallen into.

As we pulled up to Alzado's, a sedate brick building located next to the Beverly Hills Luxury Car Showroom, a place that specialized in Rolls-Royces, Porsches, and Mercedes-Benzes for the stars of La La Land, and on the same block as such standout restaurants as L'Orangerie and L'Ermitage, my mood was A-plus positive.

We pulled up directly in front and handed the car over to a valet. Inside the front door, a luxurious feeling of dry cool air replaced the muggy Los Angeles noon hour. We were greeted by Blutrich's two partners, Richie and Steve, who were expecting us. The restaurant was officially closed at that hour and all around us the staff was in a state of competent frenzy, preparing for the early-evening dinner crowd that had made Alzado's the most popular nightspot in town.

As our hosts gave us warm Hollywood greetings, my first impression of the place was that it was very high-class. Clearly a lot of money had been spent on lighting fixtures, carpets, and other accoutrements. It all had a very stylish feel to it. I noticed Lyle Alzado himself sitting at the rear of the bar, apparently engrossed in a sandwich.

Even in the dim light I could see he was a gigantic figure. His arms burst out of a black T-shirt as if they were about to explode. He was forty-one-years old and training to make a comeback in the National Football League. The legendary owner Al Davis had agreed to give him a chance at a comeback with the Raiders. He was training with the master power lifter Fred "the Squat" Hatfield.

Jeff knew Richie and Steve, as well as Lyle, from the days he'd spent at the club during the changeover from Manhattan West. The three were very congenial and warm as they introduced me to the football legend.

Lyle hardly looked up from his sandwich as Richie explained that I was a friend of Michael Blutrich's who was interested in investing in the club. He hardly moved from his stool as he extended his hand for a firm but lukewarm handshake. I thought he was pretty rude.

It was an interesting scene. Richie had a thick Bronx accent that revealed his background, and Steve was from Yonkers. Lyle was born in Brooklyn and grew up in the Five Towns section of Long Island, and Jeff, like me, was from Queens.

We were five New York City guys, three thousand miles from home, sitting at the helm of the hottest nightclub in Los Angeles. I tried not to show the sense of electricity that was running through me. I knew it was best for any deal I would ever eventually negotiate that I never let on what a great opportunity it was. It was best to appear nonchalant, but it was a challenge. I was pumping on all pistons.

Richie and Steve gave me a quick tour of the place. I think they believed I knew a lot more about the actual workings—that is, the pots and pans—of a restaurant operation than I did. As they took me behind the bar, then showed me the kitchen, storage areas, and office, I absorbed everything they said. I figured they had everything under control at Alzado's, and in the back of my mind, as always, was my gentlemen's club. It too would need a bar, kitchen, and offices. This was turning into a real educational experience for me. As a businessman I always knew that beautiful women with perfect breasts were not enough. A successful club needed a successful business operation behind it. The wonderful Club A might have survived years longer if its business had been in order. And I knew firsthand how a poor back-office operation was destroying Chippendales even as horny women packed the place night after night.

Following the brief tour, Jeff and I took a quick ride to the Hyatt on Sunset Boulevard, where we showered and changed. We were both running on pure adrenaline and could not calm down enough to pass the afternoon at the hotel before heading back to Alzado's to catch the evening's action. So we took a ride around Beverly Hills. Jeff, who knew L.A. pretty well, acted as tour guide.

He piloted the Lincoln around Rodeo Drive and Sunset Boulevard near the Beverly Hills Hilton. He knew the homes of some big entertainment industry moguls and pointed them out along the route.

But my mind was somewhere else entirely. I was working overtime thinking up all the possible angles for my club that might grow out of my involvement in Alzado's.

Primarily, I was being offered an opportunity to get in on the ground floor of a great nightclub/restaurant phenomenon. In a short time it had become the ultimate Tinsel Town hot spot. Actors, actresses, models, wanna-be's, agents, and beautiful people of all sorts flocked there every night. The owners had a plan to take the concept national, and from where I stood that looked like a good idea.

Secondly, I had to consider where all these new contacts might take me. I was beginning to think that I should approach Michael with my gentlemen's club plan. My mind raced with the possibilities that might lead to.

That evening Jeff and I dressed in our New York version of California casual—he in a sweater, jeans, and bucks, and me in a black sport jacket, button-down black shirt, jeans, and loafers—and headed back to the restaurant.

At seven forty-five it was still relatively early in the evening, especially by New York standards, but a crowd was already forming outside the building. About fifty people, most younger men and women, well dressed in expensive jeans and chinos and silk blazers, stood behind velvet ropes attempting to get in for dinner. Richie was at the front door and came through the line to greet me. The scene brought back memories of Steve Rubell and that fateful night twelve years earlier when I was led through the begging masses into the Kingdom of Heaven that was Studio 54. No longer did I float in that purgatory of the streets known to the less fortunate as "Studio 86" and "Outside Looking Insville."

Right inside the door Richie introduced us to his girlfriend, Cathy Moriarty, who was living up to Blutrich's advance billing and pitching in that night as hostess. Cathy's greeting was genuinely warm. She looked stunning in a tight, knee-length black sequined dress, and we made some small talk about how she had risen from obscurity in Yonkers to Hollywood stardom after her smashing role as Vicky La Motta. I could not help but think how wonderful it would be to have someone like her greeting guests at my club. My mind flashed briefly to Kelly and her promise to wear a latex suit for me on my birthday. I had a funny vision of her dressed like that, standing at the entrance of Alzado's asking people if they had reservations. I imagined her in that latex suit walking people to their tables. I laughed to myself at the picture. What an impression she would make on the diners. Maybe it would work in New York but probably not L.A.

One of Cathy's assistants, a beautiful young girl who had "Aspiring Actress" written all over her, interrupted the chat to take us to our table.

The table had been reserved for us in the back of the large room and gave us an extraordinary view of everything going on at the bar and the other tables. I was impressed by the careful effort Richie and Steve were going through to make sure I came away with the most favorable opinion possible of the club. They were two smart guys. They had their act together.

The restaurant was not yet filled to capacity, but most of the tables were occupied by the Beautiful People. They were tanned, relaxed, well dressed. The bar was primarily populated by model and actress types in their early twenties and their male counterparts. They were called MAWs by the L.A. crowd, an acronym for Models, Actresses, Waiters, and it was not considered pejorative. They were living the life that almost every major star lived before he or she made it big. They were working hard, and part of their work was to see and be seen in the town's glory spots. Alzado's was high on that list.

There were blondes, brunettes, redheads, all looking physically fit and showing a lot of leg and skin. Many were as good-looking as the women in Rick's. They all had flashing white teeth and were either drinking Perrier water or cranberry juice. These were not the types to consume large amounts of alcohol, thus limiting the amount of money that could be made from them. But a cranberry juice cocktail, without the vodka, still went for upward of $4, so the profit was there. And of course, that crowd did draw the heavy drinkers and big spenders trying to pick them up.

As rock music pumped through the speakers hidden around the room, I began to notice some familiar faces. They were actors and actresses who were commonly featured as supporting cast members on television and the movies. They were successful, but not household names.

After studying the crowd I noticed Lyle's memorabilia scattered on shelves and cases set into the walls of the club: trophies, plaques, photographs, and uniform items. There were also some football jerseys that had been lent to the club by his friends. Some were signed, like the one from San Francisco 49ers quarterback

Joe Montana and the Buffalo Bills number 32 once worn by O.J. Simpson.

On sale at a small souvenir counter were shirts emblazoned with the slogan "Alzado's: A Rock and Roll Sports Bar." It certainly was. And did it ever rock with its great music, hearty food, and Beautiful People.

I went to check out the men's room so I could eavesdrop on some of the conversations. Names like William Morris, ICM, and Paramount floated through the air, dancing on the melodies of the background rock music.

We ordered penne and vodka sauce and a really good Caesar salad. Then we finished it off with a tiramisù that was so extraordinary we revisited it piece by piece throughout the night, backed up with iced espresso. No booze for me that night. I wanted to drink in every bit of the scene without alcohol. I wanted my mind clear so I would remember everything precisely as it was.

Word got around that Jeff and I were "part of the outfit from back east that owned Alzado's" and after a while the MAWs began stopping by our table. It was a head trip and a half. I did nothing to dispel the notion that I was an owner, even though I still had not signed on the dotted line. With each new group of girls—they usually came to us in pairs or threesomes—offering their names and praising our club, I could not help but imagine how they would look dressing up New York's ultimate gentlemen's club.

Around midnight Lyle Alzado arrived larger than life and to great fanfare. He was like a conquering hero when he walked in and made his way through the now overflowing crowd. To my surprise he headed straight to our table.

This time he was not abrupt or cold toward us. He even made a half-assed apology for his earlier rudeness, saying he had been on a break from his grueling training and was in a surly mood.

Lyle convinced me he was genuinely glad to meet me. He sat down and we talked about different ideas for his restaurant. I said that the sports/celebrity scene was just what America ached for. I was on record as believing that the celebrity sports bar, with its star power, had the sex appeal and the potential to confer immortality on ordinary lives that people longed for. A chain of Alzado's, I told him, would be a highly marketable venture, national in scope.

I spoke about how drawing celebrities into a club, even if you comped them for their food and booze, was the way to attract a crowd of average Joes coming in with the hope of spotting, or maybe even speaking to, a star. And the average Joes were the clients that would eventually create the profits. This had been proven years before at Studio 54.

I pointed to a couple I'd met earlier. Their names were David and Susan and they were from Omaha, Nebraska. He was in L.A. for a job interview at NBC News, and they had read about Alzado's in a syndicated gossip column. So they decided why not come over for dinner in the hope of catching sight of a star. Their bill for dinner and drinks would come to more than $100, and they were glad to spend it. Back home it was a sure bet they would tell their friends about seeing Cathy Moriarty, Lyle Alzado, and a host of stars like, "You know him, he was the detective on *Hill Street Blues*." Those friends would visit Alzado's when they were in L.A.—or even better, when a link in the chain opened in Omaha.

As the night went on the "A" list stars began arriving at the restaurant. Lyle got up to greet his flavor of the month, a *Playboy* centerfold named Cindy. She was about five foot ten and had a pair of knockers that were bursting through her white T-shirt. Her nipples were totally visible; I could not keep my eyes off them. After a brief introduction they left to mingle with the crowd. Jeff then went to pursue a petite brunette at the bar who had introduced herself to us earlier.

Mickey Rourke and his crew of phony Hell's Angels took over a corner of the bar and were quickly surrounded by admirers, drawn to them like flies to fertilizer.

These were not the same genuine Hell's Angels I'd once had to deal with as a bouncer at Max's Kansas City. Those guys, with their leather colors, and fearsome attitudes, scared customers away and caused a lot of fights. Rourke's crew was more wanna-be's with very expensive Rodeo Drive biker outfits and sneering attitudes more reminiscent of acting class than Alphabet City.

I turned my attention away from Rourke and his asshole friends just in time to catch a party of four sitting down at the table next to mine. One of the four was Clint Eastwood, unassuming and casual as he took his seat. Over the years I have been in the company of many rich and successful people, but none impressed me more than Eastwood did that night. He was in great shape and exuded an easy confidence. With him was his son Kyle, actor Jeff Fahey, and another man whose identity I never learned. In the background my favorite song, the Eagles' "Hotel California," was playing. I cannot remember feeling more exhilarated in my whole life. I just looked around me and felt so mellow that I did not want the moment to end.

I did my best to remain cool and unimpressed by Clint's arrival. I did not stare at him. But the room did take on a different feeling with him in it. Later the cast of HBO's *First and Ten*, the sexy football soap opera, came in, adding to an already incredible scene. By this time I had made up my mind to get involved in Alzado's.

As if on cue, Carlos, the headwaiter, came by my table to ask if everything was copacetic.

"This is a great scene," I said.

"Just another Friday night in Alzado's," was his reply.

We stayed until closing time. As we left, the street outside Alzado's was filled with the thundering sound of about forty motorcycles revving up and screeching off. It was a surreal scene that made me think of Bob Seegar's "Hollywood Nights."

On the way back to the hotel, Jeff and I hardly exchanged a word. We did not have to. The evening had been a tremendous success. We both knew there was something special about Alzado's.

I was really charged up and could not sleep. I kept running pictures of the beautiful young actresses I had seen in Alzado's through my mind. I decided to grab a cab and try to catch up with Tina.

The club she was working in was right near Los Angeles Airport. It might have been a step above the Pussycat Lounge, but it was a small step. I paid a $3 admission fee and had to walk through a turnstile to get in. Inside there was a beautiful Latin-looking girl, with dark skin and small pear-shaped breasts, dancing totally nude on a stage that wrapped around the entire front portion of the bar. Men were sitting on stools along the bar and when they offered money the dancer would sashay over to them, lie down on the floor, spread her legs, and give them a great look at what she ate for breakfast. I will say she was very beautiful.

Other women were circulating through the bar asking men who were sitting at small round tables if they wanted a private dance. Something I considered a turnoff was that there were groups of two or three girls standing around, talking to each other and ignoring the men at the tables. It was not a very well-managed club.

I soaked all of it in as I took a seat at one of the tables. By this time I was an expert at appraising strip clubs. I could have started a side business. "Wanna know how your club is doing? Are your girls producing at their greatest levels? Call Jay B. for a quick and affordable appraisal."

In the rear of the club it appeared to my expert eye that some friction dancing, à la the Harmony, was going on. In general the girls were pretty attractive—not Houston caliber, but very presentable.

A waitress quickly approached and asked what she could get for me. She was wearing tights under her leotard, which I took as a sign that she was not a nude dancer. There was a menu of drinks on the table; all were different concoctions of soft drinks, since hard liquor was not allowed at L.A. bars if the girls were totally nude, same as New York. I ordered a diet Coke, which listed at $4.50, and asked if a girl named Tina was working that night.

I was a little disappointed when she said she did not know any Tina, but my spirits improved in a second when Tina showed up at the table.

"Jay, I thought that was you," she said, a bright smile on her face, which reminded me of the first night we'd met back in Rick's.

"Oh, I'm so glad you're here. You want a private dance?" she asked.

"Not right now."

"Oh, please. Come on, I would like to dance for you. I can't stay here if I don't dance."

I was tempted. My blood was boiling over from all the flirting at Alzado's, and I was curious about the scene in this place. On the other hand, I did not want a commercial relationship with Tina, and I told her so.

"Oh don't worry about that," she said, "nothing really happens."

So I allowed her to lead me to the rear of the bar where there were a few tables partitioned off by thin walls. I sat on one side of the table and Tina went to the other. A large sign on the wall behind her read, "Private Dances $12. Tipping is appreciated."

When the music changed, Tina pushed some hidden button which turned on a glowing pinkish light and began a slow, snake-like dance, during which she removed her one-piece leotard.

Naked, she twisted and turned toward me, never getting close enough to touch. I noticed she had not yet gotten her boob job, but she was truly a beautiful girl with a perfectly proportioned figure. It would be a shame to insert silicone into her soft, youthful breasts, I mused. One thing I'd never noticed about Tina before was that her nipples were different. One was inverted. I thought that was cute.

I was very embarrassed when she bent backward and thrust her pussy toward me. It was worse when she got on the dirty mat that passed for a carpet and did the kind of floor work I had just seen done by the Latin girl on the stage. This might have interested a student of gynecology, but I found it distasteful, and it certainly robbed Tina of her special appeal, which was a girlish innocence. I could not wait for the song to end so her dance would be over. I liked Tina, and I thought she was humiliating herself for $12. Through the entire three-minute dance a silly smile was frozen on her face.

When I took a closer look at her, which was difficult under the very dim light, I thought I noticed a bruise on her arm and her hair clearly had not been recently washed.

When the music stopped she asked if I would like another dance.

"What I would really like is to talk to you for a while. I want to tell you about my club plans," I said.

"Well, I can't talk on duty. It would cost you twelve dollars a song."

"So, when do you get off?" I said. "I'd like to spend some time with you."

"Oh, I'm sorry, honey," she said in a totally phony tone. "My lover is waiting to take me home." She nodded toward a table, almost totally in the dark at the very rear of the club, where a gray-haired man, wearing a black suit, black shirt, and white tie, sat nursing a drink. He obviously had been watching us.

I was overtaken by a feeling of despair. This wonderful girl was sinking deeper and deeper into a world of abusive relationships. I knew there was nothing I could do about it.

"Call me when you are in New York," I said as I handed her $50 and left this shit-hole club.

The following day, I worked out in the morning and later had lunch with Jeff. After lunch we drove to Santa Monica to meet some of his friends who owned a pastaria on the Third Street Promenade. There was something about Jeff and pasta. This group was related to the famous Ferrara family that owned the superlative pastry shop in New York's Little Italy section. Their place was a nice, neat little eatery but nothing to impress their East Coast relatives with.

That evening we were back in the club. The scene was substantially the same, but this time Jeff had invited some of the many friends he had in Hollywood. These were mostly behind-the-scenes types, like the casting director for *General Hospital.* A group of serious young actors and actresses joined us. They were on the cusp of making it big, and all they talked about was "the business." I was a little put off by all the self-absorbed conversation. On Wall Street, where the stress and rewards could be just as demanding and lucrative as those of Hollywood, we did not have to constantly remind one another what business we were in.

Jeff had a great many solid contacts in L.A. His services as a psychic were much sought after in a land of such insecure people, who were in demand one day and in the toilet the next. They were always after him to help them gain some perspective on their futures. He gave them private readings in his New York office, in their Hollywood home, or sometimes by telephone. Some would even call from the set of their latest project, wanting to know if they should date a certain director or consider reading a certain script.

I remained mum about my own credentials as a professional motivator and just listened to their tales of doom and Jeff's assurances that things would work out all right for them.

Before we left the restaurant, I came up with the idea of shooting an impromptu video for use as a sales pitch to prospective investors. Jeff got a freelance crew over pretty quickly, and we taped Lyle walking around the place with his *Playboy* girlfriend, who revealed a bit of cleavage and endorsed the club while having a drink at the bar.

Twenty-four hours later I was back in New York and on the telephone with Michael Blutrich. I was no longer playing it cool. I told him honestly about the wonderful time I'd had and how I thought the Alzado's concept was a gold mine of an idea.

I said he could count me in on any investment deal aimed at expanding Alzado's into an international theme restaurant. My role would be to seek investors, to the tune of about $2 million. We would license the Alzado's name and get a small percentage of the Los Angeles club. But our main focus would be on opening new Alzado's in other cities. Initially, we thought, Boca Raton, Florida, and Westchester County, a wealthy New York suburb adjacent to the city, would be good jumping-off places.

We were having this discussion a significant period of time before the opening of Planet Hollywood on Fifty-seventh Street in Manhattan, which would kick off a trend in theme restaurants—and I was not even a psychic.

When I hung up on Blutrich I relaxed for the first time in three days. A feeling of well-being came over me. I knew I had made the right decision. The nightclub business was *my* business. I saw Jeff and Blutrich and Lyle Alzado as the people who would enable me to make my own dream possible. Once again I saw sports and sex mixing in an exciting setting. If only it were mine.

Playboy 360

With Geraldo

In Doubleplay with Mark Thompson

Me and current partner Eric Kloper in Mind Gym

Alzado's in L.A.

With football great Lyle Alzado in Alzado's

Ring announcing

Scores

New York Daily News photo

Demi Moore in Scores

New York Daily News photo

Dwight Gooden in Scores

New York Daily News photo

Ethan Hawke in Scores

CHAPTER 12

The Presentation

I was no sooner back in New York than Blutrich had me on a plane for Mexico. He knew I had some real estate and restaurant contacts down there and we both agreed that Huatulco, a beach resort about 250 miles south of Acapulco, would be a perfect place for the first Alzado's outside the United States. It was like a travel agency's poster of a beach paradise. Beautiful sand and blue skies and water were the order of every day.

I spent two weeks down there meeting with Mexican investors and a fellow I had met years ago who was the general manager of the Club Med in Huatulco. He was very enthusiastic about my Alzado's proposal. We both thought a restaurant/sports bar right on the beach would draw big crowds of jet-set vacationers and would be a perfect place for romance and sexual adventures.

I met a fantastic girl named Mona who grew up in a small village near Huatulco but had the style and grace of an international jet-setter. We spent some great hours on the beach together—in the water, on the sand, and in a little hut we found in an otherwise deserted area. She introduced me to the movers and shakers in the area, and they all agreed a restaurant like Alzado's would be a natural hit. We could picture the beautiful women who were drawn to Lyle Alzado wherever he went playing volleyball on a court right outside the restaurant. We also talked about how great they would look on the topless and all nude beaches in the area. We thought the place could be called Alzado's on the Beach.

I hated to leave the paradise on earth that Huatulco represented but I was anxious to get back to New York and see how the business end of things was proceeding.

By the time I returned Blutrich had set up a company in which Jeff and I would participate. My role was to find funding. We were looking for at least $2 million and to initiate some outside promotion. Jeff would continue to use his varied contacts to help push the project along. His was a vital role. Don't forget, Jeff first brought me to Blutrich, and I was about to make this deal happen. In a way he was responsible for everything, and I was thankful.

Blutrich and I met almost every day. There was a lot happening. I was bringing people in to look at the business plans and talking up the idea with media contacts I had met through my motivational work.

By that time Alzado's was getting a lot of ink as the number one club in L.A., surpassing Bar One and the just-opened Roxbury on Sunset Strip. With all the activity, I was still trying to pick the right time to mention my gentlemen's club to Blutrich. I was more sure than ever that the people we were now dealing with were the types that could make it happen.

Another of Blutrich's many interests was the sport of professional boxing. He was a licensed promoter in New York State. It was an interest we shared; I was a rabid boxing fan and had done some boxing as a teenager. I was actually pretty good—I could dish it out and I could take it. But I never considered making a living in the squared circle.

One of my fantasies was to be a ring announcer. I admired the late Johnny Addie, who introduced most of the great fights during the heyday of Madison Square Garden. He was one guy who could say he was in the ring with Joe Louis, Rocky Marciano, Sugar Ray Robinson, and all the rest of the legends of boxing during the forites, fifties and sixties.

When I told Blutrich about this fantasy he responded in his typical aggressive way. "You want to be a ring announcer. Okay, I'm promoting a fight at the Westchester County Center and you can announce the main event."

I could not believe my ears, but I knew that when Michael Blutrich said something, it happened. So I began practicing my ring delivery in the shower and I perfected a kind of style that combined the authority of Johnny Addie with the smoothness of Michael Buffer, the most popular of today's ring announcers.

Within ten days Blutrich got me licensed, and we drove up to the center in his limo. I had no experience as a boxing promoter, but I was a professional public speaker through my motivational training, so I had confidence that I could bring it off.

The Westchester County Center was a huge old place that was used for everything from auto shows to beauty contests. That night it was host to a card of six fights—five prelims and the main event, which I was going to announce. There were about three thousand people in the seats, a large crowd for fights in that place.

I was a little nervous as I stepped into the ring, but I grabbed the microphone like a pro and went through my routine, just like I'd practiced it in the shower.

"Ladies and gentlemen, good evening and welcome to the landmark Westchester County Center, where boxing impresario Michael Blutrich is proud to bring you an evening of fistic excellence."

My voice echoed through the nearly empty warehouselike building as I continued, "this is the main event of the evening. This event is sanctioned by the New York State Athletic Commission, the honorable Randy Gordon, chairman."

I went on to introduce the two pugs, one in the blue corner, one in the white, and finished with the flourish, "And I'm your ring announcer, Jay Bildstein."

The applause seemed thunderous. Gordon, a former television boxing commentator, came over and said I was "one of the greatest ring announcers" he had ever heard.

"Why don't you give up whatever you are doing and pursue it full-time," he said. I was flattered. I was on cloud nine—a fantasy had come true but I was not about to switch my dream of G-strings for one of jockstraps. We all had a good laugh, and I decided to raise the issue of my gentlemen's club to Blutrich on the ride home.

He had heard a little about my idea from Jeff, but he was not prepared for the pitch I delivered during the ride back to New York City. I explained everything to him. I started with the day I first got the idea, on Black Monday 1987, a day he was very familiar with, and I continued through the trips to Houston and my misadventure with the Chippendales crowd and *Dear Diary*.

I told him about the women I had met. I talked about Alicia, and Lana, and Kelly. I explained the differences between the lap dancing they did at the Harmony, the topless dancing that was done in the Pussycat and most other New York bars, and the table dancing I had seen done in the fabulous Rick's Cabaret. He interrupted for a second to ask how well I got to know some of the girls.

"Not very," I said. "So far I've been all business. Besides, most of them are pretty fucked up." I told him about my experience with Tina, starting in Rick's and ending in that dive near LAX.

I continued on about how I planned to get around the New York liquor laws by having the girls wear transparent pasties that would allow them to dance close to the customer because technically they were not topless, yet would enable the customer to see their nipples.

I told him about my concept of having a sports motif in the place, with televisions showing ball games and a small basketball court on the premises. I explained that I had already, with Jay Cummings, scouted out some prospective sites. I conceded I did not yet have a name for the place, and told him Cummings had suggested Mitts and Tits. I even told him that I had to move fast because M. J. Peter was thinking about opening a similar type club in New York, and he would be formidable competition.

Finally I laid on my theory about safe sex in the nineties, "the Age of AIDS." The men will come, look, not touch, not be touched, and go home with their libidos on fire but their consciences clear. "Their wives will be grateful to us," I said, only half joking.

When I finished my soliloquy he merely shook his head and said, "You've got to be kidding."

Then he was silent again as we drove the last fifteen minutes to my apartment building. I was exhausted. I felt like I had just thrown the dice and I needed an eight or I would go bust.

As we pulled up in front of my building he said: "Boy, now I've heard it all, a giant topless club: sports and women under one roof. I'll think about it."

But as I got out of the car I could tell that I had made a positive impact. I realized he'd never cut me off, never laughed at the idea. He'd absorbed everything I said and finished with an agreement to think about it. At that moment I did not need Jeff the Psychic to let me know I was on my way. My club was about to become reality. Soon, I knew, the most beautiful women in the world would be calling Jay Bildstein boss. And I would be "the King of Clubs."

CHAPTER 13 The Deal

As the weeks passed the situation with Alzado's got stronger and stronger. We were a happy bunch. I was carrying my share of the load by bringing high-powered investors into Blutrich's fold. He was happy seeing his plan for an international chain taking shape, and Jeff was more and more excited about making the transition from full-time psychic to restaurateur. He was fascinated with the idea of becoming a chef. Also, much to my satisfaction, I had become good friends with Lyle Alzado.

As things turned out, we had much in common. We were both workout freaks, we loved sports, and we shared an interest in boxing. Of course, while my interest in sports was as a fan and businessman, his was as a great participant. He'd once even fought an exhibition match with the great Muhammad Ali. What a thrill that must have been.

But still and all, I was haunted daily by the possibility that my gentlemen's club was going nowhere. Blutrich had not mentioned it since that night he'd dropped me off after my debut as a ring announcer.

One morning I invited Blutrich and Jeff to join me for a workout at my club, the Executive Fitness Center on the roof of the Vista Hotel, high atop the World Trade Center. (It was the Vista that was shut down when terrorists set off a bomb in the Trade Center garage in March 1993.)

I was a power lifter and weight freak, but that day with Jeff, whose idea of a workout was tossing a salad, and Blutrich, a stocky 190-pounder whose cherubic looks could never be taken seriously in gym shorts and sneakers, the three of us boarded the treadmills for our early-morning sweat.

The view from that gym was fabulous. It overlooked the World Financial Center and the part of the Hudson River that begins emptying into New York Bay. Historically, it was one of the most important geographic sites on the face of the earth. For hundreds of years, before airlines replaced sea travel, it was truly the entrance to the New World.

I was glad for the workout time, having put on some pounds as Blutrich and I'd gone from restaurant to restaurant, where most of New York business is conducted. We had become regulars at the Palm on Second Avenue and at Smith & Wollensky on Third, as we presented "Alzado's Rock and Roll Bar International" to various investors.

These meeting meals usually consisted of filet mignon, creamed spinach, French fried potatoes and onions, bread with plenty of butter, salads with blue cheese dressing, and cheesecake and espresso for desert. While we did not always leave the table with a deal, at least we had eaten well.

So, as we walked the treadmills, I was evangelizing about how important it was to work out regularly. I know I have a superior attitude about the shape I keep myself in, but it is one of life's pleasures for me.

Just as I was getting Jeff and Blutrich to swear off the fried potatoes, one of the trainers from the gym came by to say hello.

Her name was Lacey and she was a petite version of Ellen Barkin. She had blonde hair cut very short and a great small, hard butt. She had these real nice breasts, the kind they call "perky," and her nipples were always very visible through her tank top. That morning she was wearing tight shorts that left little to the imagination.

Lacey was a real flirt, and she started paying a lot of attention to me. I could see that Jeff and Mike were really taking her in with their eyes. They were very impressed that I knew her, and I could tell they were curious about just how well I knew her. I decided to keep them guessing.

Lacey and I traded workout information, and at one point she asked if I would begin regular workouts with her. "I'd like to hang out with you because you work so haaaarrrd!" she said, making sure my two pals heard the come-on. They both cracked up.

When we left the gym and headed to Blutrich's Mercedes for a ride to his Park Avenue office, Jeff began asking me all kinds of questions about Lacey. Was she married, how well did I know her—stuff like that. If he was such a good psychic, of course, he would have known the answers, but I passed up the occasion to break his chops and instead began talking about a gentlemen's club filled with women who looked like—in fact, even better—than Lacey.

I turned my attention to Blutrich when I said: "You know, I saw dozens of girls in Rick's Cabaret in Houston who make Lacey look average." All the way uptown I ranted on in my missionary mode about my club plans. "You want to be around beautiful women, help me get that club open," I said.

I asked Mike to swing past the Pussycat Lounge, and once again I told the whole story of Black Monday. Jeff just asked what kind of food I would be serving, but once again Michael Blutrich was absorbing my every word.

Then, for the first time, he mentioned that he had a client who was a real devotee of table dancing clubs. My radar locked on and I asked for more information. But Blutrich was playing it close to the vest.

The only thing he could remember was that the guy was located in Orlando, Florida, and that when he'd had a meeting with him down there they had conducted their business in some club like the kind I was talking about. But he could not remember its name.

Blutrich soon changed the conversation to Alzado's, and as we drove through midmorning traffic up to his office I once again realized I'd made an impression on him. But I wondered when he was going to act.

Later that day, back in my apartment, I got a call from Lyle. He was in New York and wanted to talk about serious financial problems he was having. He needed some moral support, someone to tell him that if he stayed on course things would work out.

Lyle was staying at the Sheraton Centre's Presidential Suite as Blutrich's guest. I went up there to see him, to try to calm him down a little bit. For all his great success on the athletic field, Lyle was still a little immature when it came to dealing with a lot of things in life, especially romance and finance.

Up in the suite he was like a kid in a candy store. The place was so impressive; it had about nine rooms. Lyle said he felt like the King of Siam. But as he talked about his money problems he sounded more like a pauper than a prince. He clearly had been victimized by a series of unscrupulous businessmen who'd taken advantage of his trusting nature.

He said he was, at first, suspicious of Michael Blutrich, but had grown to trust him, and he also felt that I was a straight shooter. He mentioned how previous business partners would stick him with hotel and restaurant bills rather than picking up the tab for a suite in a New York hotel, as Blutrich had done.

Eventually, we talked about working out; he was reputed to be one of the strongest men who ever played in the National Football League, and I was no slouch as a competitive power lifter. I do not put myself in the class of a Lyle Alzado, but I once bench-pressed more than 400 pounds, and that was at a time when I weighed only 198, and my training routine did not include steroids. Many athletic coaches have told me over the years that I would have made a good linebacker if I'd just been a little meaner.

Lyle promised to invite me to work out with him at the famous Gold's Gym next time I was in Los Angeles.

Later in the evening his ex-wife, a pretty blonde named Cindy who lived on Long Island with their son and Mark Yackow, a prominent banker friend of Blutrich's and Lyle's manager, joined us. After a brief business meeting about the restaurant, we went to Smith & Wollensky, where Blutrich was waiting, for dinner.

I learned later that the entire scene, the Presidential Suite, the dinner at S&W—was all staged for Yackow, who was a rabid sports fan and wanted to meet Lyle. At the restaurant our table was besieged by fans who wanted the great player's autograph. Each time a fan came up, Yackow would repeat how he'd love to get involved in a sports bar operation. I could see how Blutrich was playing him, subtly convincing him that he could not live without the opportunity to invest in Alzado's.

About one week after that dinner, I was in my apartment looking over a proposal for a marketing plan for Alzado's when Blutrich called.

"Hey, Mickey, what's going on?" I asked.

"Uncle Jay, I have something I want to talk to you about. Can you get up to my office this afternoon?" he said. "Uncle" was a term of affection Blutrich used when dealing with people he liked. While he was only forty-five, about ten years older than me, and he looked about thirty, Michael had some Old World qualities that made him endearing. So, when he said “Uncle” I knew something good was happening, and I pressed him a bit.

“”What’s up, Mike? I’m a little buried in this marketing proposal right now,” I said.

“Well,” he answered, “I think I’ve got a way to do your gentlemen’s club.”

I sat silently, in total shock, for about ten seconds, then said, “I’ll be right over.”

With my heart pumping wildly and my mind racing, I ran for the door. After three years of trying, I knew this was it. I grabbed a cab in front of my building and gave Blutrich’s Park Avenue address. Along the way I realized I had not even bothered to change out of the jeans, sneakers, and sweatshirt I’d been wearing around the house. I flashed back quickly to the first time I met Blutrich, in Grandpa Al’s restaurant, and how I purposely dressed down so as not to appear impressed by him. Now, he was about to turn my life around, to make my dream come true.

I ran past the doorman of his building, dodged the security desk—they knew me anyway—and brushed past the elevator starter, who was offering a “Good afternoon, Mr. Bildstein.” I half ran into Michael's stately office and totally ignored his efficient secretary as, desperate to hear what he had in store for me, I went right into his private office.

He was on the phone with a client, and I threw myself onto the leather sofa. While they talked, I scanned the walls, which were jam-packed with autographed photos of the rich and famous. There was Stallone, Alzado, Cathy Moriarty, Martin Landau, Larry Holmes, Mario Cuomo, and of course “Grandpa” Al Lewis. All the pictures carried messages of the warmest sentiments to “Dear Michael.”

Michael hung up and immediately turned to me. “Boy, you got here fast—you must really want to do this club,” he said with a big smile.

“You have no idea,” I replied in the understatement of the century.

“Well, remember I told you about a client in Orlando who was in insurance and was a big-time financier?”

Of course I remembered. He was the guy who loved table dancing clubs.

“”His name is Steven Stevens,” Blutrich continued, “and at one time he was involved with the people who started the Hard Rock Cafe. He’s always interested in new restaurant ideas and clubs, and he thought your concept was a winner.

“Now, I have to tell you, this guy knows topless clubs. He’s a refined gentleman from Britain and he loves great-looking women. The first time I ran your idea by him, he did not react at all. Then when I mentioned it a second time he told me that he wanted to meet you. He said he was thinking of financing a gentlemen’s club in Florida.”

This news was so good that I found myself speechless, a very rare occurrence.

Stevens, according to Blutrich, thought the idea of mixing women and sports was stupendous. He’d asked if I had a team ready to get rolling and Blutrich had given him an emphatic “Yes!”

“How serious is this guy?” I asked.

“Very serious—he had me on the phone for one hour. He really wants to meet you.”

Blutrich then picked up his phone and dialed Stevens’s number.

Within seconds I was talking to Steven Stevens in his Orlando office.

He got right down to business. “*How many square feet do you need for your club*?” he asked.

“At least ten thousand.”

“*Where will you get the girls?*”

"Some local, but most from Houston and Florida."

"*What is your proposed location?*"

"East Side, in the sixties. There's a great spot just under the 59th Street Bridge."

"*What is your expected first-year revenue?*"

"A hundred twenty thousand a week, maybe as much as six million a year—and that is a worst-case scenario."

"*Who is your major competitor?*"

"At the moment there is no competitor doing this kind of club in New York, but M. J. Peter, who you probably know from Florida, is looking for locations."

He fired questions at me like reporters at a press conference. And I returned them with equal ability, drawing on my three years of research and some of my experience with the ill-fated *Dear Diary*. I had learned an awful lot about being a smooth politician from watching Blutrich work, and it was paying off in this telephone call.

Stevens confessed that he was not a man who was easily impressed but that I had impressed him. He told me about a club he visited in Orlando named Rachel's. He said it was a businessman's hot spot and it was making money hand over fist. He expressed surprise that such a place did not exist in New York City.

He explained that he was considering some loans for a Florida group but that Michael had spoken highly of me and that my plan seemed more comprehensive. He suggested we meet in person, and with that we said good-bye.

After I hung up, Blutrich explained that he had only gone through my idea with Stevens once the Englishman had opened the door by telling him how much he loved Rachel's. That was shortly after the night at the boxing matches, the first time I mentioned my dream to Blutrich.

But the master attorney, Blutrich, did not press Stevens on the subject. He just let it hang out there until Stevens brought it up again on his own, thus proving his sincere interest. Then Blutrich reeled him in. It's a technique salesmen call the negative sale. You use reverse psychology to ellicit from someone something you wanted all along.

After Stevens asked for the fourth or fifth time about my plan, Michael, feigning beleaguered surrender, "gave in" and put us in touch.

Blutrich thought we were in the right place at the right time. He thought a deal could be struck with Stevens, who would provide the financing in the form of loans.

We decided that we would spend the next week working out the formal plan and putting it on paper. Michael suggested that a friend of his, Irv "Blitz" Bilzinsky, be brought in as a partner since he already had a piece of a club in Westchester and had a liquor license in his name. That would be critical, because with a huge establishment like I planned the State Liquor Authority would insist that there was experience in running a club behind it.

We decided to go to Orlando to meet Stevens the following week, which was mid-December 1990.

CHAPTER 14

The Name Game

I eventually agreed to almost everything Michael Blutrich included in our business plan. After all, who was I to argue? He was putting all the pieces in place, something I had failed to do in the previous three years.

Blutrich, Blitz, and I met for dinner. The two of them had been friends and partners in various ventures for a few years, and Blitz seemed to take an immediate liking to me.

He said he did not want to take an active role in the deal, so we agreed that Michael would become the attorney for the project and eventually corporate counsel for the club and any expansion that might arise out of the concept.

Meanwhile Steven Stevens was calling every day. One of the things he was most concerned about was a name for the club. He felt strongly that the right name would be an invaluable selling point, both to investors and eventually to paying customers. Mitts and Tits was not among the names we were considering.

So I locked myself in my apartment one night, determined not to leave until I had come up with the right name for the greatest gentlemen's club in the history of the world.

I ran over all the special characteristics the club would have: televisions throughout the room so sports fans could catch the latest scores; pop shot basketball and air hockey for them to run up scores against their opponents; and the most beautiful women in the world for them to dream about scoring with. Sports and screwing. Scoring!

Scores! That was it! It had come to me in a flash—a flash that took three years. It had been right there in front of me all the time. I knew it was right. Of all the decisions I have ever made in my life, the one I have never second-guessed was Scores as the name for my club. It was a true stroke of genius.

Scoring was what the club was all about, and the right name would reflect that. Scores, Scores, Scores; I ran the name around and around in my head, over and over again, and it worked. I imagined the marquee outside with Scores on it. I conjured up gossip items mentioning Scores. "Sexy Demi Moore was enjoying the company of a tall blonde at Scores last night as she continued researching her new film about strippers." I even drew a mental picture of my checkbook with the logo from Scores adorning the checks.

The following day, as Blutrich and I flew down to Orlando, I told him my idea for a name and he immediately bought into it. He agreed it said everything we wanted to say in one word.

Steven Stevens's office was in a modern building at the edge of a light industrial park outside of Orlando. We waited in the lobby for three long minutes before a receptionist ushered us into his conference room. A minute later Stevens, sandy-haired, six foot one and stocky, walked in. He was wearing a blue suit, white shirt, and Armani tie. He was about forty-five years old and looked like he kept in good shape.

This was the moment of truth.

Quickly, we launched into talking about my idea. Once again, as he did on the telephone, Stevens grilled me over every nuance, every detail of my concept. Finally he asked the question I knew was so important to him.

"What would this club be called?"

"Scores," I said.

He loved it instantly and launched into his own spiel about how it was a great double entendre and how it spoke to everyman's "inner nature in lusting after women and conquest, à la sports." Well, that's what he said.

With that out of the way, he suggested we head over to Rachel's for lunch. We made the fifteen-minute drive to Orlando's hottest men's club in Stevens's black Jaguar.

Rachel's was a fine place. While not quite as elegant as Rick's Cabaret, it was very similar in tone and atmosphere. It had a main table dancing area that was set in a square, a small dining area which offered a buffet lunch of cold cuts and salads, and upstairs, a VIP area for high rollers.

It was very well-appointed, miles ahead of what was available in New York although still not up to my Scores concept. It was too small and seemed cramped. I expressed that to Stevens, who agreed, in his clipped British accent, with my "thematic correctness"—whatever that meant.

I noticed that while I was talking to him, Stevens was like a pickpocket in Times Square. His eyes were alive, darting left, then right, then staring ahead, he clearly loved the Rachel's scene as he gobbled up the sights of beautiful women, mostly undressed.

I was not as impressed. Having been in Rick's and Baby O's, I was more accustomed to the scene and was trying to keep my mind on business. Blutrich, on the other hand was an absolute table dance virgin and was amazed by the scene in front of him.

After a buffet dinner which was just so-so, we took a look in to the VIP area, then headed down to the main dance floor. We stood at the entrance to the table dance area for a moment or two. Stevens jabbed me in the ribs. "Are these girls amazing beauties?" he said. He was awed by the scene before him. His interest in owning a table dancing club obviously went far beyond the financial rewards.

By this time in my excellent adventure toward owning a club, I had developed a well-tuned eye for topless beauty. I was able, in a flash, to judge the overall sensuality of a club and to sum up the looks of the girls. The girls of Rachel's were stunning, and I noticed some incredible large-busted girls operating very close to the customers. They had a style of bending toward the clientele and letting their nipples just barely brush past the men's lips. It was immediately clear to me that those lips were allowed to get even closer, perhaps even allowed to touch those perfect nipples. That was something I did not see in Rick's or Baby O's and did not expect to allow in Scores.

"This is a hot place," I replied to Stevens's jab. "But I have seen better-looking girls. And I am sure Scores will offer a much better selection."

Meanwhile, as Stevens and I were delivering our critique, Blutrich made his way into the table area and grabbed a choice spot for us. He was alive with anticipation. His eyes were bugging out of his head and he had a fantastic smile in his face.

We were hardly settled in the comfortable easy chairs when a very young-looking dancer zeroed in on Blutrich like a smart bomb aimed at Baghdad. She went right up to him and stood between his legs.

She had this white blonde hair, blue eyes, and a supertanned body, thin as a wire with very well-developed abdominal muscles, which were totally exposed over her string bikini bottom. I noticed a wisp of blonde pubic hair showing out of the side of her bikini. That was something very rare, I thought. Almost all the girls trimmed their pubic hair to a small triangle, unless, like Tina, they worked in all-nude clubs, where more of a bush was encouraged.

If there was a top to match the bottom it was nowhere in sight as she placed her small, perfectly shaped breasts about a millimeter from Michael's face and said her name was Nance and that she would love to dance for him.

She kind of emphasized "Nance" and "dance," to exaggerate the rhyme. It was a very cute technique that added to the allure of her young-girl look.

Blutrich, the hotshot New York lawyer, just sat there slack-jawed and looking silly, while Stevens took out a $20 bill and stuffed it in the elastic band that through some miracle of engineering held the tiny bikini bottom in place over Nance's crotch.

The music was Madonna's "La Isla Bonita" and Nance really had her moves down pat. She twisted and turned inside of Michael's lap, across his chest, a hot breath away from his wide-open mouth, offering every bit of her perfectly toned body for his breathless inspection.

When the music ended, Stevens slipped another $20 into Nance's pants and asked her to come back later.

Blutrich was exhausted. In the little more than three minutes that the song had lasted, his active imagination had taken him through every twist and turn known to modern lovemaking.

He said he had not felt so sexually stimulated in years. Immediately the talk turned to our club and how he now really understood what appeal it would hold for the high-powered stockbrokers and media types we'd be catering to.

I then went into my standard pitch. Blutrich's reaction was typical, I said. I went on about how he was just the kind of customer we would be shooting for. He was a high-powered attorney who needed some safe way to recharge his batteries. New York City, I told Stevens, was full of men like Michael Blutrich, Jay Bildstein, and Steven Stevens who would flock to the right kind of club.

"Believe it or not," I said for the gizillionth time, "there is no place like Rachel's in New York. The city's gentlemen swingers are starving for a club where they can live out their fantasies."

"Okay, count me in—I'm on board. Let's get things moving," Stevens said.

His words shut me up. After three years, I was getting the kind of commitment I needed, from the kind of person who could deliver it. It took a beat or two for the reality of the moment to sink in on me, but when it did I lit up like a Christmas tree.

"Gentlemen, the dances are on me," I said as I waved for Nance and a few of her friends to join our group.

After a fun afternoon of girls and some serious drinking, Stevens drove us to Orlando's airport, where we mixed with the Disney World crowd as we exchanged warm goodbyes. On the flight back, Michael's face was buried in an action-adventure novel, which he read to clear his mind, but I kept interrupting him for reassurance that Stevens was serious about coming on board.

The failure of *Dear Diary* was still playing heavily on my subconscious, and I needed some kind of security blanket before I could put it out of my mind.

Blutrich was, like many good attorneys, a speed reader. He had developed his own technique of rifling through pages and absorbing about 75 percent of all he read and 100 percent of the important stuff. So, for the entire flight north, he thumbed through pages, calmed me down, thumbed through some more pages, reassured me again, then went on reading. Finally, somewhere over Maryland he lost his patience and asked me to leave him alone about *Dear Diary*.

"Forget that Chippendales crap," he said. "You're on your way now. Just please leave me alone for a while!" That was about as stern as you ever saw Michael Blutrich, and I got the message. For the next four hundred miles I just looked out the window and imagined beautiful women dancing topless among the clouds. Had I become obsessed with this dream? You bet, and it was great!

The next morning, I got to work building a management team. The first thing I did was to call Larry Wolf. We had fallen out of touch since the demise of *Dear Diary*—it was almost a year since we'd talked—and he admitted to being a little surprised to hear from me.

He told me he had just come back from Fort Lauderdale, where he had gone to work for M. J. Peter. It turned out that after we went our separate ways, Larry realized he'd been bitten by the topless bug and tried to cut some deals with Peter. None of them worked out, but he ended up taking a job with him as an advertising consultant. The job gave him a real insider's view of the Florida topless scene and what made it so successful. Along the way he had also become close with many of the best dancers, the headliners who worked in Peter's clubs throughout Florida.

He told me about one named Tyler who was considered to be the top dancer in the country, both in looks and technique. That is, she had a way of making men fall in love with her, to the point that they showered her with money and gifts in return for the least bit of attention.

Tyler looked like Pamela Anderson Lee, the *Baywatch* beauty, and she made thousands of dollars a night. Larry said he made a serious play for a relationship with her and while that never worked out, he'd learned all about her.

She was an all-American girl whose father was very domineering. When she started dating he went berserk. He apparently could not stand the idea of another man, even a teenage boy, touching his daughter. So he began making life difficult for her, not allowing her out of the house, not letting boys speak to her on the telephone. It was a real sick relationship. Larry thought he was probably even molesting her.

Finally Tyler began rebelling by running away. First she worked in a topless bar as a waitress. Eventually she graduated to dancer. Of course, when the men got a look at her beautiful body, she quickly became a star attraction. She moved into table dancing, and wherever she worked she quickly became the number one dancer. She sounded wonderful, a perfect catch for my club. But I was beginning to wonder if any of these dancers had their heads screwed on right.

It turned out that I called Larry at an opportune moment, because he had recently decided to give up the club business and go back to advertising in the Big Apple. He had returned to the city just the day before I called.

I felt a touch of resentment that Larry had tried to make a deal in Florida without including me, but I quickly overcame that, plus the awkwardness of my not having kept in touch, and filled him in on Scores. I told him about Michael Blutrich, Steven Stevens, Alzado's, Rachel's, and even Jeff the Psychic.

I was very up front with Larry. I told him that as soon as the project was back on I thought of him immediately. I explained, however, that he could not be a partner because those positions were going to the heavy investors.

"Larry," I said, "I want you to come aboard as the project manager for the deal and general manager once the club opens."

He agreed to come to Blutrich's office the next day, and before lunch we had an agreement.

We had two orders of business to attend to right away. First a business plan for Scores had to be drawn up, and second, but just as important, a location had to be nailed down.

Larry had some very valuable inside information on that front. He knew that Peter had taken options on two New York locations but had eventually "gone bad" on both of them. One of the sites was the Sixtieth Street building that had once housed the legendary Club A and more recently was the home of the Great American Clubhouse, which had also gone under. It was owned by an eccentric New York real estate giant named Abe Hirschfeld, a Holocaust survivor who made zillions in New York and was one of the city's most endearing characters. He had once run for mayor and had even owned the *New York Post* for a few years, keeping the great tabloid alive in its darkest hours.

The entire building was leased from Hirschfeld by the Bally's Company, which ran the Vertical Club in part of the building and subleased the rest of the space, including the area we had in mind for Scores. The building was actually called the Vertical Club Building.

Larry also got in touch with some of the dancers he knew and raised the idea of their coming to New York to work for us. We knew we would not find the dancers we needed in the Pussycat Lounge. The best lookers were in Florida, and we needed them in New York.

Most were skeptical. They were accustomed to hearing propositions from businessmen. But a few trusted Larry and indicated they would come up to work for us. They all agreed that if Tyler went to New York they would follow. Where Tyler went, rich men with corporate credit cards were sure to follow.

Larry and I spent the last week of 1990 touring the city's topless bars, just to make sure nothing had changed and that an upscale gentlemen's club would still be breaking new and fruitful ground.

The one place we avoided was the Pussycat. Alicia's words still burned in me. I was still angered over her calling me a failure and a phony. I just did not want to see her, no matter how much her insight might have helped the Scores deal. I know this was a stubborn attitude on my part. But I'd once had strong feelings for Alicia, and I guess I thought she should have supported me no matter what I decided to do. Looking back on it, I wonder if her putting me down was not the best thing to happen during my quest for Scores. It certainly got me hopping again.

Another awkward situation involved Jeff the Psychic. Although he was not part of the Scores project, we were deeply involved in connection with Alzado's, so he was always around Blutrich's office when Larry and I were there.

I knew he did not really care for the Scores concept, but if the club was going to have a restaurant, he wanted to be running it. There was friction between Larry and him, you know, the old guard versus the new guard; that kind of thing. Larry saw food as an accommodation to the patrons rather than a major profit center, like booze, and while I agreed with that, I still wanted top-shelf dining.

Jeff was an aspiring chef and, although the jury was still out on his culinary abilities, he did appear to have an extraordinary knowledge of food.

In the end I decided to play the politics of inclusion and brought Jeff aboard as the dining manager. That way Jeff did not infringe on things Larry cared about and did not get involved in what the girls wore or did with customers as long as they left them a little money to pay for a good meal.

By mid-January, Larry and I had inspected the former Club A/Great American Clubhouse site at 333 East Sixtieth Street. When we arrived it was completely boarded up and the electrical service was turned off. It was clear that Peter's organization did almost no renovation work on the place and had just left it in complete disrepair when they abandoned the project.

As we walked through with only flashlights to show the way, we could see wires hanging out of the ceiling, broken walls with jagged edges, and an uneven floor throughout the main area.

In the back of the house, the storage and the kitchen area, things were a total mess. The eight walk-in freezers reeked of urine and other human waste; the building superintendent said homeless people had broken though a hole in one of the outside walls, and then made the freezers their homes.

He told us he'd almost had a heart attack the first time he came down to the freezers and found a homeless couple living inside one of them. He was managing to keep them away, but it was an ongoing struggle. He was thinking of buying German shepherds to patrol the area. The rest of the kitchen looked and smelled equally bad.

Despite the unattractive atmosphere, Larry and I knew the location was perfect for the club we wanted to open. The space was fully equipped with a complete kitchen and plenty of other things we would have to buy if they were not there. It had lots of storage space plus a basement and sprinklers, as well as the HVAC (heating, ventilation and air-conditioning) that had been installed.

Other than that, the rest of the interior would have to be razed, and the four walls that contained the club would have to be rebuilt. But that was mostly cosmetic work. The structure was sound; the kitchen, sprinklers, and HVAC, which represented a great deal of investment money, just needed to be cleaned up.

So, as disheveled as the 333 East Sixtieth Street site was, it still presented a tremendous opportunity. Larry and I left the "space," as it would be called until Scores opened, bantering on about all the possibilities it offered.

We looked at a few other places, like Reins, which was previously the location for the new Playboy Club on Lexington Avenue a few blocks from the Waldorf-Astoria, but we eventually dismissed it because it was underground. That was something Jay Cummings had taught us as being very undesirable. The more we looked at other places, the more the Sixtieth Street site seemed to be far and away the best.

As far as Cummings goes, by the way, I had decided not to bring him in on this deal because he was another one who had dropped me like a hot potato when *Dear Diary* went south. He also was once again heavily involved in his real estate work. We did not need him to help find a site, and we did not need his expertise once it came to contracts, because we had Blutrich and his friend Blitz to handle all that kind of work. So, in contrast to my situation with Larry, I put sentiment aside when it came to Cummings.

Another thing that the space had going for it was the fact that, while it was in a high-class residential neighborhood, its location on the bridge access street made it less of a target for local tenants who might not approve of what was going on inside.

Also, the Bally people were being hurt by the space's going vacant, and there was a rumor that the Vertical Club might also be going belly up, so we figured everyone involved would be motivated to make a good deal with us.

As my thirty-first birthday approached in January 1991, all the pieces were falling into place, including Blutrich and his legal team; Blitz to provide the liquor license; Stevens to finance; Larry with his creative and advertising mind; Jeff on the food; and the girls from Florida anxious to take a bite out of the Big Apple.

Let the games begin!

CHAPTER 15 Roids

Our plan called for getting Scores opened by December 1991. Only half kidding, we agreed that Halloween would be the best time because it was a great night for a party. Halloween was a very big night in New York. The gay community had its parade through Greenwich Village, which had become a national institution and was broadcast around the country. Many of the city's sexually oriented clubs used it as an occasion to allow their patrons to act out different scenes—tied, of course, to their willingness to wear costumes.

In places like the Vault, an S&M club in the city's meat market district, corporate executives and their suburban wives got the chance, on Halloween, to mingle with real hard-core masters and mistresses behind the protection of Halloween masks.

In my opinion the S&M scene was gaining in popularity because it offered a sexual adventure pretty much without the threat of AIDS. Intercourse was not the focus for these people.

That was something the scene had in common with my gentlemen's club concept. Fantasy, aided by costume, atmosphere, and most important, attitude—although in Scores, instead of whips and chains, dungeons and dominatrices, there would be easy chairs and silk lingerie.

So I began to ready myself for coronation as the King of Clubs. But, keeping in mind the scalding defeat of *Dear Diary*, I knew that I could never relax and had to keep the heat on Blutrich and the others to make sure they did not get distracted by another project.

Steven Stevens became the main player on our team, because he'd had prior dealings with theme restaurants like Hard Rock Cafe and because he loved the Scores concept and saw it as a moneymaker. The fact that he was personally caught up in the sexual nature of the venture did not hurt a bit.

I continued to provide the overall vision, promotion, and marketing fuel for the company, now known as Scores Entertainment Inc.

We turned out to be right about the space, and much to our great luck it held a treasure trove of equipment that could provide strong collateral for our corporate loans. The fact the owner of the Great American Clubhouse left behind the entire kitchen turned into a windfall for us, with its salvage value of about $500,000. When the M. J. Peter group came in, they had a chance to sell off the kitchen, but instead they left it the way they found it. More good luck for us.

There were assets of great value to be taken out of the space, and I have often wondered why no one took them. On one of our walk-throughs, a kitchen expert, told us that the freezer boxes alone were worth about $60,000 each, and we had four of them. But whatever the reason these things were still there were, they worked in my favor, and in the depressed economy of 1991 I had plenty of value to back up my requests for loans.

The previous renters had also given the landlord fits as they constantly changed their plans, began renovation, stopped, got started again, backed off, and finally quit. So Hirschfeld and the Bally's people—through their lawyer, a great guy by the name of Irwin "Tex" Seeger—were anxious to get some business done with people like Michael Blutrich.

In the end they were so eager to help us get started that they did not demand key money, which in the right economy could have been as much as $2 million for that space. They also did not demand a security deposit, because they would have had to keep it in escrow and not use it for their own financial dealings anyway.

Thanks to their misfortunes with previous owners, a depressed real estate economy, and their trust of our organization, the landlords gave us a deal that under any other scenario would have been preposterous.

We eventually got the keys to the door for three and a half months' rent, which came out to about $100,000. We got a ten-year lease and two ten-year options.

Good fortune was smiling upon me. After more than three years, my belief in the inevitability of something good coming out of my persistence had finally kicked in: I had a genuine financier, a powerful attorney, and a dream deal on a space for Scores. Who could have asked for more!!!

Also, Alzado's was going full steam ahead. A nationwide chain was coming closer and closer to reality. In early February, as Stevens neared the final financing deal on Scores, I headed west with Jeff the Psychic to hire a corporate salesperson for Alzado's, someone who would generate a catering business. We would also meet some friends of Jeff's who were opening a club called Fleetwood's with rock legend Mick Fleetwood of Fleetwood Mac.

I had met a candidate for the sales job through a mutual friend. She did similar work for a brokerage firm in Los Angeles connected with Michael Milken. She was a gorgeous blonde, very sharp, who really knew her business. A real mixture of brains and beauty—I had met a few women like her during my quest for Scores, Alicia and Kelly among them.

During our stay I took Alzado up on his offer to work out together at Gold's Gym in Venice Beach. We had talked a lot about fitness regimens in our telephone calls. I savored the opportunity to lift weights with an NFL powerhouse. Jeff came along just to watch.

I had not been training hard in some months but strength was my strong suit, so Lyle was pretty impressed when he saw me bench-press 275 pounds for seventeen reps. I actually surprised myself with that performance. I guess my ego took control of all my other bodily functions and carried the day for me. After spotting for me, Lyle surprised me by declining to do any pressing himself. I was disappointed, especially since I'd performed at a level I expected would be in the same league as anything he did. He said it would put him out of sync. I wasn't sure what he meant by that but I did not press the issue. When they saw he was not going to lift, the small group of gym rats who had gathered to watch drifted away. I guess I had not impressed them enough to keep them interested.

We moved on to some easier exercises—light curls and some aerobic stuff. I always thought a person of my bulk looked foolish doing certain aerobic movements, so I was amazed by how graceful Lyle appeared. But again I was surprised, this time by his shortness of breath and relatively easy selection of exercises.

I found I could keep up with him, rep for rep and pound for pound. The only explanation, I figured, was that he was just humoring me. After all, he did not need to show off for me; Lyle was a guy who picked up the biggest fullbacks in professional football and threw them to the ground like rag dolls. But here I was, keeping up with him. It did not make sense, but I enjoyed the ego boost and the looks from the other gym rats, especially the women.

After the workout we went to Lyle's apartment in Manhattan Beach and then to the Firehouse, a restaurant favored by many of the bodybuilders and professional sports trainers who thrive on the Hollywood "body beautiful" scene. Lyle was treated like a hero by the Firehouse crowd, but his mood was subdued. Several of his fans interrupted our meals and offered to pay our check, but I insisted on taking care of it. Lyle was not accustomed to putting his hand in his own pocket. He once told me he went for a month without paying for anything: food, drinks, clothing, transportation. Lyle was very astute at capitalizing on the special place Americans hold for professional athletes.

Alicia used to comment about that. She wondered why we did not reach out to great musicians, painters, and dancers the same way. Of course she was not talking about topless dancers, although many of them never paid for their own food, clothing, or transportation either.

On the way back to the hotel, Lyle began talking as he drove. He spoke in way I had never heard him do before. He seemed to want to unburden his mind of something that was bothering him.

I began to understand his subdued mood as he admitted to Jeff and me that he had used steroids continually for more than twenty years. He told us that some of the biggest stars in Hollywood were on "roids." He said they were guys who made it to stardom as action heroes like underdog boxers who eventually win the championship, and heroic cops, and Vietnam commandos. Roles like that.

Alzado hated that group of stars. He knew many of them personally because they sought his friendship, believing his toughness and tremendous physical ability would rub off on them. He called them "phony tough guys" and wished they would leave him alone.

There was a real sadness to his tone. The car filled with a kind of grief. I remember feeling concern for Lyle, whom I had come to admire and respect over the past few months. Looking back on that car ride, I feel I had a premonition of the sadness that was to come and affect all our lives. Jeff seemed overcome by the gloom as we pulled up in front of Ma Maison, the Hollywood insiders hotel that had become our headquarters.

As we got out of the car I tried to cheer the big guy up by telling him I was going to need some help auditioning dancers for Scores. I said we would need to rent a suite at the Beverly Hills Hilton and have scores of girls come up to show us their moves.

Lyle smiled at the thought, but his mind was on something else. I leaned across the front seat and placed my hand on his massive biceps and said: "Lyle, anything you need, just call."

He looked right in my eyes and replied that I was a good friend. It was a sad parting, but I did not dwell on it. Lyle Alzado had a right to be down in the dumps as much as anyone else did.

The next day Jeff and I did some work at Alzado's and then rented tuxedos for the opening of Fleetwood's that evening. Before we went back to the hotel we stopped to see if the place was ready.

I was shocked to see that with only six hours left before opening the site looked like it needed six days of work. Ladders were up all over the place. Painting was still being done. The door on the men's room was not on straight and there apparently was a major problem going on behind the bar.

When we arrived later that evening, though, it was as if by magic everything had come together into a completely finished, ultraelegant blues and rock supper club. It was real Hollywood glamour. Great food was passed around on platters served by fine-looking women in tuxedos. There were about six different types of shrimp and something I loved that involved bacon wrapped around a piece of sweet sausage. It was one of the few things I ate that could be considered "not good for you."

Anyway, the evening went off beautifully, with dozens of rock stars like Bonnie Raitt and Sting and Jerry Garcia showing up. I sat next to Rod Stewart the entire night. Talk about drawing power—people, even other famous people, could not leave him alone. It is really true when stars complain about a lack of privacy. But that is the price they pay for fame and oodles of money, and I don't feel particularly sorry for them. I was also able to enjoy the company, that evening and on a few return trips to L.A., of a twentiesh California beach girl who at first mistook me for one of Stewart's agents and then just fell in love with my rap about being a New York nightclub owner.

Of course, as I sat through the revelry my mind was wandering back and forth to Scores. The atmosphere in Fleetwood's was something I wanted to capture in my club: glamour, beauty, a sexual buzz that ran through the place, thanks mainly to the large number of hot rock stars and their girlfriends. The only difference was that in Scores the atmosphere would exist every night. A person would never be able to walk in and not be surrounded by beautiful women. I anxiously awaited my moment in the sun.

Unfortunately for its owners, Fleetwood's did not enjoy many days in the sun. For reasons that I was never able to learn, they were never able to obtain a permanent liquor license. When the temporary license they were issued for opening night ran out about a month later, they had to survive on their menu alone, and it was not that great. So Fleetwood's is an impressive but short entry in the history of nightclubs. I am really happy I was able to be there that opening night. I also learned an important lesson about having all your ducks in a row, e.g., making sure you are fully licensed before you count on nightclub success.

On the flight back I was haunted by memories of Lyle. He seemed so down; I was very worried about him. Other than that, I considered it a very successful trip. Now it was time to get on with Scores.

Blutrich soon finalized the financial arrangements with Stevens, and right after that I signed the lease with the Vertical Club at their offices. That was a momentous occasion for me. It culminated three and a half years of dreaming, envisioning, working, and planning toward the place that would be Scores. I put disappointment and frustration behind me. We were off to the races.

There is no such thing as a secret in New York, and the very next day after I'd signed the lease I began getting telephone calls from contractors, food service people, promotional service companies, and even some women who wanted to sign up as dancers. In one stroke of the pen on a lease I had become an accepted nightclub owner.

Jay Bildstein, that kid from Queens, was taking on the legends of Studio 54, Visage, and the Copacabana. I even had the lease to the site of the fabled Club A. Of course, the challenge now was to become a *successful* nightclub owner. To that end, I was totally focused on the task ahead. There was much work that needed to be done before the doors of the greatest gentlemen's club in the history of New York could be opened.

Larry and I set about to line up the appropriate contractors, as well as the architects, interior decorators, and everyone else we would need on our team.

I mandated a protocol that before a decision could be made on any general contractor we would bid the job to a minimum of five companies that did that kind of work. The winner would have to pass a very strenuous background check regarding his finances and references. I did not want any surprises popping up after we opened that would endanger our licenses and permits. And I wanted a firm that was known for getting the job in on time. We were shooting for the holiday season, figuring to make much of our initial investment back before the year ended.

With the help of Larry Wolf and Michael Blutrich and the stories of failures caused by poor planning, like Fleetwood's and John Juliano's troubles with the Copacabana, I proceeded aggressively, but with great caution.

We eventually settled on the general contractor that Donald Trump often used, and our architects were also interior designers, a couple named Bob and Alice.

The months of March and April were filled with blueprints and a massive cleanup of the space, with plumbers, electricians, and demolition people always coming and going. It was a very exciting time. All the workmen who came into the space got caught up in what we were trying to build. And true to form, they all had advice and nightclub dreams of their own. One carpenter offered to build a secret room in my office where I could audition the dancers. "You know—the *real* audition," he said.

Another workman would not leave me alone about a girl he knew who danced in a two-bit topless joint in Brooklyn. He assured me she was the most beautiful girl, "with the greatest tits I've ever seen. They're at least 44 double D," he told me. He said he had no personal interest in the girl but that if she happened to need a manager he would volunteer his time.

One morning, at about 6 o'clock, a man hired to lay carpet was waiting at the front entrance with a very pretty, very young girl at his side. She was wearing a long raincoat, which I found peculiar as it was late May and the sun was shining. When my cab pulled up he opened the door and led me to the girl.

"Mr. B., this is my niece Annette. She's very beautiful and she's a great dancer. Will you give her a tryout?" he asked.

This was something I was not prepared for, especially at 6 A.M. in the middle of the street on a beautiful spring day.

I politely said good morning and offered that I would gladly give Annette a tryout in a few months when we started hiring.

But my answer was not good enough, and the carpet layer and his "niece" followed me into my makeshift office. We were no sooner through the door than he pushed Annette in front of me and she, with a coy smile on her face, opened her raincoat. Underneath she was wearing . . . nothing. She was totally nude and exposed to me, and she had a body to be proud of.

Now, I took a closer look. She had beautiful blonde hair and I could see the evidence that it was real. Her breasts were large, and because I don't think she was a day over seventeen, they did not need any artificial enhancement to point proudly toward my admiring eyes.

I did not know what to do or say. Uncle Carpet Man broke the ice by offering to "leave you two alone" while I made my decision.

The offer brought me back to the reality of the situation, and I recovered my composure. The girl was gorgeous, and I felt she would probably make a good member of my team of table dancers. "We're not ready for hiring yet," I stammered. "Just leave me your number and I promise to call you in when we are."

Annette seemed relieved when "Uncle" handed me a business card and promised to get back to me in a few weeks. "After all," he said, "I'm working here; I'll know when you're ready."

My life was changing very dramatically. Something I had not given a lot of thought to was my personal dealings with the dancers, and I have often regretted not anticipating the problems those relationships would cause.

At the end of April, Michael, Larry, Jeff, and Mark Yackow, and I piled into a stretch limo and headed down the Garden State Parkway to Atlantic City, the East Coast gambling mecca on the beach. We were off to see the George Foreman–Evander Holyfield fight for the heavyweight championship of the world. I was not going to be the ring announcer, but I thought it would be a great night anyway.

We were having a great time in the limo, boozing and talking about women, when the radio reported a story about Lyle Alzado being hospitalized in L.A. with a brain tumor.

The car fell silent. I was stricken by the news. Lyle had just married a beautiful twenty-four-year-old girl. Jeff and I had been invited to the wedding in Oregon but our work on Scores had prohibited us from going. In telephone conversations, Lyle's mood had clearly improved a great deal since the last time I'd seen him. I had not been able to get in touch with him the last few times I'd tried, but I'd attributed that to his new bride and the excitement of the honeymoon period.

The rest of the trip passed in a gloom for all of us. We did not care who won the fight, and we all passed up the chance to attend an orgy in one of the promoters' suites.

Lyle was soon found to be terminally ill.

Over the next few weeks, as he deteriorated, we had to make some hard business decisions. The business at Alzado's dropped off as soon as his situation hit the public; no one wanted to party in a place whose owner was dying from brain cancer. Soon the only customers were the plastic surgeons, actors, agents, and other Hollywood glitterati who arrived in droves on motorcycles, causing more problems with the surrounding community than they were worth.

When Lyle began speaking out against steroid use in television public service announcements, investors in Alzado's International began withdrawing their money. Nobody wanted to make money on the back of this beloved man.

Blutrich decided that when Lyle passed away we would quietly shut down the restaurant and after a decent period of time reopen it under another name. This became my project.

CHAPTER 16 Florida Girls

There was a message from Tina on my answering machine when I returned home from Atlantic City. In an almost incoherent, slurring voice she said something about how I was her only true friend in the world and that she would be coming to New York soon and would definitely be calling me. "Keep the sheets warm," she said as the message ended.

What a depressing situation. I really did not know much about her, but for some reason Tina struck a chord when I met her that night in Rick's, and her adventure in upstate New York that led to my bailing her out of jail was a good story that got a lot of yucks when I retold it. So I continued to have a warm spot in my heart for her and welcomed her call. But I also realized that there would always be some kind of grief on the other end of those calls.

Tina was drifting deeper and deeper into a world that eventually I would see many dancers drift into. It would be easy to call them losers, but with just a little compassion you could view them as victims. They were frequently girls who had been abused by their parents, emotionally and often physically, and who would search for years for a father figure to give them the kind of love they yearned for.

Usually drugs and booze helped fill the void. Often the women, as they became older and more cynical, became hunters themselves, and preyed on weak men who would mistake their affection for love. I saw many girls latch on to rich older men, who would indeed act out the role of benevolent, loving father for many years. I also knew that in many cases they latched on to men who treated them just as their biological fathers had, beating them and raping them.

Once in a great while a girl would find true love, someone who would actually help her along the road to normal life, with kids and a mortgage. I hoped that would happen to Tina, but I did not see myself in the role of her savior.

I was more interested in business; Alzado's had to be saved, and Scores had to opened. We were just about to open the first expansion of Alzado's in Westchester County, New York, a project that gave me great credibility regarding my Scores venture. The Alzado's marquee was a proven winner, until the announcements of the hero's illness. There was no use fooling ourselves about drawing customers as long as Lyle lingered near death—a report that had become a fixture on the nightly news shows once he spoke out against steroid use.

Lyle told me over the phone one night that he was embarrassed to visit the restaurant on La Cienega. He was down to 185 pounds and had lost his hair from chemotherapy. He had no inclination to play the host. While he wanted the Alzado's franchise to survive his death, he did not have the strength to help that happen. And none of us had the heart to push him. We were determined to do our best for his estate.

Larry, who was not involved with Lyle, sugges
to scout women for Scores.

He was right about that. L.A. is a magnet for beautiful women. Even in the not so upscale strip joints like the place near the airport where Tina worked, there were always beautiful women around. There were a lot of Eurasian women and some beautiful Mexican girls, as well as the traditional California beach girl types. Also, it was not unusual for young actresses to work as strippers and table dancers while waiting for their big break—acting ability was also a valuable trait in a good table dancer—and they covered a wide range of looks.

Larry did not believe in the concept of "build it and they will come." He believed that you had to "build it, promote it, and market it, and then they will come." He was right, and having beautiful, promotable girls staffing Scores was a keystone for our projected success.

Larry was confident he could attract some of the girls he met in Florida. A few days before I left for L.A. he arranged for a meeting with a Florida girl named Dawn and a friend of hers named Tom, who had been a manager of clubs in the south for seventeen years. We flew them to New York because we knew we would have to maintain a constant recruiting system to assure ourselves of a 10-plus staff.

It was the first time in New York in many years for Dawn and Tom, so we really laid on the hospitality. We put them up in a suite at the Sheraton Centre and arranged private sightseeing tours of the Big Apple. We took them to dinner in Little Italy and for after-dinner drinks at Elaine's.

My eyes were on Dawn the entire night. She was brunette, with the look of a *Vogue* model. She was about five foot eight and wore heels that made her look six feet. She had these incredibly high cheekbones and wide, bright green eyes. She was very thin and did not have much of a chest, but she exuded class and I could see how men would flock to her.

Larry and Tom both noticed my attraction to her. When she went to the ladies' room in Elaine's they said in unison: "Jay, if you think she is great you should see Tyler. She's the girl you have to have."

Larry had mentioned Tyler before, the Pamela Anderson Lee look-alike who got into dancing to piss her father off.

"She's the blonde bombshell to top all blonde bombshells," Tom said.

Dawn came back to the table as Tom was describing Tyler and she jumped right in. "Oh, you're talking about Tyler," she said without a hint of jealousy.

Dawn went on to say how she never saw anyone make men melt in their pants like Tyler did. I thought this was incredible testimony coming from a girl who might have considered Tyler a rival. But I realized it was onc topflight pro talking about another—something like Dan Marino praising Joe Montana.

Most important, Tom pitched in, Tyler was like the pied piper of table dancing. The other top-rated girls would follow her anywhere. She was admired by them all. If she wore a red dress, all the girls would start wearing red dresses. If Tyler flirted with the law by flashing a little beaver, then all the girls would take the chance. When Tyler stopped, they would stop. I knew we needed this woman. It would be like a very good football team acquiring a Hall of Fame quarterback. It would put Scores over the top.

I liked Tom and Dawn very much. He was a laid-back Texan, tall, about two hundred pounds, a former professional kick boxer who looked like a sandy-haired version of Clint Eastwood. He had made a very successful career managing high-class topless nightclubs. He knew all aspects of running a club. Larry attested that he was well liked by the girls on the circuit, who trusted him and knew they did not have to kick back money or sex to get a fair shake in his clubs. I decided that Tom would make the perfect operations manager for Scores. Before they returned to Florida, he'd accepted the job, and Dawn had agreed to dance for us and to help recruit other girls.

Before they left New York the four of us went to visit a new club called FlashDancers that had opened on the site of the former Kit Kat Klub, a seedy topless bar. The space had also seen life for many years as one of those dime-a-dance halls, which in a sense were forerunners of the gentlemen's clubs.

It was located in a crude downstairs area of a run-down building across the street from the Ed Sullivan Theater, which is now home to David Letterman's show. The place had the feel of a basement and the aesthetic appeal of the Pussycat Lounge—in other words, none.

As the Kit Kat Klub it had been dead for years, surviving only with a couple of B-girls doing the champagne hustle. But as FlashDancers it was alive once more. Business was booming as some very attractive girls danced topless on a stage and at a few tables scattered around the crummy place.

As soon as Tom and Dawn walked in the girls stopped what they were doing and rushed over to us. They all knew Tom and Dawn, and because Larry and I were with them, we were also greeted with what I have come to know as the traditional showgirl's welcome. They swamped us with shrill giggles and wrapped their arms under ours as they sensuously scratched our backs through our suit jackets. At the same time they would go to a tiptoe position on one foot and lift their other gorgeous leg so that the heel of their shoe almost touched their firm ass. The greeting was offered to males and females alike. I would eventually receive thousands of hugs like that and hate it each and every time. It is as contrived as the "air kiss" that Hollywood phonies offer each other.

Anyway, the scene in FlashDancers once again convinced me that table dancing would be a big winner in New York. What they offered there was only an approximation of what I had in mind, and it was doing great business.

While Larry and I did have a momentary thought that our idea had been stolen, we also realized that we would be filet mignon to their White Castle belly busters.

We took a big table at FlashDancers and ordered some drinks. Quickly I was approached by a black woman named Jezebel who had one of the most incredible bodies I had ever seen.

I let her dance for me, then Tom, who seemed to know her and invited her to sit with us. She was pretty friendly, the presence of Dawn at the table probably establishing some kind of openness that a group of men could never accomplish alone.

Jezebel told us she was, of all things, Belgian, and that she'd been living in New York about two years. She was wearing a white sequined dress that contrasted beautifully with her coffee-colored skin. She had long, perfect legs and the highest, tightest butt I had ever sat next to. Her face was not the greatest, but that body put her on the first team of all the girls I ever saw, in Houston, L.A., Florida, or, eventually, Scores.

I nodded to Larry that she had an "atomic" body and we agreed that she was a must-have for Scores. I figured Scores would need a minimum of fifty dancers a night, seven nights a week, so taking into account illnesses, unexpected quittings and firings, I thought I would need at least seventy-five of the most beautiful girls constantly ready to dance at Scores. They would be the crème de la crème of girls from across the country. While my experience with good-looking girls in New York was not great, I did know there were some, like Gigi in the Harmony, Lana at the Pussycat, and now Jezebel in FlashDancers. And, of course, there would always be room for Alicia if she ever wanted to dance again.

Before we left FlashDancers, Tom had extracted promises from the best-looking girls to come to work for him at Scores. It cost me about $300 in dance money to buy the time to allow Tom to make the pitch, but if just half of the girls kept their promise, I knew, it would be money well spent.

Two days later Jeff and I flew to L.A. to visit Alzado's and recruit some girls for Scores.

Within twenty-four hours I realized the restaurant would have to be closed and reopened in a new concept. Its only customers were bikers, who were enraging the neighborhood with noise, and a few hookers who had made the bar their headquarters.

Brainstorming with Jeff, I figured the best thing to do was to keep Alzado's a sports bar under a different name and use it as a kind of minor league team for Scores. I came up with the concept of a sports bar that featured beautiful women, as opposed to Scores, which was a topless bar that featured sports.

I knew the neighborhood around Alzado's would not allow a full-fledged topless club, so before I left L.A. we put together a plan for a club called Double Play which featured three big-screen televisions and a dozen smaller monitors around the room. We decided to take out Lyle's sports memorabilia and to replace it with a more general sports theme. The other attraction would be fabulous looking waitresses in tight short shorts and T-shirts tied right under their breasts.

In addition, we put in a small basketball court and scheduled some girls who were born to wear bikinis in best-body and wet-T-shirt contests. The best part of the plan for me was that the waitresses hired for Double Play would become a talent pool for Scores in New York, just like the Columbus, Ohio, Yankees feed their best talent up to the New York Yankees.

Before we left L.A. we hired a new management team and interior decorators and placed an ad for waitresses.

Florida girls, Hollywood girls, New York girls—this was the part of the job I liked. The King of Clubs was on a roll. For the rest of the spring I flew back and forth from coast to coast, and occasionally to Fort Lauderdale like a regular jet-set entrepreneur—which by now, of course, I was.

By the end of June, Alzado's had been transformed into Double Play, and we were ready for a gala opening night. With Tom's help we selected six strippers from Florida to work as bikini and shot girls for the grand opening. The shot girl's job was to walk around, barely dressed, with a large bottle of a vodka-and-juice combination, which she would pour into a customer's mouth while she straddled his chest. The shot girl at Scores would eventually develop this act into high comedy.

During this period I came into direct contact—in a business sense—with the strippers for the first time and got to see how scatterbrained and unreliable many of them were.

We sent first-class airline tickets and hotel reservations to six girls in the Fort Lauderdale area, but only four showed up at LAX to meet the limo we sent for them.

The other two just cashed in the tickets and never joined us in L.A. at all. Two of the four who did come checked into the hotel but never contacted us at the restaurant. As far as we know, they just disappeared from the face of the earth.

One of the remaining two, a girl named Drew, was insubordinate and refused to recognize me as her boss, and within an hour after her arrival at the restaurant, when she would not wear the T-shirt we had made for her, I had to fire her.

But there's always a bright side, and in this case it came in the magnificent shape of Janet, the one remaining Florida girl. She was a godsend. Built for speed at five foot five and 105 pounds, she had a great big smile and a body that looked like it was born in an aerobics commercial. She had an infectious personality that seemed to light the whole place up. Janet could even make the bad-assed security staff crack a smile.

She was a Jewish girl from Bayside, Queens, not far from my old stomping grounds, and began dancing after she and her mother moved to Florida.

Also helping to save the day was a photographer named Denis, a Florida native who moved to California for the talent pool of available glamour models. He had shot some layouts for *Playboy* and *Penthouse,* but most of his work was seen in biker magazines like *Easyriders*. Those models were of a slightly lower caliber but were generally pretty sexy.

Denis was the photographer who shot the very famous poster titled "Hauling Ass," which featured four women in the back of a pickup truck, wearing high heels and with their butts exposed except for their tiny T-bars. It became the number one selling non-celebrity poster of all time.

Some of his models signed on with us as waitresses. One was a bubbly blonde from Hawaii named Beth whose father was an original Hell's Angel. She was 110 pounds of pure dynamite, with a great butt. She had a deep, golden tan. We had to fight the crowds off one day when we had her shoot baskets wearing a tiny bikini on the street outside Double Play.

Another stunner who helped us out was Jennifer. She was about thirty years old and well-known in the entertainment business as a highly skilled makeup artist. But she enjoyed the excitement of working table dancing clubs and was very willing to pitch in as a Double Play bikini girl. Jennifer was a witch who belonged to a coven and had done some time in a women's reformatory. She was very smart and had restaurant ideas of her own. She wanted to open a fast-food vegetarian drive-through.

She had a friend named Candy (I often thought they were lovers) who was a five-foot-ten showgirl type with blonde hair down to her waist and fabulous legs. But she did not have have the personality of Jennifer.

We hired a Swedish girl who had posed in *Playboy*. This gave her a superior, aloof attitude, but she was a hard worker and was one of the few beauties who would do a shift as a waitress if we were short.

Despite all the personality problems, I realized that we'd ended up with a pretty good group of bikini girls and waitresses. They were fantastic-looking and were getting paid only about $50 to $100 a shift. I knew then that I would never have problems recruiting the right kind of girls for Scores, where the money would be much greater.

We set opening night for the night of the Lakers–Bulls NBA championship game. Larry flew out to handle the advertising, and his genius paid off immediately when he placed an ad in the *Hollywood Reporter* called "Catch This." The ad showed a flawless beauty posing bent over, wearing a catcher's mask, chest protector, high heels, and G-string. It announced Double Play as a sports bar sporting beautiful women. It drew 450 calls the first day it ran, and the phone never stopped ringing after that.

We had a big party the night of the Tyson-Riddick fight and I hosted an *Up All Night* segment on USA Network where we had all kinds of stars, like Fred Travalena, Lou Ferrigno, and Bo Swenson.

Over the following weeks stars like Jean-Claude Van Damme, wrestler Jesse "the Body" Ventura, and the wonderful actress Elisabeth Shue, whom I fell in love with in *Adventures in Babysitting* and who hit it very big in *Leaving Las Vegas,* showed up regularly.

I ended up staying in L.A. longer than I intended and did not get back to Scores until late July. You can imagine my exhilaration when I walked into my apartment my first day back and put on the television. There on MTV was comic Pauly Shore doing a segment that was a take off on Double Play. As he walks past the restaurant's logo, which was designed by Larry and featured two giant breasts painted like baseballs, Shore turns to the audience and says, "Check out the baseballs."

I knew I had arrived and was ready to "score" big time.

CHAPTER 17 Tyler

No sooner was I back at the Scores site than I was presented with a major problem. It was very serious and no experience in my past had prepared me to deal with it. A group of black and Puerto Rican construction workers who called themselves "the Coalition" had appeared on the site and tried to shake down the construction foreman.

Their spiel was a demand for jobs for minority workers, but they clearly were after a payoff to make them disappear. One of the leaders approached my men with a gun in his waistband.

But our workers were an experienced bunch and just as big as some of the coalition crew. My guys told them that the boss—meaning me—would not allow unauthorized personnel on the site.

The foreman called me at home and told me there was a standoff and no work could get done until it was handled "one way or the other." I guess he was telling me that if I wanted to pay off the extortionists that was okay, but I had to do something. I said

I would be right over to handle the situation personally. I said I would throw "the Coalition" out on their lazy asses.

When I got to the site about fifteen minutes later, the incident was all over. The foreman told me that my answer was just what he'd been hoping for. He knew I would stand up to the blackmailers, so he picked four of his biggest guys and they'd persuaded the Coalition to either take their illegal act someplace else or deal with a collection of sledgehammers in the hands of some very tough, honest laborers.

The Coalition is a group of minority tough guys who would rather fight than work. Every week or so a battle breaks out—sometimes involving gunshots—between them and honest workers on construction sites all over New York. While many contractors stand up to their whining complaints, there are many who pay them off to avoid trouble. They are one of the reasons people hesitate to do business in New York. But if everyone would just stand up to them they would go away.

That was the only time anyone ever tried to shake me down during my tenure with Scores.

One preconceived threat never materialized. I'd been warned constantly by a host of businesspeople that I could expect a visit from the Mafia demanding I do business with companies they ran, companies that supplied everything from napkins to concrete. This is part of the folklore of New York, and frankly I believed it would happen. I was prepared to be approached by La Cosa Nostra. I was not sure what I would do when it happened, but I was ready for anything, because I believed if I did not stay prepared my dream would not be allowed to become a reality.

I hired two former FBI agents to handle the contact for me, whenever it came. I did not want to deal with it, because I found it so distasteful and also because I was afraid I would mishandle it and make matters even worse. Well, the fact of the matter is, the touch never materialized. I was never approached; nor were my two agents. I kept them on the payroll anyway, because they were really classy guys and because it gave others the perception that I was a no-nonsense owner who was prepared for any eventuality.

Others tell me I was very lucky regarding the mob; they say I was just in the right place at the right time. They say that I opened Scores during a period when Mafia bosses like John Gotti were under great pressure from the crime-busting U.S. Attorney Rudy Giuliani and that they had trials and indictments to deal with and were not looking for new business. They were afraid of contacts with people they did not know because Giuliani and some Mafia-busting cops like New York's Joe Coffey seemed to have a wiretap under every pillow. But whatever the reason, I apparently dodged the Mafia bullet, and I am very happy about it.

I am scrupulous in my business dealings. I do not want a penny that I have not earned through hard work, and I do not want to be associated with people who take the easy way out. It sounds very old-fashioned to say that it is much easier to point a gun at someone and demand his money than to get an education and work hard to make your own money, but I believe that to be the truth and that is how I live my life. And I have not done badly living by that code.

There was not much I could do around the construction site. The guys working there were highly paid pros, and they did not need me to tell them how to reinforce concrete or run electrical cable.

Blutrich was handling the paperwork, including the all-important licenses, and Larry was doing a bang-up job on the promotion and advertising.

So with those guys handling their ends I was able to concentrate on recruiting the staff. I was keeping in contact with all those beauties I met in L.A. and was making new contacts with Florida girls through some of the dancers I'd met in FlashDancers.

The word was spreading that I was offering a new policy regarding how dancers were to be paid. I did not realize what an impact I was to have on the relationship between dancers and owners, but I decided to allow Scores showgirls to come and go completely as they pleased.

I was banking on the expectation that I would have an overload of first-class dancers, thanks to my aggressive recruiting program. I now knew that we would have plenty of women available to work at Scores. This policy was attractive, especially to the girls from Florida, who were used to working a very scripted weeklong schedule.

I also realized that the hype Larry was spreading about Scores was so powerful that I would be able to break with the New York tradition of paying the entertainers shift pay. Topless dancers in places like the Pussycat Lounge were generally paid $15 to $20 per dance set, which usually lasted about fifteen minutes. So in those clubs a girl could earn, if she was a headliner, maybe $200 a night plus whatever tips were offered up to her on her perch above the customer. There was no table dancing.

At Scores, as in the Florida clubs, the girls were going to dance on the stage and among the customers at their tables. My whole concept, and I had seen it work in Florida and Houston, was that the girls would make enormous amounts of money from the customers. So, we were to operate on the system that the entertainers actually leased their space from the club, for a token $5 a night, and, while they did not get paid for showing up, they got to keep all they earned from the customers. In the following months I would see some of the top girls leave the club with garters stuffed full of money and a date with a customer to go shopping along Fifth Avenue the next afternoon. Stories of girls getting gifts, such as furs, cars and even houses would become commonplace. On television talk shows some showgirls claimed to make more than $2,000 a night. It was well worth the $5 house fee and remained worth it even when it was eventually boosted up to $25.

The owners of Scores Entertainment Inc., of course, would make their money from the enormous amounts of liquor and food that would be sold.

As Scores became more and more successful the girls were asked to tip the make up artists, the deejay, and the indispensable woman known as the house mom. It was not a problem—there was plenty of money to go around—but I learned eventually that I drew the ire of many of New York's successful topless dancers, who were content with the $200 or $300 they were paid for just showing up each night to dance in clubs where men had to keep their distance. Not all the girls thought the potential of Scores-type money was worth the extra work they had to do—diligently maintaining their good looks and perfecting a unique personality in order to persuade corporate execs to part with hundreds of dollars a night.

Larry had lined up the legendary Tyler to make a commercial for Scores that would run on cable television stations. It would be the first time a topless nightclub advertised in New York. We focused on the sports channels, figuring their viewers were the men we were trying to attract.

I had heard a lot about Tyler but had never really seen her. When Larry screened the commercial she hit me like a ton of bricks. It forever convinced me that what is often talked about as "chemistry" between people is a real thing.

My heart actually pounded watching Tyler on the screen. She was, as I'd been forewarned, a better-looking version of Pamela Anderson Lee. She was a bona fide sex goddess. She outclassed Jayne Mansfield by a country mile. She was everything Larry and Tom had told me and more. The effect she had on me was particularly strange. I had been pretty successful maintaining my aloof image. I had broken down only a couple of times, once with Alicia and of course with that wonderful morsel Gigi in the hapless Harmony. But just the video image of Tyler was turning me to mush.

She was a platinum blonde, not even brunette, which I favored. Watching her in the ad, I swore that whatever it took I would get her to come to work in Scores. She was the personification of what I had dreamed about as the prototypical entertainer for my club. Long before I had a site, or a liquor license, or even a name for the club, I pictured someone like Tyler as being the main draw. I told Larry to go ahead full steam with the commercial and to make sure Tyler became a Scores dancer.

The effect she had on me was even more dramatic considering that during those days I was meeting beautiful dancers at the rate of about four an hour as they showed up to ask for jobs.

The dancers would come up to my new offices on Park Avenue, and the interview would be done in a highly professional manner. There were always a few people in the room and usually at least one woman. I could not take the chance that a rejected dancer would make up a story of rape or extortion and destroy the reputation of Scores before it even officially opened.

We scrutinized the applicants for more than just beauty. Let's face it, they were all beautiful. But we were also concerned about their attitude. All the girls had to strip down to their G-strings and we then examined them in an almost clinical manner. We were on the lookout for unsightly skin blemishes, moles, scars, or even the hint of any illness. We were concerned about how they smelled and how well their hair was done and if their fingernails and toenails were manicured. Many of the girls showed up in street clothes with the sexiest lingerie underneath and occasionally one showed up in an evening dress, which I always found strange, because we started the interviews at 8 A.M.

Some of the girls were quite charming as they explained that they were actresses looking for work between auditions. Others were prostitutes who made it clear they would kick back profits to a cooperative management. Some were very aggressive and offered more than money for the opportunity to work. Some would strip before I asked them to. Some would not be wearing panties. I thought about calling Alicia to ask for help in lining up the girls, but I found I was still—irrationally, I admit—holding a grudge against her for her remarks that day at the Pussycat.

The other thing we were doing with the girls was trying out the transparent pasties I had invented to circumvent the New York State Liquor Authority laws. The law said that topless dancers had to be at least six feet from and eighteen inches above their customers. That law was the main reason New York was so far behind the rest of the country when it came to table dancing. If you think about it, New York is usually the trendsetter in most types of entertainment. But in sex-related business it is way behind, thanks mostly to its antiquated laws.

Anyway, we had great fun trying out the different types of pasties we wanted the girls to wear in order to make them "untopless dancers."

We tried all kinds of concoctions from plain old Scotch tape to special surgical-type adhesives, and the girls were good sports about dancing around in them to see if they would fall off when they perspired or bent over too far. See-through latex was the final solution. It was hard to determine if the girl was wearing anything over her nipples, and that was the way we wanted it. With that equipment she could get up close and personal with customers.

The day I knew that Tyler was coming for her interview, I was more nervous than the girls who auditioned for me. I made a special effort to look good myself that day. I worked out especially hard in the morning and wore a brand new Armani suit to the office. Tyler was expected at 10 A.M. but she kept us waiting until almost 5 P.M. The anticipation made a nervous wreck out of me and I hardly paid any attention to the girls who came earlier.

When she showed up in the flesh I threw the interview process, out the window.

I looked at her in stunned silence. Her body was a potent weapon. I realized that she had probably used it all her life to get her way with men. I understood why M. J. Peter called her his favorite dancer. My willpower was fighting a losing battle with my libido as she sat in an easy chair wearing a simple black business suit that through the talents of an excellent tailor managed to reveal each and every one of her magnificent curves. When she crossed her legs she showed me a spot of bare flesh just above her nylons. I almost choked on my coffee.

Three days earlier, when I had called to invite her to the interview and arranged for a first-class ticket for her, I was warm and friendly. But now I was scared. I was afraid to be too friendly. I knew this girl could wrap me around her little finger if I gave her an opening. I decided to act as cold as a nuclear winter.

I was smitten by her, but I was a businessman, so there was no way I was ever going to fall prey to her charms. For Scores to make it big I needed Tyler as badly as a diabetic needs insulin. I needed her and the women—and men—who would follow her to Scores. But I had to be in charge.

So I spoke to her in abrupt sound bites. I asked her where she was from, if she was married, where she had worked, why she wanted to come to Scores. She answered the questions: She was from Florida; she worked all over, in Michael Peter's clubs, both all-nude and topless; she was not married, but she did have a boyfriend; she wanted to come to Scores because she was working in a club called L.A. Woman in Nyack, New York, about twenty-five miles north of the city and had heard that Scores was going to be the best club in America and she thought she could make big money.

As she answered, she got up from the chair and began to remove the jacket she was wearing. She began to unbutton it, but

I put up my hand to stop her. "It won't be necessary to strip," I told her. "Your reputation precedes you."

My gambit had an immediate impact. I have no doubt that Tyler had never met a man before—including, from what I heard, her father—who did not try to take her to bed. My decision to deal with her on a different level was clearly appreciated. She softened a great deal and lit up in a genuine smile as she sat back down in the chair.

"I would like to offer you the position of head recruiter and star performer at my club," I said. "You will get a contract and be considered part of the management team."

Now it was her turn to be stunned. She sat in the chair and looked me over. She looked around the office, checking out the other people and seemingly absorbing every inch of the place in detail.

Then she brightened again and said she would love to have a contract and did not see why we could not work something out. I told her we would put some papers together and get back to her in a few days. Of course, the contract was not just for her protection; I still remembered the Florida girls who'd stiffed me in Los Angeles.

As Tyler left the room I totally undressed her with my eyes. What a gorgeous woman.

We eventually agreed to pay her $500 a week and put her up in a midtown hotel. She was thrilled with the arrangement. No one had ever before treated her as an equal. So, with five weeks to go until opening night, the King of Clubs had signed the premier topless dancer in America.

Within days, Tyler was bringing girls around for Larry and me to interview. She brought her friends Jane, Nicky, Lalani, Avery, Meegan, and Holly. Sometimes they were their real names; sometimes they were names adopted for the stage. We remained vigilant in our recruitment standards as our days became a blur of perfect breasts, thighs, and rear ends.

At the same time, I was searching for a public relations firm that would be able to spread the name of Scores around the world. I was surprised at the reaction I got at many of the firms I approached. Basically they said they would be happy to take my money but did not honestly believe they could do much for Scores.

They told me that topless clubs were as old as dirt and that since the media reporters and writers were as often women as men, they did not think they would be able to adequately cover the comings and goings at Scores.

I gave them my entire pitch about sports, women, AIDS, food, booze, everything, but I could not get a public relations firm to sign up. I explained how Scores would become a celebrity hangout. None of them seemed to get it. One guy said he thought I'd been smoking banana peels.

I was getting the same song and dance I'd gotten from the first investors I had approached before Steven Stevens came into my life. Undaunted, I determined that I would approach columnists and reporters myself if I had to. I knew we needed good press to make the club work, to give it a wholesale legitimacy and star appeal.

Eventually we signed with the firm of Capalino, LoCicero, Marino and Tan, a political public relations firm with ties to the administration of former mayor Ed Koch.

Larry had a friend who worked there, and while it seemed they might not be equipped to do entertainment-type work, we figured they probably would be useful battling any potential community, legal, or political uproar when we opened. After all, while our entrance was in the shadow of the 59th Street Bridge, we were also just a stone's throw from Sutton Place.

Eventually we took out full-page ads in the *Daily News* and the *Post*, when, two weeks before opening, we launched a $60,000 strategic marketing plan to blast Scores into the public consciousness.

By mid-October I became obsessed with the fear that something would go wrong. I set up triple redundant recruiting for dancers and waitresses. Tyler proved to be as good as her advance billing and brought twelve of the hottest table dancers in the world to New York. She even managed to find Jezebel, who had disappeared from FlashDancers, by using an ad in the *Village Voice* personals.

In addition to all this there were the girls from Double Play, who were constantly sending their friends to audition for me, some of them the winners of hot body contests on the beaches of Santa Monica and Malibu.

Physically the site was ready for opening, with all the mahogany and stained glass installed. Some of the walls were painted wine bottle green, others had Ralph Lauren paisley wall paper on them. Someone said the club looked like the Polo Lounge in the Beverly Hills Hotel. The half-court basketball court was installed. The golf machines were being tested; a pool table and air hockey table were in place. The Squirrel System, which monitored booze served at the bar, was almost fully installed, and booze and champagne were being delivered on time. Everything was right on course for our Halloween opening.

Jeff the Psychic dropped out of the operation around that time, saying he had another lucrative offer. Personally I believe he was in over his head and wasn't equipped to run Scores' food service. We were able to get one of the owners from a popular restaurant in Tuckahoe, New York, and a cousin of Mark Yackow's to take over the kitchen operations.

I also had to take time out one day to fire Lacey, the knockout personal trainer from the fitness club. I'd hired her to do a bunch of odd jobs around the offices and the site, but because she was "a friend of the boss" she thought she *was* the boss. After she tried to push Tom around, then didn't apologize, I had to fire her. It was one of the rare times I'd mixed business with pleasure. That is usually a mistake.

We were down to one week before opening when calamity struck. We discovered that the architect had failed to file for the public assembly license. Without it, we were dead in the water. The next week was nothing but frantic phone calls. We hired a former city attorney to help us break through the red tape. Blutrich called every political contact he had. We got a meeting with the deputy commissioner of buildings. It turned out that the problem revolved around an exit door which led through the Vertical Club. It did not seem to be properly covered by fire sprinklers as a "protected means of egress."

One day before opening we fixed the problem and got a temporary public assembly permit. It was then that we realized our cabaret license had not arrived from the Consumer Affairs Department. This all-important document, which allowed dancing to be performed in a restaurant, was caught up in some other tangle of red tape. But it was too late to turn back, and we made the decision to open without the license.

There was not much else we could do. We had sent out ten thousand invitations for opening night. Budweiser was doing a promotion with us, sending in a bikini girl in a casket in honor of Halloween.

Considering the legal ramifications of opening without a cabaret license, we were trying to find some loopholes in the code. Did the code refer to dancing of all kinds or just ballroom dancing? The debate raged on, images of the mess in Fleetwood's running through my mind as I watched the workers put the finishing touches on Scores.

The girls were showing up well ahead of schedule. They were all caught up in the importance of the opening. Tyler had done a good job of instilling a special pride in them about working in Scores. The workmen had all they could do to keep their eyes from wandering towards the dressing room, where fifty of the most beautiful women in the world were walking around in various stages of undress.

Food was cooking in the kitchen. Beer was worming its way through the Squirrel System. Larry was conducting a last-minute once-over. And at 4:45, October 31, 1991, Michael Blutrich arrived with the cabaret license. "I got it, Jay," he said. What a score! We were in business.

CHAPTER 18 Scores

With cabaret license in hand, we opened the doors. Blutrich came in and sat down at the bar with the construction workers I had allowed in earlier. He needed a drink. Being a teetotaler, he ordered his usual ginger ale. For all his expressed confidence that everything would turn out all right, he had still spent a frantic day undoing the last bit of red tape that stood between a "clean" opening—that is, one with all our ducks in a row—and a risky one, where we would be at the mercy of some city official who could shut us down for the lack of a piece of paper.

My heart was racing a mile a minute as I awaited the first customers, but I was absorbing everything in a kind of slow motion. Major league hitters sometimes say that they can actually visualize the baseball frozen in air as they take their cut at it. That is how I felt. Everything around me seemed to slow down as I examined each detail of my club.

The reality was that things were pretty quiet for the first hour or so. A few businessmen from the neighborhood wandered in to see what the new sports bar had to offer. They were surprised and impressed when they saw the girls and the table dancing setup. Their hands quickly went to their wallets.

Larry and I exchanged several concerned glances during that first hour. I guess we had hoped the advertising and promotion would have created a mob scene at the door by eight-thirty in the morning. But we should have realized that New Yorkers are basically a blasé bunch. There is not much they have not seen. Every gimmick in history has been tried on New Yorkers, from P. T. Barnum's freak shows to wide-open sex clubs like Plato's Retreat. New Yorkers would not go too far out of their way to check out Scores, and they would try to be cool about it—but they *would* check us out. Larry and I agreed on that.

At around six-thirty the stream of successful young men in Burberry raincoats began. As I looked west toward the subway stop at Lexington Avenue, I saw them with their *Wall Street Journals* tucked under their arms and their cordovan leather attaché cases gripped tightly in their hands. A dozen or so made their way towards my front door. I stepped out of the way as they paid the token $5 entrance fee, checked their coats and briefcases, and stepped into the heaven on Sixtieth Street I'd given four years of my life to create.

It was a pleasure to see their first impressions. Up to that moment in their lives, those horny Wall Street guys thought the Pussycat Lounge defined a topless club. When they walked in to the main room at Scores and saw four beautiful blondes dancing on the large, main stage, then Jezebel on the champagne pedestal next to the bar and Janet on the pedestal in the game room—which contained the golf, billiards, and other sports attractions—well, their breath was literally taken away.

I stood with a group of my initial customers as they saw Tyler for the first time. The music playing was "I Touch Myself" and she was swaying, nude except for a G-string so tiny we called it "butt floss," about twelve inches away from the wide-open mouth of one of the local businessmen who'd come in right after the doors opened. The transparent pasties did nothing to diminish the sensuality of her perfect nipples. The garter on her perfect thigh was already stuffed fat with $10 bills.

The four men I was standing among could not believe their eyes. They jabbed each other in the side with their elbows, and the grins on their faces told the entire story. They almost tripped over themselves heading for a table right next to where Tyler was bending over at the waist, showing off her perfect butt to her first Scores customer.

I indulged myself for a moment and walked into the center of the room. I stood among the disco lights and the pounding rhythm and took my first deep breath in days. I spread out my arms and slowly turned around. Even if the SLA shut me down right now, I would forever be known as the King of Clubs.

I was brought back from my reverie by a few small crises—a freezer door in the kitchen was stuck, a girl walked out of the dressing room without her pasties, Coke was coming out of the ginger ale spout. They were minor glitches and I was thankful for the distractions and the chance to do something. I figured the busier I was, the less time I would have to worry that something might go wrong. By seven o'clock the restaurant was starting to fill up, and the aroma of grilled steak was mingling with the Chanel No. 5 and $21-a-throw Davidoff cigars to create the atmosphere of a high-class gentlemen's club that I'd envisioned four years earlier.

By eight o'clock we were packed wall to wall. Just about every table was occupied and the bar was full. The few tables in the restaurant that were empty, had been reserved for the VIPs whom we'd invited to come at nine-thirty.

Our ad campaign, a combination of my "Go for the gusto, take no prisoners" marketing philosophy and Larry's brilliance in putting everything together through clever placement, had paid off big time.

When the invited guests began arriving, they too were awestruck by the scene laid out before them. These guests were among the city elite. Newspaper columnists and reporters, photographers, television news producers and assignment editors, magazine writers and editors and public relations experts—all the people we would need to keep the phenomenon of Scores going strong past the first night.

Even these professionals were amazed at the quality of the girls who strolled among them, showing off their expensive evening gowns and revealing as much of their bodies as the law allowed.

One magazine editor told me he felt like the pages of *Sports Illustrated's* swimwear edition had come alive. Little did he know I had often used that kind of example to lure prospective investors.

More and more of my target-type customers began to arrive as the evening wore on. These were the men in Armani suits wearing Rolex watches and Ferragamo shoes. They paid their bills with American Express Platinum Cards, usually in the name of a corporate account, and signed with Mont Blanc pens.

The cash register was ringing. Prosperity was in the air. With New York City suffering through one of the worst economic periods in its history, money was flowing as smoothly as fine wine in Scores. A friend from my old neighborhood in Queens, whom I had invited as a VIP guest, cornered me near the bar. "Jay, you have harnessed the power of pussy!" he exclaimed.

He might have put it crudely but he'd hit the nail on head. I hearkened back to my NYU professor and his Inelasticity of

Demand theory. We would pay the price for things we needed, and we needed sexual stimulation.

I remembered that scene in my brokerage the day in 1987 when the market crashed: the stripper dancing on the desk of the "Broker of the Month," helping my boss forget his troubles of the moment by allowing him to slip $10 bills into her panties.

Now, opening night of Scores, I had brought Tyler to New York. She was dancing, virtually naked, in my club, going from table to table, raking in major money for herself and for the club. Her friend Jane—who had a distinctive look, with short-cropped blonde hair and enormous tits—was almost as much in demand. One guy for whom she danced up a storm would not let her go to another table.

Lalani, a Hawaiian girl whose long, silky black hair played off her brown skin like hot fudge melting ice cream, had six guys at the bar hypnotized as she placed herself between their legs, swaying and sliding to the disco beat and whipping that hair over their bodies. I noticed that when a song ended her customer would always order a drink—he needed it to cool down. That's how the system was supposed to work. He stuffed Lalani's garter with $10 bills and ordered expensive drinks that went into my pocket.

Across the room, Holly, a redhead with a supertight ass and perfect boobs, who looked like a young Raquel Welch and wore a flesh-colored T-bar that made her appear totally nude, was leaning her breasts toward the yearning lips of a local police reporter named Phil, who was known to stand up to Mafia hoods but was clearly melted butter in the hands of this exotic woman.

Holly's friend Meegan, a higher-octane version of Bridget Fonda, was on the smaller stage, which was surrounded by many of the guys who'd first come into the club three hours earlier. They offered up $5 bills each time she got on the floor and, with her back turned and her butt in the air, spread her legs just a little bit so they would think they were seeing something they were not supposed to. She was a real pro dancer, one of the few who could make almost as much on the stage as working the tables.

Jezebel, who was second only to Tyler in looks and appeal, was working one table with four men sitting around it. She was making a fortune as they literally threw money at her in return for a display of her charms. Another black girl named Avery, a Robin Givens look-alike whom Jezebel had brought to the club, was doing just as well in the game room. She wore a leather dress and a dog collar around her neck and patent leather five-inch heels. When she took the dress off she had a tiny patch of leather covering her crotch. Her dancing evoked the eroticism of a dominatrix, and the men loved it. Occasionally, on stage, over the coming months, she and Jezebel would act out a little S&M scene to the tune of Madonna's "Vogue." Some girls said Jezebel and Avery acted out the real thing in their private lives. Whatever happened in their private lives was their business. As far as I was concerned, I was thrilled to have those two girls working in Scores.

When one of my security guards joked that Jezebel had a face like the basketball player Scottie Pippen, his partner replied, "if Scottie Pippen had a body like that, I'd fuck him." The two were embarrassed when they realized I'd overheard the conversation. At first I laughed, but then I used the occasion to make a little speech that I hoped got spread around to all the staff.

I told them they should keep their sleazy remarks to themselves. "Scores is not a dive of a little strip joint. It is the greatest gentlemen's club on the face of the earth, and we all have our roles to play. Be professional at all times," I told them.

They might have thought I was insane, but from that time on I never caught any of the staff making disparaging remarks about the dancers. We all knew that the dancers brought in the bread and that they were to be treated like the important stars they were. Jezebel could bring in that security guard's weekly pay in one hour in the form of a magnum of champagne or two ordered by a customer who wanted to show off for her.

My need to tell off the security guard was an example of how uptight I was that opening night. I was sure the police or State Liquor Authority would be coming in and giving me a violation for some infraction, real or imagined. I had heard that the local community was not thrilled when they learned what was to be going on inside the new "sports bar." They, of course, were wrong when they thought it would be more than lovely ladies dancing for well-behaved gentlemen, but perception was everything and I knew they perceived us wrongly. I was hoping that the few local businessmen who came in with the early arrivals would set everyone straight, but I was not counting on it. The hard time given Alzado's by its neighbors annoyed with the motorcycle noise was fresh in my mind. I was obsessed with the fear that Scores would attract the biker crowd. I even refused to hire girls with tattoos because they were typically worn by biker girls. Occasionally I would allow one with a small tattoo to work, but she had to cover it with Derma-Blend, the theatrical body makeup.

Also, other topless bars had run into picketing and city council resolutions when they tried to open in certain neighborhoods. So, while all around me men were having the time of their lives enjoying the fruits of my labors, I was still worried something bad would happen. I believed in the Boy Scout motto "Be Prepared."

To that end, I had five gunslinging former law enforcement officers hired just for opening night. They were big, tall guys, in good suits, who could not be intimidated. They were used to dealing with all kinds of bad guys, from mafiosi to drunken heavyweight champions.

I decided to bring them in when one of the girls heard some rumblings that the other club owners in town were going to try to disrupt my gala opening. I'd known there was already a level of jealousy over what I was doing on Sixtieth Street. The other owners knew I was going to put a dent in their pocketbooks. They had it very good for many years, with no one trying to open a club that was different in style and class than the places like the Pussycat Lounge. Well, that period of grace was over.

As it turned out, we had absolutely no trouble that night other than a stuffed toilet in the men's room, and that probably was a total accident.

I made one trip to the dancers' dressing room, at around ten o'clock. The girl's were as pumped up as I was. They were all infected with the excitement of an opening night and shared my belief that something special was happening in Scores. By this time I was used to walking around among the naked girls. Often in the dressing room they would remove all their clothes, even the G-strings and T-bars and take a break.

The girls paid no attention to me as they adjusted their transparent pasties, did their hair and make-up, splashed on some body lotion, or filed a nail. I tried to respect their privacy by not looking directly out them, especially not at their breasts or crotch. I would look up at the ceiling or down at the floor even as I spoke to a specific girl. It was while looking at the floor that I realized how unattractive the feet of most of the showgirls were. You'd see a girl, even one almost as gorgeous as Tyler, with perfect hair, the face of an angel, breasts like a sculptured goddess, and thighs to rest your head on, and invariably she'd have ugly feet. It was a result of having them stuffed in impossibly high heels for at least ten hours day and then dancing on them to boot. Even when they were off duty most of the girls wore high heels because it made their butts look better. I saw many of them going to the supermarket in sweatpants, T-shirts, and high heels.

But always, when I was privy to their locker room preparations, I saw them as analogous to professional athletes who depend on their physical abilities to make a living and take very special care of the tools of their profession. The well-fitting G-string was as important to a Scores dancer as the right pair of sneakers to a member of the New York Knicks. I was always impressed by the efforts the girls made to stay on top of their game.

Something that always gave me a chuckle was what they did with their pubic hair. They all kept it very well trimmed so it would not stick out of the the G-strings in an unsightly manner. Some trimmed it in the shape of a heart, others a triangle, and still others, in just a straight bar down the middle of the crotch, which we called a Hitler's moustache. Very rarely did a girl shave herself completely because she might find herself working in an all-nude club, and dancers were required to show "pubes" when they worked those places.

At about midnight the Budweiser promotion began. A real coffin was wheeled into the middle of the club in a smoky fog created with dry ice. When a gorgeous beauty in a string bikini that did nothing to hide her obvious charms, popped out, the place broke into hysterical cheering and applause. In the entranceway, Larry and I stood, turned to each other and shook hands.

One of our lawyers walked in with a deputy mayor and a city commissioner who wanted to see what all the fuss was about. Several of my business associates, including some who'd taken me to the Pussycat for the first time, came at my invitation. They were all gaga over what I had accomplished. Some female friends I'd invited were in shock at what they saw, but they too were taken aback by the beauty of the women.

I guess I have to admit it was a pretty decadent scene. Gorgeous women in high heels and T-bars, were gyrating to songs like "I Touch Myself" and "I'm Too Sexy" while all around men ate filet mignon, drank $600 bottles of Cristal champagne, and smoked $50 cigars.

In the sports area, while some guys were shooting baskets on the half-court and others played pool, near-naked beauties paraded around them. I coined a phrase that night. I called the scene an "orbfest." There were basketballs, pool balls, and women's breasts everywhere you looked.

As the night turned into morning, my radar went into alert mode when I noticed one girl without her pasties and another kissing a woman guest on the lip. I decided to have a quick meeting in the dressing room to go over the rules once more. I gathered as many of the girls as possible, not wanting to take any away from paying customers, in the cramped room.

I said I realized that we had all been caught up in the exhilaration of what was happening tonight and that I wanted to quickly go over the ground rules we'd discussed when each dancer was hired. I had to be vigilant, I said, because there were people who would like to see us go out of business.

I reminded them never to be parallel with the floor when they danced on a table. I said they had to keep a foot away from the customer. That was almost impossible to enforce without the customer's getting up and leaving, and the girls knew it. The men realized they could not touch, but for the money they were willing to spend they wanted to be able to be close enough to inhale the sexuality transmitted by the dancer.

I reiterated that they could only touch a man if they were putting their hand on his shoulder to balance themselves as they took off their dress. They could table-dance two at a time for a customer, but they had to face the man. They could not dance for the entertainment of each other and they could not simulate sex. They could not touch their own nipples or their crotch. They could not accept business cards or phone numbers and they could not make dates. I did not want them confused with prostitutes.

It was very important that they did not ask the man to "buy a gal a drink." That and similar phrases were considered by the SLA to be trademarks of a B-girl who conned guys in the champagne hustle. The SLA called that practice "clipping"; that is where the term "clip joint" comes from. It was also something I knew about from firsthand experience years ago in the Horse's Rail.

"I worked four years for this night and I do not want to be shut down by carelessness," I lectured. The girls took my speech in a good-natured way. They knew I was very nervous about the law coming down on me. They found me unusual in this regard because they were more used to dealing with owners who were shady characters and were not afraid of the law. I'm sure they wondered why I didn't just make the proper payoffs and let them get on with hustling guys out of small fortunes. Still, they listened, then went back on the floor to do their thing.

When I came out of the dressing room Blutrich was waiting at the bar to see me. He had noticed that I was not as relaxed as I might have been. He told me to chill out a little. "I'm your attorney," he said, "and so I know better than anyone that you are now the king. Try to enjoy it a little more. Don't worry so much."

The club stayed packed to capacity, which was 550, until 4 A.M., when we closed. We had to practically push the customers out of the door. I never was sure how much money we took in that night. We kept records, of course but we had a lot of freebies among the media and other invited guests for whom the bartenders were under orders to be especially generous.

But exact figures did not matter. I was sure that Scores was in for the long haul. The club had delivered on its promise of high-class entertainment in luxurious surroundings. No one had a complaint. If there were men who came in expecting to leave with something more than it turned out they'd been offered, they kept their disappointment to themselves. As a business venture, I was sure, we had scored 100 percent.

Among the staff, everyone had a great night. Tyler said it was the highlight of her career. She had done plenty to bolster her reputation and had been exposed to a whole new group of faithful followers.

Two dancers approached me and gave me big hugs and kisses. They said they had never worked in such a fun and profitable place. They asked if I would like to come back to the hotel with them. I'm sorry to this day that I couldn't. I could not believe they were not as exhausted as I was. I went home and collapsed in bed. My last thought before passing out was an anxious one. I pictured Scores the next night, empty except for me and Tyler.

CHAPTER 19

Sexual Power

My anxiety was eased as soon as I showed up the next night, a Thursday following Halloween. There was a small crowd outside the entrance waiting for the doors to open at 5 P.M. They'd been treated to a free show of watching the girls arrive. They'd gotten a good look at them as they stepped out of their taxis and limos and strutted their stuff through the front door. The girls loved that scene, which they did not really get in Florida or Houston, where few people walk from place to place and crowds in the street are rare.

Clearly the word on Scores had already spread as the Halloween revelers returned to their offices and told their friends about the hottest new place in town.

As the club filled up that evening I began, for the first time, to heed Blutrich's advice and relax a little bit. I took a seat at a table in the VIP area, which we called the President's Lounge. I was no longer a frenetic ball of energy. I was now the cool, calm, and collected club owner. I took on the attitude of Humphrey Bogart as Rick in *Casablanca*, the greatest film ever made. However, unlike him, I would not drink in my own club, and I would certainly not get involved with either the entertainers or the customers. (Well, if Ingrid Bergman walked in I might consider rethinking my position.) I ordered a combination of cranberry and orange juice and club soda and enjoyed watching the skilled barmaid squirt it out of the expensive booze gun.

On the stage was a dancer named Shannon who danced under the name Brandy. It was getting harder and harder for me to remember the girls' real names. I could not really understand why someone would not want to use "Shannon" as a stage name; I'm sure it was not her real name anyway. Maybe it was because they had split personalities. Shannon was the nice girl from the sleepy Midwest town. Brandy was the stripteasing slut.

When Shannon noticed me, she came down from the stage and made a beeline for where I was sitting. She parked herself in the chair next to mine and swung around so her taut and muscular legs were draped over my lap. Her five-inch white pumps hung over the side and an ankle bracelet swung seductively back and forth as she moved her foot. I noticed a tattoo of a small scorpion on her ankle.

Gently I removed her gorgeous legs from my lap and asked her why she had not covered her tattoo with Derma-Blend the body makeup. She immediately put on the face of a little girl pouting and told me she had gotten the tattoo because her boyfriend liked it.

"But then he started hitting me so I broke up with him, and now I'm stuck with the spider," she murmured softly.

"Well, you know I hate tattoos, so make sure you go down to the dressing room and cover it up," I said. I really had no inclination to fire her over a small scorpion on her ankle.

"Yeah, sure, sure, you know, he beat me up just like my father used to," she said, suddenly offering more information than I wanted to know. But I felt a tug at my heart for her. She was not a spectacular beauty, but her five-foot-seven, 125 pound body caught the attention of most men. She was a brunette, which I favored, and she had great green eyes that I suspected might have been contact lenses because the color was so perfect. (Why shouldn't she have been wearing contact lenses? After all, she was carrying a package of silicone in her tits that made them stand out straight even as she slumped in her chair telling me her tale of woe. Changing the color of her eyes was hardly a big deal.)

It wasn't that the girls of Scores were so good-looking. Rather, they all had a "good look." And they did whatever was necessary to attain that look. In addition to the obvious boob implants, they used hair extenders, capped their teeth, and had collagen injections. Some even had their lower ribs removed to create the perfect stomach. And believe it or not, a couple of the girls had butt implants. They did what they thought they had to do to compete in the world of the major league showgirl.

Shannon was going on about how all men were just after the same thing and why shouldn't she take advantage of it. I was actually starting to feel sorry for her when she spotted a man she knew and without another word jumped up and skipped across the room to dance for him. I noticed that as quickly as she'd turned on the poor little girl act for me she was able to switch into the hot broad mode for her customer. Don't get me wrong, though: While I know she was acting the helpless victim, I did believe what she was saying about her boyfriend and her father. It was a theme I was hearing from these girls on a regular basis.

My first days at Scores, starting about a week before we actually opened, set my tone with the girls for my entire stay as its owner. It was a period of time fueled by a sense of myself as a person possessing an enormous amount of sexual power. The most beautiful women in New York were constantly kissing my ass. It was as if I were the president of the United States or even a major rock star. Showgirls were always grabbing me, kissing me, asking me out, inviting me to bed or even for a quickie in my office. When they hugged they invariably grabbed my crotch. It was wild.

If I had not learned some lessons during my four years of studying the topless scene I might have surrendered to the almost irresistible temptation. But my fear of not succeeding as a businessman, of having the club shut down or of losing business because of some scandal or distraction caused by sex, kept me on track. I managed to maintain my composure and self-control.

When I did not return their hugs and did not caress the offered thighs and breasts, the entertainers soon realized that I was in the business for the business end of things. They came to appreciate the fact that I'd treated them in the same manner I'd treated the brokers who once worked for me. I wanted everyone to score big at Scores, and that would only happen if we kept our minds on business. If a girl did not want to play by those rules, it was fine by me if she went to work someplace else. There were plenty of places where a manager might accept a blow job in return for changing a girl's shift, but she would never make the money she could make if she played it straight at Scores.

Now, don't get me wrong. I was plenty turned on by these girls; only a robot would not have been. But I disciplined myself not to show it. Sometimes I thought my entire body would explode. But I hung tough and reminded myself that the attention and affection being showered on me was artificial.

I called it the Johnny Bravo Syndrome after an episode of *The Brady Bunch* that I recalled from my youth. In that program Greg, the eldest Brady kid, was scouted by an agent who said he could make him into a rock star named Johnny Bravo. By the end of the show Greg finds out, to his disappointment, that the only reason the sleazy agent wants him is that he "fits the suit" a producer had made for his show's rock star.

It had nothing to do with Greg's talent, just as the adoration I was receiving had nothing to do with my charm and good looks. I was the King, the Big Cheese, and the lust the women were sending my way was because I "fit the suit" as the boss man. I'd like to think that some of it might have been genuine attraction, but I could not dwell on that thought—it would have only led to trouble.

I much preferred the girls like Jezebel—who just came in, worked her shift, and went home—to the ones who would invite me to go out to after-hours clubs or early-morning breakfasts.

During that first week of business, we had twelve superstar girls whom Tyler had brought up from Florida and thirty others who we found working in New York or who had answered an ad we placed in the *Village Voice*. There were three or four others who came in from Southern California via my Double Play connection and another four or five who showed up for an audition when they heard about Scores through word of mouth.

Because we really needed the Florida girls to get us going, we paid for their airplane tickets and put them up in the Roger Williams Hotel on Madison Avenue. They called it the Roy Rogers Hotel.

The girls were getting $10 a dance and we were charging a token $5 fee to get through the door just as a way of making sure the guys had some money in their pockets. We kept the prices low at first, figuring it would always be possible to raise them once we proved successful but that it would be much more difficult to drop them to stimulate business if we'd had to do that.

At about ten o'clock on night two, a ruckus broke out in the main room. I was on my way there when I heard a girl scream and a table crash to the floor. As I got there I saw a man trying to pull one of the dancers off the champagne pedestal, which was next to a giant bottle of champagne, the largest bottle sold.

This big guy was trying to yank a girl named Shawna, whose real name was Alice, off the pedestal by her arm. I got there before security, and reacting as quickly as I had back in my days at Max's Kansas City, I grabbed the guy's arm and pulled him away from the girl. But instead of punching the offender out like I might have done twelve years earlier, I acted like the sophisticated owner I was. Calmly, I asked him to follow me to the bar. Thankfully, he did. I had not traded a punch in anger in a decade, and did not want to.

Taking the diplomatic route, I said, "Look, pal, you can't be grabbing women off the stage, as desirable as they may be. Sit down. Let me buy you a drink."

I signaled the bartender for two club sodas, and the guy thanked me and said his name was Steve. He said he was Alice's boyfriend. It took me a second to remember that Alice was Shawna, and I nodded in understanding.

"I don't want her dancing here," he said. "I warned her that I would come and get her." During our brief conversation Shawna had positioned her 40 double D silicon boobs about four inches from the face of a customer at the bar, who was showing his appreciation of her talents with $5 bills. I was hoping Steve would not notice, but he did, and as I tried to reason with him he suddenly bolted from his barstool and this time grabbed Shawna/Alice by her hair.

This time I decided not to be the one to intervene and remained in my seat while the security guys did what they were paid very well to do. They acted very quickly, pulled Steve away, and ushered him out the door. Shawna/Alice went back to showing off her boobs.

As I lifted my club soda Tyler came up beside me with a warning about the girls. Some of them, she said—not the girls she'd brought up from Florida, but some of the others—were "dirty-dancing."

She meant that some of the dancers were touching the customers and maybe giving them a peek at what treasures lay beneath the fronts of their T-bars. The worst thing that could be happening was that they were letting the men touch them under the T-bars or letting them touch or kiss their nipples. I was not naive enough to think that a skilled dancer and an experienced customer with money to spend could not work out such an arrangement. But I could not let it happen, especially so early in the history of Scores when I had this paranoid conviction that every law enforcement type in New York was determined to shut us down.

I called Tom over and told him what Tyler suspected. He assured me that he would check it out and take care of it, even if it meant firing someone. I was pleased with the way everyone was doing their jobs—security, Tyler, Tom. Larry called it staying in their own lanes: sticking to what they knew and taking care of business there.

Friday, day three, was another fantastic day. Business boomed, but it was marred by a major brawl that broke out when a dancer named Angel, a girl about five feet tall and ninety pounds with a tremendous mane of wild raven hair, spit in the face of a Wall Street type who'd tried to put his hand down the front of her T-bar. In response Mr. Wall Street slapped Angel, which brought the security team full steam from the discreet perches they used to watch out for just such happenings. As my guys escorted Mr. Wall Street to the street a bunch of his friends began complaining loudly that they were being too rough. By the time they got to the street, it was a full-scale brawl and blood was flowing.

The Wall Street crowd, all totally boozed up, let their beer muscles get the better of them and started battling with some men who were waiting in line. There were about ten customers, all well-dressed guys in expensive suits trading punches with Scores security when the police from the 19th Precinct pulled up. In that precinct it was not unusual to find men in expensive suits fighting in the street, and the officers were calm and professional as they restored order.

It was interesting that almost all of the fights that broke out in Scores were initiated by so-called gentlemen or executive types. The "candy store cowboys" who would sometimes come in from Brooklyn and Queens rarely got into fights. If something happened that angered them they were cool enough to take it outside or to write it off completely.

Usually even the guys who'd expected to score would not cause scenes. I would see men like that leaving every night. You could tell by the look on their faces that they felt they'd just thrown a few hundred dollars down the drain, that they'd spent and spent and had not even gotten a feel. Those guys would leave angry and probably not come back, but they would not start fighting. It was always the boozed-up executive types who imagined someone giving them a dirty look or insulting them that sent the security guys running.

When a police lieutenant pulled up to the scene, Blutrich went to talk to him but was intercepted by one of the Wall Streeters, who spit in his face. I don't know what all the spitting was about—it was not the way battles were fought outside Max's—but I am glad there was no shooting or stabbing.

Blutrich remained as cool as a cucumber as the saliva dripped down his cheek onto his suit. He had great composure, perfected during his days as a trial attorney. It took almost an hour for everything to settle down. Nobody was seriously hurt, so the police let everyone just go home to sober up. I went home exhausted again.

Angel later told me that she made a fortune that night and that one guy offered her $100 if she would spit on him. With an endearing wink she told me that she "would never do anything like that." Angel turned out to be one of my favorite girls and an all-time-leading moneymaker at Scores.

Saturday was more of the same businesswise but without the

fighting. On Sunday, my vision of building Scores around sports paid off. When we opened at 1 P.M. many men from the neighborhood came in to watch the football games. Without the games it would have been a slow day. The girls did not do as well as on previous days, but the bar turned over plenty of cash.

On Monday night we were once again packed to the rafters. Scores was now the biggest sports bar in New York, and anyone who ridiculed my determination to add eight big projection television screens and forty smaller monitors to the mix of girls had to eat their words. We captured a sports fan audience and turned them on to table dancing. Tom was annoyed when I asked him to pull down a screen between the main stage and the audience, but he had to admit I was right when the game came on and guys started screaming for the girls to get out of the way.

So the scene unfolded with Monday Night Football on the screens (no volume—sorry, Frank), booming dance music, and showgirls performing all around (while being careful not to block the views of the game.) My theory of sports and women was a home run.

On Monday night I also got my first taste of the kind of entree I would have now that I was a big-time New York club owner. Bo Dietl, a legendary NYPD detective, came in that night with a good friend, the owner of Adam's Apple, the famous singles bar. At this time Bo was a private investigator and there was a book out called *One Tough Cop,* which told the story of his exploits with the NYPD. I recognized him when he came in, because the book had received a great deal of publicity. He and his friend wanted to see what all the hullabaloo on Sixtieth Street was about.

They stayed to watch the game, and Bo even demonstrated the fingertip push-ups that had helped make him a legend among tough cops. He was a great guy. He ran outside to his car and got a copy of the book, which he autographed for me, and before the evening was over he invited me to be his guest at Rao's, the exclusive Italian restaurant in East Harlem where reservations were made three months in advance. Bo and I got along very well. Over the next few years we enjoyed some great Italian dinners together in Rao's.

That week was Tyler's birthday. We sent her flowers and balloons and had a cake for her. I threw a nice little party for her in the President's Club that all the girls appreciated. Tyler and I sat in a quiet corner and had the first personal conversation of our relationship. She told me her real name was Katie Holiday and that she was originally from Rehoboth Beach, Delaware. We spoke quietly for about an hour, during which Tyler pretty much told me the Cliffs Notes version of her life.

She told me her parents moved to Alabama near the Florida border when she was sixteen. She was a champion cheerleader in high school and after that won many beach-related contests like "Best Bikini Body" and some events sponsored by a national suntan product. She graduated to working in Thee Doll House for M. J. Peter, and she reiterated what I had heard about how the more her father complained about her lifestyle the more daring she became.

She was blessed with large, beautiful breasts that she'd needlessly enhanced with silicone. Eventually she moved to Fort Lauderdale and Pure Platinum, the totally nude club, where she quickly became famous for her great looks and personality and began to make big money.

All of a sudden, as she was talking, Tyler began to cry. She was sobbing uncontrollably. I figured it had been brought on by a combination of too much booze and too many memories, but one day I was to find out that she really was a troubled young woman. I put my arm around her and we exchanged an emotional hug. I think there was a feeling that we cared for each other, but, of course, I signaled myself that that was a dangerous emotion around a woman like her.

As we were talking the club opened and Tyler spotted a friend of hers who had come up from Florida to celebrate her birthday. She turned the tears off, put on her showgirl smile and got up to join him. She left me thinking about how complex the dancers' lives were. Nothing was as it seemed. Their breasts were fake, their names were phony, even their so-called real names were probably not real, and behind the aura of their fabulous beauty, more often than not, lurked ugly memories.

As I wandered back to the main room, I was confronted by one of the most exotic women ever to grace the lineup at Scores, or anywhere else for that matter.

She was striking, with high cheekbones and full, pouting lips. She had a really slim waist and a chest that stood out like headlights on an old Buick. Looking like a Latin spitfire, she was dancing on one of the pedestals, a very sensuous dance, in a black ultrasheer full-length robe, G-string, and black high heels. When she let the robe fall I could see a gold chain around her hips, which I thought was a very sexy touch.

As she danced in just the G-string, she began squirting a foamy white mousse into her hand, which she then rubbed sensuously on her body. It was a great turn-on, and even I was awestruck by the act as she rubbed the mousse all over her darkly tanned body. Her hand traveled slowly over her large, sculpted breasts, then down her torso, and over her hips and legs. She made mincemeat of the men who were watching her. She was toying with them, and they loved every sexy second of it.

When the song ended I called her over. She put on the sheer black robe and with a big smile came over to where I was standing. Standing next to her made me weak-kneed. This was chemistry doing its thing, percolating through my bloodstream. I felt I could faint looking at this woman's body. She had the greatest ass I had ever seen, every bit as hot as Beth's at Double Play, maybe better. Her face and body exuded eroticism. She reminded me of the legendary fifties pinup sensation Betty Page, but she was even more sultry.

She told me her name was Marina and I asked her to step into my office.

Once inside I sat behind my desk and said, "Marina, I would appreciate it if you did not put that cream on your body while you dance. I want to make it perfectly clear. NO CREAM!!"

"Who the fuck are you?" was her response.

"I'm Jay Bildstein and I own this club," I retorted.

Never one to be upstaged, yet realizing she'd made a mistake, Marina shot back, "Why can't I put on the mousse?" My lame answer: "Because it could be perceived as lewd and lascivious."

That almost made her laugh.

"Where the hell do you think you are?" she said. "This is a strip club. Let me put on the cream; come on, the guys love it."

But I did not yield. Much to my relief as a professional, I stood up to this very special woman who had ignited feelings in me that I had previously been successful in keeping down.

Marina was a dynamo of erotic sensuality. She turned out to be very, very smart and the most genuine woman I ever met in the topless business, or any other business for that matter. She was the real McCoy when it came to the perfect mixture of brains and beauty, and she is the only person I met through Scores who is a friend to this day.

Marina: heart of gold, outrageous body, brains and beauty. I like to call her Marina, the Queen-a My Club.

CHAPTER 20 Marina

During our first week a dancer named Marcy came by the club at around three in the afternoon to pick up some clothes she had left in the dressing room the night before. I had not even noticed Marcy until now. She was just another perfect 10 in a room full of 10s and was more quiet and introspective than the other showgirls.

She was not one of the girls who were always looking to hug me and grab my crotch or to throw themselves on the casting couch that they were sure existed.

I was deep in conversation with a reporter for an entertainment magazine who was doing a piece on topless clubs around the country when Marcy came over and grabbed my arm.

"Mr. Bildstein, could you come with me for a moment? There is someone I want you to meet," she said.

Marcy was wearing jeans and a sweatshirt and her usually well-coiffed hair was hidden under a Yankees baseball cap. She looked cute, but nothing like the showgirl she would turn into in about three hours. Most of the guys thought she looked like Melanie Griffith.

I was a little annoyed at the interruption, especially because I was not even sure who she was, not having exchanged one sentence of conversation with her since she'd come to work at Scores. But I wanted to give the magazine writer the right impression of me so I asked him to excuse us and I let her lead me out into the street to where a stretch limo was parked.

In the rear seat of the gigantic car sat a little boy wearing a Yankees jacket. The window was rolled down and he was leaning out. He broke into a big smile when he saw Marcy dragging me toward him.

"Mr. Bildstein, this is my son Mark. Mark, say hi to Mr. Bildstein. He's my boss. He owns this whole place," she said.

Mark sent a shy smile in my direction, then backed off as Marcy opened the door to get in. I said: "Hi, Mark, it's nice to meet you." He was a cute little boy with a mess of blond hair and a really curious expression. But he was too shy to shake the hand I offered him.

I saw a man sitting on the other side in the rear seat and when Marcy saw me notice him she said offhandedly: "This is my boyfriend, Al." Al did not even look in my direction, and that was fine with me.

Marcy closed the door, and they drove off to parts unknown while I returned to the club. I found the scene very touching. I was proud that Marcy, a major league showgirl, would think so much of me that she wanted her son to meet me. And I also thought it was nice that she'd made the effort for her son to meet her boss. It was no different from a secretary in a large corporation wanting her children to meet her boss. I returned to the interview feeling pretty good about the little family I was growing around Scores.

I have relived that scene a thousand times since that day, because it became part of one of the greatest tragedies I have ever been part of.

A week after Marcy introduced me to Mark we got word at the club that she had been involved in a terrible car crash on a highway in Westchester.

We later learned that she was stoned or drunk while driving home one night and had rammed her car into the rear of a hot dog wagon parked along the highway. The accident left Marcy a quadriplegic.

She was brought down from Westchester to Bellevue Hospital, about a mile south of Scores, for treatment. The other girls were really generous to her with their time and money. They went to visit her, and for almost a year they made regular contributions to a fund that helped pay her hospital bills and provide for Mark. I do not know if Al chipped in, but I hope he did.

The news of the accident left me distraught. I felt a real involvement with the girl because of that touching scene the previous week. The day she was moved to Bellevue I related the incident to Tyler. We were sitting in my office and I could not talk about it without crying. I could not hold back the tears.

I sobbed on and on. All the emotions of the past month that I had been holding back seemed to burst forth in a torrent of tears. Tyler came behind my desk and put her arms around me in a sincere hug—no fingernails scratching my back, no knee searching for my crotch.

That was a turning point in our relationship. Previously I'd tried not to show any emotion in front of her for fear that she would use it to turn me into one of the sniffling sycophants who followed her everywhere just for a smell of her perfume.

But at that moment I was inconsolable. Shannon's words from last week, when she'd told me about her boyfriend and father beating her, ran through my mind. I was on an emotional slide into a cavern of despair as I began to see the other side of the body-beautiful business. I finally regained my composure and returned Tyler's hug. It was a tender moment, even if she was acting.

Eventually, I heard Marcy made some physical progress and that she and Mark ended up back in Florida with her parents.

I walked around the club during those first weeks in a constant fog of emotional ups and downs. Business was busting out all over, it could not have been better, but I was beginning to have my first doubts about life with the showgirls. I did not want to be a part of their problems, but it was impossible to stay away from them. They all had great looks and magnetic personalities, and I was a man with a healthy combination of hormones. I don't care what anyone says, you never get used to seeing women who look like Tyler and Marina walking around naked.

Marina proved to be a calm port in the stormy seas of Scores. I noticed that she took all the emotional turmoil in stride and that she was not part of the often hysterical atmosphere that surrounded many of the girls. She seemed to keep her business to herself and appeared much more stable than the others. I began to seek her out for conversation, and it was from her that I started to learn about the secrets of the showgirls. Marina had her head on straight. She knew where she came from and she knew where she was going. She also was one of the girls who despised what I had done to the New York topless scene.

My success, Marina often said, caused the downfall of the girls who had been able to make a good living in the old fashioned topless clubs.

Marina was dancing with Tyler in L.A. Woman in upstate new York when she heard I was bringing the Florida girls to New York City. She was one of the most desired topless dancers in the area, demanding a minimum of $175 just to show up to work at a topless bar.

She was originally from Chicago, the cherished daughter of a working-class family, but when she broke off with her boyfriend she moved to Florida to escape the bad memories. Once there she started dancing in topless bars. She made the circuit from Fort Lauderdale to Miami, avoiding table and lap dancing clubs, and eventually took her name from the most common sign along the highway—Marina.

The wonders of plastic surgery provided her with two of the most beautiful breasts on the face of the earth, and a woman she met while on vacation in Acapulco persuaded her to try the topless clubs in New York, especially the working men's spots on Staten Island. That was around 1988 and the bars were called bikini bars. The girls liked them because they were kept safely away from the men by the SLA regulations. They could remove their tops but not their bottoms. On her first night in a bar called Scarletti's, Marina made $700 dancing to Top 40 tunes.

"I'm really an exhibitionist," Marina used to tell me. "I love to take my clothes off and dance nude in front of men. That is, I like it when they can't touch me."

For Marina and many other girls, the old-fashioned topless bars like the Pussycat Lounge were perfect. They could earn good money and had control over their interactions with the customers. She loved her verbal sparring with the guys. "They would always point to my fabulous boobs and say, 'Are those yours?' My answer was always the same; 'They're not yours,'" she would tell me with a chuckle. "I must have used that line ten million times, the guys loved it."

Another of her favorite and most often used lines was what she would say to me when I called her at home.

I would say, "Hi, Marina, what ya doing?"

She would invariably reply, "Not you, honey."

The corny one-liners gave her a wisecracking image that contrasted with her stylish good looks and made a much more human character out of her. It was easy to like Marina.

Marina liked dancing the day shift because she knew most of the men were there on their lunch break and would have to leave within an hour or so. This did not give them much time to be a pain in the ass. In Scores a man could stay all night and, if he chose to, make a girl's life miserable for hours.

"The topless bars put the power in the girl's hands," Marina says. "I could choose who I wanted to talk to and I could really get to know a man if I wanted to without constantly fighting off his hands. In Scores and other table dancing clubs a girl has to ask a man if he wants her to dance for him. A girl could be rejected, and I do not like that."

During her years in topless bars, Marina had actually met four men whom she had serious relationships with. One of them liked her so much that he promised to open a club just for her and her girlfriend Jody if they would agree to headline there. They thought he was kidding until about a year later he hired them to work at a suburban site that is still going strong.

It was a topless club, but of course that was no problem for Marina, who proudly says, "I have a problem keeping my top ON!"

Marina had firsthand knowledge of how things changed when Tyler and I brought up the girls from Florida. Because I was not paying them to work—rather, they were paying me $5 to "lease" space in my club for them to carry on their business—the other topless bar owners seized the opportunity to either reduce the amount they would pay or cut it out altogether.

When Marina heard about Scores she figured she might as well check it out, because she realized the salad days of being a topless bar headliner were over. Although eventually, because I saw the value of having one stable girl in the stable, I did pay Marina something just to show up, it was nothing like she was used to. Until Marina told me about it I had no idea of the resentment this policy caused me among the girls who were working successfully in New York when I opened Scores.

Tyler, she says, was the other major factor in changing life for the girls. Marina began to open my eyes about her.

"All of us are con girls," she said. "You know the movie *The Grifters*, about the con men and women? Well, that is what we are—we're con girls, and Tyler was the best.

"The Florida girls were all on the con. I don't blame them for it. But it is better to know what they were all about."

Over the weeks we spent drinking coffee and talking, Marina explained to me how the girls spot really rich men by looking at their shoes. I realized she was right when she told me the girls knew it was not unusual for a man to spend $500 or $600 on a suit, especially if he was a corporate executive type. But the girls knew if he spent $300 on his shoes, that meant he had real money and was generous with it.

Those were the men the girls would seek out in the club. And if they found one they would keep it to themselves. (Guys they would avoid were the ones wearing a lot of jewelry.) They called it the "Guido effect." The competition for the big scores was intense.

I began to watch the Florida girls at work. I could see them make eye contact with certain guys who seemed to be bigger spenders than others. They, more than girls from New York and L.A., would often spend the whole night with one customer. I totally believed their stories that they got as much as $4,000 a night from some of those guys.

I began to talk to the girls about that stuff, and my eyes were really opened. Shawna told me about a man she met her first week in Scores. He paid for for about ten dances in a row and then just asked her to sit with him, which of course cost him $10 every time the song changed.

Around 3 A.M. he asked Shawna if she would visit one of the discos in town with him. "I just said I could not leave. I told him I could make another five hundred dollars if I stayed until closing," she told me. "No problem," said her customer as he handed her $500.

Marina told me how those nights on the town would lead to an early-morning shopping trip along Fifth Avenue. "That was the biggest score for a girl. If she got a guy to take her shopping on Fifth Avenue between Fifty-fifth and Fifty-ninth Streets, that was a home run." Marina did not have to tell me that included in that stretch of territory was Tiffanys' and Bergdorf Goodman's.

But I was surprised when I learned that the girls did not automatically jump into the sack with the big spenders. They did not have to.

Marina explained, "Many of these guys are just looking for company. They want to party in New York and be able to go home with a clear conscience. Of course, they want to party with the most beautiful girls. It's not about fucking. These guys could all afford to order up the top call girls to their hotel rooms. But that's not what they're looking for. Of course, if a girl thought she had to go to bed with a guy to make sure he returned to Scores the next time he was in town then she would give him the fuck of his life. No big deal. It's business."

From day one in Scores I saw many relationships develop between very wealthy men, some of whom were highly placed executives in corporations that were household names, and showgirls. As I predicted, there was a need for these sophisticated situations, which suited both parties to a T. The men got what they wanted in a safe environment, and the girls got what they wanted because everyone knew the rules.

Marina danced only occasionally at Scores. She was turned off by having to get too close to the men. And she did not like the level of competition with the other girls. The Florida girls, especially, were known to compete ferociously. If one girl got her boobs enhanced to 42 D, the others would pump up to 44 double D. If Tyler wore a black dress, everyone would start wearing black dresses.

When I started seeing the girls get collagen injections in their lips and liposuction in their already perfect thighs, I knew the atmosphere was dangerously insane.

For all her low-key attitude, Marina lived anything but a low-key life. She saw plenty of action as one of the most desirable women in New York. One time she was invited to a playboy's birthday party on the island of Elba, where Napoleon was sent to exile.

"You know how you get directions to someone's house for a party. They say take 'so and so bridge' or 'route so and so.' Well, these directions told you at which airport to park your private plane and where to moor your yachts. You know, if you had a twin-engine plane you had to go to a certain airport and use a certain runway, if you had a jet you had to go somewhere else. The directions included radio frequencies and everything. This was a well-heeled crowd.

"As for me, a guy flew me in, and all they wanted me to do was walk around naked all weekend. I never even unpacked my bags. I just took off my clothes in my room and headed for the fabulous beach. Oh, yeah, I had to dye my hair and bush blonde. I loved it. I got a gift of a Rolex before I left. One of the girls got a Jeep."

Marina never minded walking around naked. Her dancing was designed to make men think she was totally nude. Her favorite costume was just a man's tailored shirt and a flesh-colored, oyster shaped cup that fit over her crotch. It was custom-made in Paris; some kind of spring mechanism kept it in place, and I want to tell you it was effective. With transparent pasties and that little cup, she really did appear completely naked. And considering her body that was quite a treat.

I might have slipped off the deep end without Marina's wise counsel during those early days. But I was honest with her and she was honest with me. That is how we have been able to remain friends. Nowadays she is working as a photo stylist and as an assistant to a famous film director. She is still a knockout. When she walks into the East Side restaurant where we often meet for dinner, heads still turn.

CHAPTER 21 Lady in Red

About ten days after we opened, the famous comedian Jackie Mason came into the club. Things had been going great guns. Music was blaring, the disco lights were flashing—we were really in a groove. Marcy was still on my mind, but success was overtaking remorse.

I sat with Mason for about an hour. He was with a fairly attractive older woman but was unabashedly ogling all the girls. He was hilarious, having some remark to make to each girl who came by to ask if he wanted a dance. He rejected them all, but with a smile.

That same evening a group of pro ballplayers, including the great Leonard Marshall of the football Giants, also came in. The athletes really helped to dress up the place. They could be loud and aggressive with the girls, but it only added to the party atmosphere. The girls did not like them so much because most of them were not big spenders. They were more accustomed to other people picking up the tab.

I was indeed living out my dream, and while it was more of a mix of emotions than I'd expected when I got into the club business, it was one hell of a good life!

I was hobnobbing with the glitterati. I was the king who owned a club that was the hottest spot in town. I was swimming in the Nile.

But as often happened during those days, no sooner was I enjoying the fruits of my success than I would be brought down to earth by some shocking event. In mid-November two of my dancers were the victims of a horrible crime.

When their shifts ended at 1 A.M. the two headed for the Cat Club in the East Village to party the rest of the night away. Many of the girls found it hard to go straight home. Their jobs were very physical and demanded a high energy level, so it was hard for them to just go home and curl up in front of the television set. They worked in a boiling cauldron of erotic energy. This was one of the reasons many of them, I learned, engaged in bisexuality.

At first when I discovered many of the girls were having sexual relations with each other I thought it was a reaction to being turned off to men. Well, that was the case with some of them, and some of them were actually lesbians. But often they would go back to the hotel room or apartment they were sharing and get it on with each other as a means of burning off the sexual energies they'd spent all night cultivating. They found it a safe way to experience pleasure and did not see anything immoral about it. They called it "recreational lesbianism."

On more than one occasion I was invited by two or more girls to join them in their rooms. They figured that if there was more than one of them it could not be construed as a love affair—just "recreational sex." I figured if there was more than one them it might kill me.

Anyway, the two girls who went partying that night, Nancy and Gina, were more interested in working out their tensions on a dance floor and maybe meeting some cute guys.

According to all reports they both got very drunk and left at closing time, then got into separate cabs that were waiting outside the club.

What they could not have known was that the cabdrivers had a plan of their own. Using their radios, they signaled four or five other cab drivers to meet them in a dark, isolated spot at the foot of the Manhattan Bridge. When they pulled up, the other cabs drove in and blocked the rear doors of their cars. It was a practiced maneuver that had apparently used by the group of scumbags on more than one occasion.

Each girl was attacked in the back of her cab. They were repeatedly raped and sodomized for about three hours, until the sun came up over lower Manhattan. When the rapists were finished they took the girls' clothes, jewelry, and money and left them in the street. They were found by a homeless scavenger, who covered them with his raggy jacket and sweater and called the police.

They both needed a hospital stay to recover. About one week later Gina came back to work. She was still covered with bruises and scrapes and needed a quart of makeup before she could appear on the dance floor. Nancy dropped out of sight and was never heard from again.

I noticed Gina out on the floor, oscillating back and forth between nervous laughter and blank stares. She was scaring some of the customers. Some of her friends at the club finally convinced her to go home to her folks in Brooklyn for a few weeks and chipped in some money so she would not feel the pressure to work.

I was always amazed at how generous the girls could be to each other when necessary. They might cut each other's hearts out in competition for an easy mark, but they invariably pitched in when one of them was in trouble.

Gina never came back to Scores. She went to work at Show World, a scumatorium on Forty-second Street where she starred in a lesbian love act. I'd thought that women only migrate to better work environments—the top being Scores—not worse ones, but the rape had left her in really bad emotional shape. Now she works as a hard-core dominatrix, apparently exacting her revenge on willing customers.

My head was still reeling from the rapes when a dancer named Laurie cornered me in my office and asked if I could lend her money for an abortion. She said that when her boyfriend found out she was pregnant he had a fit, smacked her around, and said she'd better do something about it.

Well, I could not believe that Laurie, who earned a lot of money in Scores, could not afford her own abortion, but I sympathized with her plight. While in college I'd had the unfortunate experience of being asked by girlfriends to pay for abortions on two occasions. I did both times, although I have often thought that the second girl was scamming me, because she would not let me go to the clinic with her. Anyway, I certainly understood why Laurie wanted to have the abortion and I was not in a position to moralize or lecture her about it. I gave her a couple of hundred dollars and told her not to worry about paying it back.

That turned out to be a mistake, because the word got around and some of the girls thought I was a soft touch on that issue. A week would not go by without a girl asking me for money for the same thing. If I believed them I helped them. If I did not believe them I proved to be a harder touch than they expected.

So within one month I had garnered the triumph I desired but had also been hit over the head by two genuine tragedies and a host of lesser ones. That was something I'd never considered during my four-year climb to the top. Marina had warned me that this life was not going to be all glamour and cash, but I thought surely Marcy's accident and the rapes of Gina and Nancy had to be a year's worth of bad luck that had just been bunched together in my first month.

The end of November was a far more uplifting time. Bo Dietl invited me to Rao's with a group of his friends that included a big Hollywood producer. It was an incredible feeling, for me, to be in that extremely exclusive restaurant with such a high-powered crowd.

I brought Tyler as my date, and she was the center of everyone's attention. She wore a short, red clingy dress with white stockings and red high heels. To say she turned heads would be a gross understatement. Everyone who saw her almost dropped dead in their tracks, and these were rich and famous people accustomed to being around great beauty.

My taking Tyler out for the evening sent a tremor through the rest of the girls at Scores. They were jealous; all of them wanted to be seen around town with the boss. Even my friend Marina made a sarcastic remark about me "going out with Tyler." I shot back, "It's just business," and I meant it.

The fact was, Tyler was an incredible promotion for Scores. That night at Rao's everyone wanted to know who she was and where they could see her. The evening was an outstanding success. I was the king holding court. Everyone had to hear what this guy with the most beautiful girl in the world had to say. I expressed myself about Scores and anything else I wanted to talk about, from the state of the economy to the difference between silicone boobs and those filled with saline solution.

The food and the company were great and Tyler proved to be a wonderful dinner companion, witty and charming. When I was dropping her off at the Roger Williams Hotel she invited me up to her room for a nightcap. I accepted, and we got into a pretty hot little scene. She did a private table dance for me as I sat on the edge of the bed She stripped out of that tiny red dress and turned her butt toward me as she bent over to peel off her stockings. Wow! Talk about hot! I did not let it go further than that, though. She thought I was nuts when I got up off the bed. It was hard, but I had to keep reminding myself that it was business.

Being with a woman like her it was easy to forget everything else and just focus on getting your hands and lips on her body. Her sexual charms were a potent drug. She teased me to the point of explosion, but I did not want to become one of Tyler's victims. (Though I have to admit that there are times I wish my discipline was not so effective.)

Bad things, alas, continued to happen. Despite my commitment to security, burglars managed to get through the gates that covered the rear exit. They managed to get into my office and break through my heavy-duty, fire-resistant safe. They probably thought they were about to uncover a bonanza of cash, and if they did, they left disappointed. Most of our business was done through credit cards, and we continually deposited small amounts of cash in the night depository.

All the thieves got was some petty cash used to set up the registers at the bar and front door. Still, the burglary was a distressing situation, especially when we found that someone had made the burglar's job easier by having disconnected the alarm system. It may have been coincidence that the alarm did not go off, but more likely it was an inside job. No one was ever arrested for the crime, so I would never find out the truth.

By early January, Jay Bildstein and Scores were the talk of the nightclub business. Other club owners began to show up to check out what Bildstein had wrought on their dingy, dank, dark world of topless entertainment. I had an advantage on about 90 percent of the other owners in that I knew much about their clubs, having studied them for four years, but they knew nothing about me or my club. They were surprised when I welcomed them to Scores and revealed that I knew their names and which bars they owned. I had done my homework in a fashion that they could not imagine.

A funny incident occurred when the owners of a relatively new club in Queens named Goldfinger's came to Scores. Goldfinger's was a cut above the average topless joint. It was not in our league, but it was trying hard by offering decent-looking girls and staying clean. There was talk on the street that the Goldfinger's owners wanted to open a club in Manhattan.

The owners came to Scores to size up their competition. They were a party of four people: the two owners, a stunning blonde named Amy Lynn Baxter, a former *Penthouse Pet* who was apparently doing for them what Tyler had done for me, and a gigantic guy who looked like their bodyguard.

I was sitting alone at a table in the nearly empty President's Lounge, my arms spread wide onto the adjacent chairs. I was the king surveying my kingdom, and that is the picture the group from Goldfinger's saw as they entered through the double, stained-glass doors into the plush President's Lounge.

At that moment a loud, familiar voice boomed out, "Jay, Jay Bildstein! Wow, how have you been?"

I stood up to greet the giant bodyguard who had called my name. As he stepped forward in excitement the two owners and Amy Lynn stood there with blank expressions. We patted each other on the back like long-lost cousins, which we almost were.

Actually, he was the cousin of Cathy from the temporary services firm I continued to do consulting work for.

"It's good to see you, Larry," I said.

"Great to see you too, Jay. You mean you are the owner of this place?"

"Of course. Don't you remember the plans I told Cathy and you about?"

He said he remembered vaguely but had not connected me with Scores. He then launched into a better public relations pitch for me than a team of $300-an-hour publicists could have. He told his three companions the I was a top motivator, sales expert, and an all-around great guy.

I made no effort to interrupt him, as I noticed his spiel had the effect of deflating the two owners, who had come to size up the interloper so they could better plan how to cut him down.

But I played the generous host and invited the entire group to join me at the table. I signaled a waitress to bring food over, and she quickly delivered a tray of chicken tenders and sweet and sour shrimp. I ordered drinks all around and when everyone settled in I said: "So what can I do for you good people?"

Before they could answer Amy Lynn remarked that the lounge looked like the Polo Lounge of the Beverly Hills Hotel—just what I loved to hear.

The two owners, John and Steve, began telling me how they had come to see if I would be interested in teaming up with them in an alliance to recruit dancers.

They said they were in the early stages of opening a club on West Twenty-eighth Street—the worst location I could imagine for an upscale club. It was an area infested with streetwalkers.

They told me they heard M. J. Peter was back in New York and was planning to take over Stringfellow's on West Twenty-first Street in order to turn it into Pure Platinum. They saw Peter as major competition—they were right about that—and thought I would be happy to join with them against him.

They thought that having two upscale competitors in Manhattan would jeopardize Scores. This was a moment of triumph for me. It was clear that they viewed me as the key to keeping the great M. J. Peter out of New York.

But I did not see the business the same way they did. They had a parochial view of the nightclub game. What I saw was that two more clubs opening in Manhattan would announce a trend, a fashion, and attract more business for everybody. I knew that I would forever be known as the man who'd set that trend in motion.

They continued to try to persuade me to join in with them. As they spoke I gobbled up the shrimp and chicken, which were delicious. Occasionally I would interrupt them with, "Try some food, it's wonderful. I have a great team in the kitchen."

Eventually they got the message. Steve said that maybe they would build their club a little differently, more upscale, and take on Peter themselves. I had won. I convinced them I was the king and was not afraid of anyone, including the great Mr. Peter, and did not have to ally myself with anyone.

The owners and Amy Lynn left and Larry, who was not really a bodyguard but just a friend of the owners, stayed and had a fabulous evening as my guest.

Not too long after that meeting, Steve and John did open Goldfinger's on West Twenty-eighth Street. They offered a diet of specialty acts like Amy Lynn and some porn stars. They were never any real competition to me and did not last very long.

Pure Platinum also opened and proved to be a more formidable competitor. M. J. Peter was a classier guy, and it showed in his club. But Pure Platinum offered no sports, only women, and they were not better-looking than the Scores women. Once again my sports feature came through and proved to be the drawing card that Peter's club did not possess.

I had kicked off a gentlemen's club fever in New York, giving new life to a dying industry. Clubs all over the city tried to imitate what I had accomplished. Clubs started changing their names. Gentleman Jim's and Thee Doll House opened. Incredibly, none of them copied my sports theme.

The popular press, as I had predicted, began to take notice. The media began to cover Scores and the gentlemen's club phenomenon that it had spawned.

Wolf-TV came to the club, we began popping up regularly in the newspapers, and then we got the call from Geraldo himself and a group of the Scores girls appeared on his popular show.

My theory about society's psyche had proven correct. The club that Jay built would someday become a place where Madonna hung out and Demi Moore went to study for a part in the movie *Striptease*. But always in the back of my mind were the haunting memories of girls like Marcy, Nancy, and Gina and the tragedy they'd found.

CHAPTER 22

Fame

In January 1992, *New York* magazine, the final arbiter of what is in and what is out in the Big Apple, featured a full-page article about Scores headlined "Shirts and Skins." The article, by Meredith Berkman, said Scores looked "like an opulent supper club" and was serving "a few hundred men in well-cut dark suits and fanciful Nicole Miller silk ties or faded Levi's and Italian wool sweaters . . . seated at dark-wood tables in an enormous hunter-green room." The article described the exact feeling I had hoped to capture in Scores.

A twenty-one-year-old dancer named Kassandra, "a tall, strikingly beautiful black woman with sky-high cheekbones, huge brown eyes, and a soft, little-girl voice," was interviewed by the writer.

She explained how Scores had changed the topless scene: "It's not like biker bars anymore, like you see on TV. These are really clean. There's a difference between sexy and slutty."

I could not have written a better script. The article also featured two pictures of a blonde dancer named Heather who had quickly become one of the favorites at the club.

I had been interviewed for the piece about a month before it appeared and had expressed the point that Scores provided "safe sex" in the world of AIDS.

Just one week after we opened the great basketball star Magic Johnson announced that he was infected with the HIV virus. The news was broadcast over the sports channels that were being broadcast in Scores and it brought the club to a ghostly silence. The dancers stopped dancing and the deejay shut down the music while we all absorbed the frightening news.

So, that article really put us on the map. It was well-balanced and portrayed the club as the kind of place I had bent over backward to create. If anyone had any doubts about the fact that Scores was headed for a long run of prosperity, they were dispelled by that article.

The Monday night the magazine hit the stands we had a record crowd. We filled the President's Lounge and the main room by 8 P.M. and there was a long line in the street up until around midnight. We almost ran out of chicken tenders that night.

By that time we had also appeared on *Geraldo* on CBS. Tyler, a dancer named Camille, and I were invited on the show to talk about the current trend in topless bars, which I was credited as being directly responsible for bringing to New York.

Unbelievably, Tyler overslept that morning and did not make it to the taping on time. I began to notice a trait in her, and in many of the other dancers as well, that doomed them to failure. Each time they had a genuine shot at mainstream success, something would happen that would spoil their opportunity.

I was present when girls would be offered legitimate roles in films and even on Broadway. Invariably they would come up with some reason to miss their audition or even their first day on the job. They would catch a serious cold, or someone in their family back home would need them to return immediately, or the dry cleaner would not have had that special dress ready in time. They were afraid of success in the mainstream world. I know that if Tyler had appeared on national television she would have attracted all kinds of legitimate offers from Hollywood. She may have had to take off her clothes at first, but she would have eventually found mainstream success. Instead she overslept and blew it. She actually paged me during the taping of the show to see if they would hold things up for her. If I'd said yes she would have come up with another excuse not to make it.

Of course, she blamed the oversleeping on having had to stay up all night helping one of the other girls get over a broken love affair.

Geraldo was not very happy with me on the show. I took a stern position and refused to let him intimidate me into talking only about the sleaze factor of topless dancing. I held my ground, pressing forward my position that Scores was an upscale entertainment club. I focused on telling him and the audience about the accent on sports.

I explained to him that we catered to all the needs of men, not just sex, and I explained how popular Sundays and Mondays were at the club because of the football games on the big screens. The studio audience broke up when I related how the guys would yell at the showgirls to keep out of the way of the screens as they watched the games without the sound.

Also on *Geraldo* that day was a blonde with a perfect body named Janine who had appeared nine times in nude layouts in *Penthouse*. Appearing in a black pinstriped minidress, she talked about an act she and another girl were performing in topless clubs around the country. It was called *Blondage* and revolved around a lesbian S&M theme. When the show ended I went back to the green room to get her number but she had already left.

I would have loved to have Janine perform at Scores, but I was against featuring specialty acts because in other clubs they usually involved porn stars, and I did not want that reputation to rub off on Scores.

Not long after the *Geraldo* appearance, I saw Janine on *The Playboy Channel*, doing an all-girl love scene with Alex Jordan, a famous porn queen. In August 1995 Jordan was found dead in her L.A. home. She had committed suicide.

I followed Janine's career from the day I met her and I know she got deeper and deeper into the hard-core porno scene. I noticed that each time I saw a picture of her she was sporting a new tattoo or some part of her body had been recently pierced.

She became a living metaphor for what I saw happening to many of the girls I met through Scores. They were always pushing the envelope of sexuality. It started out with tattoos, first on a shoulder or ankle and then in increasingly exotic territory, and moved on to body piercing, which followed a similar route around their fabulous bodies.

The strict policy against showing tattoos at Scores forced the dancers to cover them with body makeup, but once in a while one would slip past the inspection of the house mother.

One time a honey blonde dancer returned from vacation in Florida with a tattoo of a chain around her ankle. Some patrons were absolutely knocked out by the imagery. But I remember one of my security guards, a retired detective with two teenaged daughters, commenting that he could not understand how "a pretty kid like that could do that to herself."

That retired detective did not see the trend as I did. He did not understand that the tattoo was symbolic of the downward slide into the depths of low self-esteem. That was the common denominator among all the showgirls.

He and I talked at length about the destructive qualities of the girls after one of the dancers committed suicide by blowing her brains out while sitting on the steps of her boyfriend's house. She left a note in her car saying that he "had treated me like all men had treated me."

I was personally involved in that tragedy, because the boyfriend was an old friend of mine whom I had invited to Scores. He became a regular and was dating the suicidal dancer for two months. When he decided to date another of the girls she decided to end her misery by firing a .38-caliber bullet point-blank into her head. The horror stories were beginning to pile up on me. I was losing sleep over them.

That summer *US* magazine wrote a tremendously positive feature on Scores. The article said it was "different and convivial." The great morning drive-time radio personality Howard Stern began to mention us in his hilarious monologues. Stern was always talking about sex in a humorous manner, and he clearly understood the appeal of Scores. A few months later he and a small group of friends showed up for lunch at the club. He might have had a reputation as a madman whose mouth was out of control, but he turned out to be one of the friendliest and most well-behaved of all the famous guests to come to Scores. He even turned down my offer to pick up the lunch tab. He's a great guy with a real understanding of the male libido.

During that winter I was moved to bury the hatchet with Alicia. I really missed her. Being surrounded by all the erratic personalities of Scores, I yearned for some rational, intelligent conversation with a woman who had control over her own ego.

I found out that Alicia no longer worked at the Pussycat Lounge but that she stopped by on Wednesdays to have dinner with the owner and visit with old friends who still danced there. So on a Wednesday night I popped in, and sure enough Alicia was there, hanging out at the bar while waiting for her dinner date.

She was shocked to see me, but we exchanged a warm hug and settled into some small talk. At first it was a little uncomfortable, but after a while we were chatting like we'd just seen each other the day before. That's the way it is with genuinely good friends. Even if you have been out of touch for years it is easy to fall back into a comfortable state with each other. When she asked what I had been up to I just replied that I was busy investing in a bunch of different ventures. I did not say a word about Scores. I invited her to go to the movies with me the next afternoon, and she accepted.

I picked her up at her loft the next day and we went to see *JFK* at the Cineplex Odeon on Twenty-third Street. After the movie Alicia said she wanted to go to a place in the Village where we used to go to have cappuccino. I was encouraged by her selecting a place where we had shared some warm moments.

But, instead, I insisted we take a cab uptown because there was a new place in town I wanted to show her. She had no idea where we were headed as the cab pulled up on Sixtieth Street.

As we got out of the cab, right in front of Scores, I said: "Oh, by the way, this is that gentlemen's club I told you I was going to open. What do you think?"

She could not respond. Her jaw hung down in utter amazement.

I led her inside and conducted the grand tour. It was a spectacular feeling to show her around. At first she did not believe it was my club, but as the showgirls, who were arriving for the early-evening shows, began greeting me, she got the idea that I had delivered on my dream.

I showed her my office, the kitchen, the champagne locker. She insisted on a peek inside the girls' dressing room. Alicia had always had an eye for beauty and she let out a long slow "Wooow!" in appreciation of what she saw.

We stayed at the club all night. We ate and drank, and several of the girls danced for Alicia, who loved every minute of it. I took her home in a limo, and on the way she told me that in her twelve years in the business she had "never seen anything like Scores." Alicia invited me in and we finally did what we had put off for so long. It was a wonderful night, and I left the next day feeling very good about our relationship.

After that evening we stayed in touch pretty regularly, and she was very helpful to me in evaluating some girls who I was not sure would work out in Scores. For instance, she had a way of spotting a particularly sexy move—it might be a flick of a perfectly pink tongue or a wink of a tiny eye—that I might miss during an audition.

Alicia was forever warning me that the girls would try to seduce me just because I was the owner and not because they really liked me—in other words the Johnny Bravo syndrome. I did not tell Alicia that I was wise to that. I enjoyed how jealous she was about all the girls around me. I wanted to be more than just very good friends.

Unfortunately something happened between us that I still cannot put my finger on. But we once again drifted apart. Alicia moved to Queens and stopped coming to the Pussycat on Wednesdays, and I got more and more caught up in the growing business of Scores and Double Play in L.A. We have not spoken in years.

Another old friend came back into my life not long after Scores opened. Bob, the connoisseur of topless clubs, came walking in one night and asked the doorman to tell me he was there.

I went out to greet him and was immediately impressed by how well he looked. He had gotten himself back into great shape, almost as trim as he was in college. His eyes were bright and his skin was clear. He showed none of the telltale signs of the aging alcoholic I'd seen when we were last together.

He told me he had seen the newspaper ads for Scores and had watched me on *Geraldo*. He was sincerely happy about my success and soon became a regular at Scores. He got right back into the swing of things, quickly reestablishing himself as a master pickup artist. He was about the only person without access to a platinum credit card whom I ever saw go home with Scores showgirls. They loved his good looks and charm, just as the girls in the Pussycat Lounge had. I guess it did not hurt him at all when he added a line to his rap about being my best buddy. Eventually, though, Bob stopped coming in, and I once again lost touch with him.

Around the time he first returned we suffered through another tragedy when one of the girls, a dancer from Georgia who was just barely twenty-one-years old, was found dead in her hotel room with a needle was found sticking out of her arm. She was close with a few of the other dancers from the South, and they blamed unsavory characters she met at the club for turning her on to drugs. That was nonsense, of course. I did not control who the girls saw on their time off and I would not allow a known drug dealer to hang out at Scores. But, as always, these girls needed someone else to blame for their own shortcomings. It was becoming a depressing routine.

To make matters worse, two Scores waitresses were killed in a car crash on their way home one morning.

I was beginning to lose faith in my theory about the redeeming social value of Scores. I had not counted on being so deeply involved in the private world of degenerate sex and drugs that so many of the girls were caught up in.

There was further bad news when a former female cashier and her two thug boyfriends teamed up to rob Scores one weekday afternoon.

She showed up at lunchtime on a day when we were not opened for lunch and asked the maintenance crew to let her in so she could pick up a check I supposedly owed her.

As soon as the door was opened the two thugs pushed their way in past the director of maintenance and waved pistols in his face. The group was so hapless that the cashier blew her cover by grabbing a pistol from one of the men and ordering the three maintenance guys and Suzy, the daytime receptionist, to get down on the floor. She even called one of the thugs by his real name, Ralph.

They pistol-whipped everyone and finally got the safe open. But the take was less than $500, which was about all the cash we ever kept on hand.

I arrived at the club just as the police were pulling up, within minutes of the robbery. Suzy was in a catatonic state. I later learned that both her parents had been killed in a similar robbery years before. She was frightened to death. She quit the following day and I never heard from her again.

The robbers were never brought to justice. About three years later one of the maintenance men recognized the cashier working in a fast-food joint. He called the police but they could never put together a case.

The media attention Scores was receiving had an unsettling effect on many of the girls. They claimed that they were being threatened by club owners in Florida, that they would be blackballed down there if they continued working for me. Jealousy and ignorance were calling the shots. The other owners refused to recognize that I had put topless dancing on the menu of legitimate entertainment.

As it turned out, the point was moot because they enjoyed dancing in New York, and especially at Scores, more than they did in the increasingly all-nude atmosphere of Florida. But threats, robberies, drug overdoses—it was all starting to get to me.

Another incident that spring made me feel like crap but ended up with a silver lining.

I had met a sharp attorney named Eric Kloper through Lacey, the fitness trainer whom I had to fire from Scores when she would not follow Tom's orders. Lacey introduced us when she was trying to promote a movie deal. She brought together a bunch of actors and writers and Eric. He was the shining star of the meeting, which went nowhere except that he and I hit if off and stayed in touch through a few low-key business deals.

One day he brought a guy and a gal to see me about an idea they had involving a club for singles. They wanted to try it out in Scores on Sunday nights, which, with the passing of the football season, had really slowed down. The idea was for single men and women and couples to be welcomed into the club. Of course, that was always our policy and couples were not unusual guests, but we did not promote the club that way.

I did not see Scores as a singles meat market, but because I liked Eric I was willing to give it a shot. One afternoon we struck a tentative deal and Eric and the guy and gal left.

About fifteen minutes later the woman returned alone. She was a voluptuous brunette, about thirty-five-years old and very sexy. She could have been a Scores showgirl. She asked me to advance her $5,000 against work she would do on promoting the Sunday night cvents.

Clearly she'd come back alone so she could seduce me out of the money. She had left her guy sitting in a car outside at the curb. She was all over me—her hands in my shirt, her lips on my ear lobes—as she tried to convince me she was good for the money. I was laughing inside. Don't forget, I had been resisting Tyler for almost a year. This woman was hot, but she was not Tyler.

Finally the scene was broken up by the police, who were called by my security guys when they became suspicious of the man sitting in the car alone. It looked to them like a getaway car and they thought I was being stuck up. Well, in a way, I guess I was.

After that act I wrote the deal off and did not try to reestablish contact with Eric Kopler. When we finally did have to do some business together I realized he knew nothing of the $5,000 gambit, and we became good friends as well as partners in many ventures.

He is a genius who masterminded a big-time music deal involving one of the greatest groups of all time. Unfortunately, it ended up in litigation and the public never received the benefit of his idea. But after that was settled, we went on to other projects.

Currently we are partners in a Manhattan motivational center called the Mind Gym.

A few days later I got a call from one of the people at Double Play informing me that Lyle Alzado had died. We held a moment of silence for him in the club that evening. It was very moving as the deejay stopped the music and the flashing disco lights were turned off while everyone took a quiet moment to remember the great athlete.

CHAPTER 23

The Final Score

Later in 1992 I sponsored one of Michael Blutrich's boxing events. It was not quite in Madison Square Garden, but it was a lot closer than the last event, when I was the ring announcer in the decrepit old Westchester County Center. For this night of fisticuffs Blutrich had set up a ring in a ballroom of the Pennsylvania Hotel, right across Seventh Avenue from the Garden.

Of course, I was the ring announcer for the fights that night, and we promoted a contest using showgirls from Scores.

The girls were outrageously sexy as they pranced around the ring between rounds holding the number of the next round high over their heads. There was one guy who kept yelling; "I can't wait for round sixty-nine"; he said it every round of every fight. It was good-natured fun and the fights, though without a headliner, were pretty good. I was great once again as the next Michael Buffer.

Following the fights we threw a huge party at Scores. Larry Holmes was fighting a comeback event on the screens, and we were packed to the rafters with boxing fans, sportswriters, and others who were just there for the girls.

Randy Gordon, the state athletic commissioner who'd told me in Westchester that I was a great announcer, was there. He complimented me to no end about what a hit Scores was. There were a number of pro fighters there, including that character Mitch "Blood" Green who once fought an unofficial battle with Mike Tyson on the streets of Harlem. It was a powerful evening.

Tyler hung on my arm throughout the night. She was totally enjoying the celebrity status that being associated with Scores had brought to her. Being a former cheerleader and having a basically, if larger-than-life, "all-American-girl" look, Tyler fit right in with the athletes and other sports types in attendance that night. She was everyman's American Dream.

We had become very close while working together in recruiting the girls and then keeping them in line regarding what they were allowed to do or wear out on the dance floor. She was a royal pain with her prima donna attitude, but behind that I sensed a troubled woman looking for a true friend.

When the crowd left that fight night, we ended up alone, cozy on the couch in my office, sipping after-dinner drinks. It was a constant struggle to resist her charms, which I knew to be fatal.

There were so many reasons I had to protect myself from giving in to her. For starters, she did have a boyfriend in Florida. She always referred to him as a "creepy degen," but she regularly sent money to him.

As we had many times before after a hard day's work, we talked about her past. She always told me how domineering her father was and how she got into stripping just to rebel against him. But that night, for the first time, she told me about how he'd turned totally cold to her when she'd started going out with boys. He could not stand the thought of another man touching her. She always stopped short of saying her father abused her sexually, but she always gave that impression. She would say something like, "dad loved me soooo much. He just couldn't keep his hands off me," and she would give a knowing smile when she said it. Despite the shadow of abuse, though, she seemed to profess heartfelt love for the man.

One day she and a bunch of her girlfriends were walking through the parking lot of a local mall when they noticed the telltale signs of two people having sex in a car parked near the rear. They decided to sneak up on the car and surprise the couple. When they banged on the rear door, the couple jumped out of their exposed skins.

But it was Tyler who was most surprised, as she realized that the man was her own father. He was screwing a woman who worked in a local dry cleaning store. All the girls knew both adults involved, and the story had spread like a whore's legs through the town by the time Tyler got home.

She never confronted her father about the incident, but she used to say that from that day on she began to lose respect for all men. She left home right after high school when a young marine corps officer whom she had fallen in love with was killed in a motorcycle accident.

That is when she got a job at Thee Doll House as a waitress and in short order moved up to topless dancer. We would often laugh at her stories of the beautiful, but awkward, girl working her way up the topless ladder.

One of her favorite stories was about the time a guy offered her "$10 to see her "beaver," and she said she was sorry, but she did not have any pets. The guy thought she was dumping on him and left in a huff.

"Believe me," she used to say, "if I knew what he meant I would have shown it to him. Well, I would have gotten him to up the ante, but I would have shown it to him."

Tyler, like Marina, was an exhibitionist and loved having men lust after her lush body. But unlike Marina, she used that lust to manipulate and dominate men.

At first I ignored the warnings from Alicia and Marina that women like Tyler were only into themselves and that she was after something from me. I thought they were just jealous. But it turned out they were right.

The closer Tyler and I became, the less work she wanted to do at the club. I had given her a couple of generous bonuses for the great job she had done as a recruiter, but she was trying to get more money out of me so that she could dance less. That was never part of our deal. I needed Tyler out on that dance floor, drawing men to her like no one else could.

That night after the fights she offered herself to me like never before, including the night she did that private dance for me in her hotel room. She cleverly tied her offer of a lifetime of great sexual companionship into a package that would end up with her a part of the management team, pulling in big bucks and doing no work—but she assured me I would be happy with the arrangement. I always wanted to believe that she genuinely liked me—after all, I would have loved to be able to have a carefree affair with her—but I realized that evening that she was trying to wrap me around her finger. I knew her deal would be one I would regret forever.

So I resisted her once more, making up some excuse about having to get up in a few hours. Over the next few days I spoke to Larry and the other members of Scores Entertainment Inc. about what we should do with her—businesswise, that is.

So we made a deal to settle her contract and she was let go. Scores seemed to bring out the worst qualities in people. All the guys wanted to be cock of the walk and the women all wanted to be queen of the kingdom.

My fixation on opening Scores had bordered on obsession, and it was not until I was immersed in it that I became aware what horrors lay behind the glitter and glamour. For every new beautiful dancer who came in, a new tragedy was revealed.

Within three months of opening the club I'd heard more stories of childhood sex abuse and maltreatment than a child psychiatrist hears in a lifetime.

The incredibly sexy and sexual women who worked in my club were victims of the most barbaric and inhuman treatment I had ever heard of. Their fathers fucked them, their boyfriends beat them. Or, searching for love, they turned to other women, who used them just as harshly.

Pretty faces and beautiful bodies hid battered souls and butchered minds. They hid twisted sex lives and often a hatred of men that was frightening.

Scores, for all its glamour and glitz, was nothing more than a sick symbiosis. It was an environment where men and women played hunter and prey. The men wanted to score; the women wanted to make a score.

There were exceptions—like Marina, with her heart of gold, whose childhood was not perfect but who kept her sanity about her and did not view men as some evil enigma.

In the middle of all this ambivalence, however, there were moments I thrived on. I met Charlton Heston's son, a great guy, Corbin Bernsen came in; and well-known New Yorkers like Joey Adams, the comedian, and his gossip columnist wife, Cindy had dinner with me there. One night John Kennedy, Jr. came in. The music mogul Ahmet Ertegun often came in with his entourage. I met every manner of sports celebrity.

As spring became summer I found myself being recognized on the street, thanks to the television reports on Scores.

One afternoon a dancer called me at the office and asked if I could come to her apartment. She said she had some business that she had to discuss personally. I was a little annoyed but I went over. It was just a few blocks away.

When I arrived, one of the other Scores girls was leaving the apartment. She had a big smile on her face when she let me in.

Inside, on the sofa, two girls, both beautiful topless entertainers who were the objects of men's desires, were making love in the classic 69 position. It was one of the most erotic scenes I had ever witnessed in person. For a few minutes, they either did not realize I was there or pretended not to know. It did not matter to me. I got an eyeful of something most men fantasize about but never get to see up close and personal. But instead of being overcome by the passion of the moment, I found it almost pathetic. My first thought was, What do these girls want from me?

Finally, Debbie, the girl who'd called me, turned her face from her lover's lap and asked me to join them. "Come on, Jay, dive in, get your clothes off; we'd love to have you," she said.

These were two women who looked like they could have just fallen out of the pages of *Playboy*. No matter what their motives in inviting me to join them were, I could have had a wonderful time. I would have worked off all the sexual tension that had been building in me since Tyler had first turned me on. I could have spent a few hours that I could remember for the rest of my life.

But I couldn't. It was not the same as the time I walked in on Liz and Mary when I worked at Max's. I was nineteen years old then, a college kid not thinking about anything but getting laid. That was before I found myself caught in a web of suicide, freak accidents, and women who psychologists would say were living out the return of their repressed emotions and revengefully mastering the trauma of their past by dominating men.

I could not take any more of the challenge of not giving in to temptations that would lead me down the dark alleys those girls walked every day. I had had enough. I could not allow myself to weaken at this point and join in their self-absorbed fun and games. Somehow I was able to turn around and walked out. On the way back to Scores I decided I had to begin the process of removing myself from the club.

In order to be successful I'd had to be in charge of my emotions, but increasingly I was having feelings of guilt. I felt I was exploiting people's weaknesses, which had never been my intention. Those two girls only knew one way to get a man's attention. I did not want to make my living on the backs of abused women or lonely, socially inept men.

When I got back to Scores I was so fed up and disgusted I felt like walking to the river and throwing in my keys. I called Eric and Michael and put the word out I would agree to listen to proposals from the many groups that had approached us about buying Scores since its opening. By this time Larry had quit, realizing sooner than I had that total involvement would lead to more emotional problems than we'd bargained for. Tom had also quit—seventeen years in the topless club business had been enough for him. So there was no one around who could talk me out of it.

It took a few weeks to settle on the right group of buyers, but exactly 365 days after I opened Scores, I completed a deal to unload it. I sold it to a group of investors who had been at opening night and had decided then and there that it was a business for them.

The deal I made with them precludes me from divulging its details, but suffice it to say I was happy with the financial arrangements. I could have made more if I stayed on. But I think doing so would have driven me into the kind of life I saw the dancers leading, and that was not for me.

The new owners have taken Scores to new heights. It became known as the place where Demi Moore studied for her role in *Striptease*. It remains the cleanest and most honest of all the topless clubs, and it still employs the best-looking women. Scores remains the number one gentlemen's club in the world. Everything I predicted has come to pass.

People I meet these days cannot understand why I got out of a business they saw as the living end, with big money to be made and great sex available at the snap of my fingers.

But they did not see it from my end. They did not know the inside story. Oh, I still think a lot about those fantastic women and from time to time I still see Marina. But owning that club turned me into an advocate for feminist issues. I still appreciate a beautiful woman but I totally disagree with supposed feminist authors like Camille Paglia, who says that stripping is an ego booster for women, that it empowers them. She says it builds their self-esteem. Others say it is reminiscent of the worship of the female pagan deity.

Those who say that are either so intellectually dishonest or misguided that they deserve to be ridiculed instead of admired as experts. They choke on their own self-importance.

On December 7, 1995, while writing this book, I was on my way to consult with a young hotshot Wall Street brokerage manager named David Murray. Outside his office building Howard Stern was doing a promotion for his latest book. He had Scores girls on either side of him as he entertained the crowd. What fun he was having.

Wherever I go, people adore Scores. I miss the action, the glamour and beauty, but in the ultimate analysis my heart breaks for the beautiful women who every day sell a little piece of what is left of their souls.

Has the King of Clubs become the King of Hearts? Hardly. I have just come to realize that true beauty is not skin-deep and that I am just not the type of person who can make money out of other people's sorrows and weaknesses.

I remember the nights of seeing men who could not afford it go home broke. I remember seeing men who could afford it lavish thousands of dollars on girls. I remember the legendary stories of shopping trips on Fifth Avenue. I remember the good times as well as the bad. I remember why I got into the nightclub business and I remember why I got out.

In the end, though, who's keeping score.